# The Redeemers

BY

## Kate Morgan

*To every writer with that one special book: Never give up.*

# THE REDEEMERS

2nd Edition - April 2017
1st Edition Trade Paperback, August 2015
All Rights Reserved

## Dark Recesses Press

6273 132A Street, Surrey, B.C.  V3X 3T2
Canada

Cover and Inset Layout and Design:     Bailey Hunter

A catalogue record for this title is available from the National Library of Canada

ISBN: 978-0-9809732-5-9

# THE
# REDEEMERS

BY
KATE MORGAN

# TABLE OF CONTENTS

# TABLE OF CONTENTS

# CHAPTER ONE

"Too bad Matthew didn't wait until summer to save the world," Annie said to the ginger cat at her feet. "The weather might have cooperated."

The Kansas City leatherworker's wife jumped as more thunder crashed overhead. "The pie can wait, Orange Beast. I have to see if this storm's going to wreck Carnival." Annie set down a half-sliced apple and stuck her head out the kitchen door. A burst of rain pelted her as mud bubbled around her doorstep. Shielding her face with one hand, she peered up the narrow street through the midday gloom.

Every shop's Carnival decorations were waterlogged. The blacksmith had stuffed several scarecrows to look like Redeemers and the first grateful survivors of the Last War. They all bent at unnatural angles now. The beautiful painting across the front of the inn of Matthew, the First Redeemer, resembled a stick of beef jerky. Annie knew it wasn't respectful to be amused at the Redeemers, but a snicker escaped her as the innkeeper's wife ran outside with bedsheets and nails to cover her masterpiece.

A flash of lightning illuminated the stone abbey in the distance. Redeemers didn't decorate for Carnival; that was everyone else's job. Simply saying 'Thank you' didn't begin to cover what everyone owed them, so every shop in every town along the Smoky River transformed itself into one big, elaborate 'Thank you.'

The wind snatched up Annie's flowered green dress and she slapped it against her legs. As she looked up, she saw movement in the bookstore on the corner. Jacob's handsome secretary had the right idea: he was pinning up their banner on the inside of the bookstore's center window. Annie didn't need lightning to read it: He'd found some gold paint for the two-foot-high '203 Years of Peace.'

Another gust of rain pasted Annie's hair to her eyes. Spluttering, she groped behind her for the towel on the counter.

"Hey, stranger."

Annie jumped again. "Sara, don't do that."

The butcher's wife stood grinning in the doorway, water from her bright red dress making a river on the wood floor. "Nice hair. You look like a drowned carrot."

Annie closed the door and tossed the towel at her. "Here. You're dripping all over everything."

Sara rubbed her long blonde hair into a neat twist and crouched to scratch Orange Beast under his chin. "I saw you checking out everyone's displays. You haven't come across the street to gossip for three weeks. I think you're keeping secrets from me."

Annie's hand moved toward her stomach and Sara pounced.

"I knew it! The minute I saw Hank buying red raspberry leaf from Daniel, I knew you were going to have a baby."

Annie grinned. "We were waiting a few months to make sure I didn't lose it. I was going to tell you, honest."

Sara danced Annie around the kitchen. "A baby, a baby, a baby. And you've only been married a year. That's incredibly fast."

"Hank said he can already feel the baby kick, but I told him that was silly."

"Men. They turn eighteen and think they know everything. Max is barely nineteen and he acts like he knows more than the Redeemers." She handed Annie the last peeled apple. "Speaking of Max, he says it's high time you and Hank came over for dinner. How does tonight sound?"

Annie sliced the apple and sprinkled nutmeg and honey into the bowl. "Thanks, Sara, but Hank went to Liberty for skins on Monday and he's two days late coming home."

"And he calls himself the most reliable leatherworker in Kansas City. How many customers have you had to soothe?" Sara snatched a honeyed apple slice and popped it in her mouth.

"Thief." Annie poured the apples into the fluted piecrust next to

Sara's elbows. "Not too many. I'm kind of worried. He's always back when he says."

"Is that why you're wearing his favorite dress?"

"It's my good luck charm," Annie said. "He says the green makes my red hair brighter."

"He's right. You know, maybe they passed around too many bottles of wine while they bargained," Sara said. "Let Hank sleep it off and you come eat with us. We'll pack up leftovers for him so he knows what he missed."

Annie laughed. "Serve him right if he misses your food and my dress. I'll leave a note in case he makes it home in time for dessert."

She opened the sideboard drawer and took out paper, pen, and ink bottle. Just as she dipped the pen into the ink a muffled knock came at the shop door. "Now that's timing."

"I'll help you unload," Sara said, and they went into the shop adjoining Annie's four-room house. Annie opened the side door, but her teasing welcome never came out. An old man she didn't know stood on the threshold.

"Is this the leatherworker's?" he said over the noise of the storm.

"Yes," Annie said.

"I have his skins." He held out a soggy receipt in a hand spotted and twisted with age.

"But—" A thunderclap drowned her words as he squelched out to a cart in the churned-up road.

Annie followed him, Sara close behind. "Excuse me," Annie said. When the old man continued walking, she ran in front of him. "Excuse me, but why do you have Hank's skins? Where's—" More thunder. "Where's Hank?" she said over it. He reached beneath the oiled leather cover on the back of his cart and pulled forward two heavy, tanned cowhides. She clamped her hands on his wrists. "Where—is—Hank?"

He stared at her hands. "I'm sorry to tell you, but he is dead."

Annie froze.

"We found his body caught by tree roots on the riverbank yesterday morning. It looked like thieves robbed him and threw him in." He cleared his throat. "The rocks on the riverbank are jagged. He was so battered—"

A small sound escaped Annie's throat.

"We tanners had him cremated this morning. Please accept my sympathy." He pulled away from her nerveless grip and climbed into the seat. Before Annie could say anything, he flicked the reins and drove off.

"Hey! Annie's delivery!" Sara called, but he'd already turned the corner, his cartwheels spraying mud.

Annie fell to her hands and knees. The wind changed, driving mud and water into her face, and with that the tears came. The next moment her chest heaved with sobs as the storm attacked her from outside and grief from inside.

Sara slogged over and hauled her up. "Come on. You're staying with us tonight."

\* \* \*

For the first time in her eighteen years, Annie didn't participate in Carnival. She lay on the bed in Sara's spare room all day crying into the sheets, the thin pillow wrapped around her head.

No one missed Carnival. Even in her misery it felt wrong not celebrating with everyone else.

The rain had stopped during the night and all her neighbors began singing and dancing in the streets right after breakfast. Annie heard everything through the pillow and the closed window. She could tell when the Redeemers appeared—the usual minutes of silence then dozens of voices shouting 'Hip-Hip-Hooray!'

She dragged another handkerchief from the pile Sara had left for her and wondered what that phrase meant. Old Jacob the bookseller hadn't been able to tell her, and he was packed with odd bits of knowledge.

Why was she thinking about celebrating the Redeemers? Hank was dead. He'd never see the baby. Never appear at her shoulder with another terrible pun to make her groan. The Redeemers might've saved the world two hundred years ago, but they couldn't bring Hank back from the dead. Who cared about the Redeemers anyway?

Annie actually stopped crying for a minute. Where had that thought come from? She knew what everyone owed to the Redeemers. Hank would be shocked if he heard her say something that disrespectful.

The tears returned. Hank wouldn't hear her say anything again. Everything they'd worked for was useless now. The special items only they offered—Hank's white leather buttons, the pierced leather belt she'd designed and everyone bought for New Year's— what was the point?

The theater musicians began their show-opening music. That meant the play of Matthew Saving the World and then the feast. Annie's throat closed again. She didn't care about any of it.

Not true. She cared about the baby. She couldn't hide in Sara's house forever. She had little Hank to think of.

But not today. Right now the only thing that mattered was that Hank was gone.

\* \* \*

Two weeks later, Annie set a plate of sausages next to the eggs and biscuits on Sara's breakfast table. "I'm opening the shop today."

Max speared three sausages. "Sure you're ready?"

Annie poured coffee for herself and Sara. "I've gotta do something."

"It's only been two weeks, Annie," Sara said.

"Hank's all I think about, Sara. I haven't slept for days. Cleaning the shop might get me tired enough to forget for a few hours." She drank half her coffee in one gulp. "Besides, if I don't reopen, people will take all their business to Liberty or Topeka."

The hall clock chimed eight times. When it stopped, Sara said, "How are you going to handle it? With the baby, I mean."

Annie scooped eggs onto her plate. "I'm only four months along. I'll be fine through the summer."

"I don't know, Annie. Skins are all heavy lifting."

"Oscar from Mike Dairyman's farm used to come help us with the dyeing. I'll see about hiring him in the fall." She looked at Sara's freckled face and at Max's broad, hairy one. "I have to think of the baby, not just myself."

Sara nodded. "I'll help you clean the place out after breakfast. The sun will burn off the mist in an hour. Perfect cleaning weather."

\* \* \*

At nine-thirty Annie propped open the shop door and hung the boot-shaped sign above it. Orange Beast dashed between her legs without a backward glance.

"So much for missing me," Annie said. "He probably thinks he's master of the shop now."

Sara opened the shutters and ran a finger across the glass. "Don't believe it. He howled every morning when I came to let him out." She wiped her finger on her apron. "How can so much dust accumulate in only two weeks? Where's a bucket?"

"In the back under the sink. I'll get vinegar from the kitchen."

"Rags, too."

"Yes, missus, anything you say, missus." Annie dived for the inner house door, tears blinding her. *Strong. I have to be strong. Little Hank depends on me.*

Annie's legs turned to wilted dandelions and she hit the floor, dust poofing around her. She shouldn't cry. She was sick of crying.

"Hey, the bucket's not there—oh, Annie. Annie, come on." Sara plopped next to her and rocked them both. "It'll be okay. You're tough, like shoe leather. You can do it."

Annie's sob turned into a laugh. "Was that supposed to be a compliment?" She reached for her handkerchief.

Sara laughed too. "It didn't come out right. But you are. My sister would be a useless lump through all this."

"Holly, the dressmaker's model?" Annie blew her nose.

"She shrieks when she breaks a fingernail. Makes me sick."

"She's beautiful, Sara." Annie wiped her eyes, grateful for the distraction of Sara's younger sister. "The minute she turns sixteen she'll marry a rich innkeeper and demand her own personal maid."

"Poor man." Sara stood and brushed the dust off her trousers. "Run some water over your face and tell me where you hid the bucket."

The kitchen pump groaned and squealed, but finally produced clear water. Annie dried her face with a towel from the cupboard, and remembered. "Try the shelf by the back door."

Sara cleaned the windows, singing a drinking song about beer and Midsummer nights. After a few shaky tries, Annie joined her on the choruses in between totaling bills.

Half an hour later, the blacksmith came through the door and blocked out the morning sun. "Good morning, Missus. Sorry about Hank. Glad to see the place open again." He shook Annie's hand. "I'm afraid I had to get my new bellows in Liberty. You were closed longer than I thought you'd be."

"That's all right, Roy. You ordered something before Carnival, didn't you?"

"Three leather aprons, Missus. But maybe Hank didn't get them done before he, that is, well—"

Annie turned to the shelves behind her. "That's right. Yes, we have them." She spread the top apron on the counter.

Roy nodded. "Wider around the upper back. Just the way I like them." He placed six one-dollar coins in Annie's hand. "Always good doing business with Hank—uh—you know what I mean. Good day, Missus." He scooped the aprons into his huge arms and dashed out.

Annie gave a crooked smile to his vanishing back. One sale completed. She could do this.

Sara said from the doorway, "That man needs a wife. He's twenty, at least."

"Not while his sister's still living with him."

Old Milly the weaver knocked on the doorframe an hour later. Annie leaned the broom against the wall and smiled at her.

"I'm so, so sorry about Hank," Milly said, clutching and patting Annie's hands. Snippets of thread dropped from Milly's sleeve to the counter with every pat. "But I'm glad you have a few childbearing years left to find a new husband."

Annie tried to extract her hands, but decided against it. If her hands were free she'd slap the woman's interfering, froglike face, which would be bad for business.

Milly's lips changed from a sympathetic pout to a toothy smile. "Do you have my order of white leather buttons?"

"Of course. That'll be two-fifty."

When Annie closed the door behind Milly, the weaver was already yoo-hooing Jacob the bookseller, who was standing in his shop's doorway.

"Sara, how does that woman stay in business?"

"Because everyone wants her basket weave linen cloth. And speaking of childbearing," Sara put her hands on Annie's rounding stomach. "Little guy, give me good luck in making a playmate for you, Redeemers willing."

Annie squeezed Sara's hands. "What if it's a girl?"

"She'll have even more sympathy for my wish." Sara walked to the house door and looked in. "Eleven-twenty. Lunch?"

"Just let me get one of the belt forms from the shop. Max's is practically worn through."

"He'll love you. Will you make a carrot cake for supper?"

"Sure. Come and tell me what color he wants." Annie led the way through the house to the worktables. She kept expecting to hear Hank's voice back here, singing his favorite working song. Or trading bad jokes with Max over a beer in the kitchen.

*I'm tough. I can do this.*

She stretched above her head. "Hank always keeps these too high. I think he did it so he could lift me up and tickle me." Annie swallowed hard and pulled down a narrow wooden box, knocking off two smaller boxes with it.

"Got one." Sara blew dust off the lid and opened it. "Kid-sized shoelaces."

The other box opened on its way down and its contents spilled over Annie's feet. "Scraps." She picked up a thick square of calfskin. "Wait. This one's a packet."

"What's in it?" Sara reached for it.

Annie snatched it away. "I don't know. Letters, maybe. It's the right size."

*Hank saved all the letters I wrote when he was away buying supplies? He always was romantic under that tough surface.*

She picked out the knot in the string holding it together. Her hands trembled a little as she unfolded four thin flaps from the center. Sara put a hand over hers, but Annie shook it off. "I'm fine." That wasn't a catch in her voice, either.

One thin piece of paper lay in the center of the soft leather square. It was ragged around the edges and heavily creased. Some of the words on it had faded and been re-inked.

*Not my letters.* Annie's heart clenched.

"What's it say?" Sara whispered.

"I can't read it. Here, come over to the window." Annie tilted it to catch the shiny black ink. "But the examination of a good conscience towards God by the resurrection of Jesus Christ, who is on the right hand of God, swallowing down death, that we might be made heirs of life everlasting."

She looked up at Sara. "What on earth does that mean?"

# CHAPTER TWO

Annie stared at the paper, then at Sara. "God? Christ? Are those supposed to be names? How do you swallow death?"

Sara shrugged. "You got me. Sounds like it's from one of those experimental books what's-her-name keeps writing."

"Who? Oh, her. She's weirder than this." Annie fingered the paper. "Why did—"

"Why did Hank keep it hidden?" Sara's question overlapped Annie's.

*I thought we didn't have secrets from each other. He must have been planning to tell me about it. Maybe it's a keepsake, with some kind of special meaning to Hank's family.*

"Hello?" Sara snapped her fingers between Annie's nose and the paper.

Annie flinched. "Sorry. It must be a secret family thing, like a word-puzzle, maybe."

"Or maybe Hank wrote poetry in secret."

Annie almost laughed. "Hank hated poetry. No, this is too well taken care of and on an expensive piece of calfskin."

Sara rubbed the leather between two fingers. "Are you sure? Oh, wait. Of course you're sure."

Annie reread the paragraph. "I know most of these words, but the paragraph still doesn't make any sense."

Sara replaced the shoelace box on the top shelf. "Can we talk about it over lunch? And Max likes dark green, pine tree green."

"Right. I know there's one in there." Annie rummaged in the belt box. "Here we go. Does he like plain or designs better?"

"Plain. Says it makes him look slimmer."

"And you want me to make carrot cake?" Annie folded the calfskin package and slipped it in her trouser pocket before setting the other two boxes on a lower shelf. "Maybe Jacob will know what this is."

Sara pointed to Annie's already full bookshelf as they walked back through the house. "He'll talk in circles 'til you can't think straight and then sell you a book on making flutes from bones or something weird."

"I meant to buy every book on those shelves, thank you." Annie locked the door behind them. "Besides, I want information, not a bargain. Jacob loves mysteries. He'll be clay on my pottery wheel."

\* \* \*

After the carrot cake was in the oven, Annie threw a cloak over her clothes and headed through the crowd in the butcher shop. Max was wrapping a ham and Sara taking the money for a rabbit. Dinner shoppers crammed the market square. The dairy farmer was just selling the last of his cheese and butter. The blacksmith's apprentice pushed past her on the front step, the skinned rabbit bouncing on his back.

Annie headed west, the setting sun just visible from beneath the edge of a heavy layer of clouds. She passed the grocer's and the weaver's and entered the bookseller's. The grocer's apprentice and the glassblower's oldest daughter sat at one of the reading tables, arguing over the latest installment in *The Weaver's Web* books.

"Jacob?" Annie called.

The bookseller's shaggy gray head popped up from behind a stack of books. A cloaked and hooded Redeemer sat next to him.

Jacob squinted at her. "Annie! Just one minute."

Annie opened that week's newspaper and watched Jacob and the Redeemer from the corner of her eye. Redeemers seldom left their abbeys, probably because they didn't want to hear people saying, 'Redeemers willing, we'll have a good harvest' right in front of them, like Redeemers weren't human. She turned to the paper's recipe page. Had she ever seen anyone speak to a Redeemer, other than a bookseller or blacksmith for business? And thanking them at Carnival, of course. She couldn't picture it happening. Saving humanity from extinction must make it hard to carry on a normal conversation, even two hundred years after the fact.

The Redeemer took a bundle of paper and three bottles of ink and left by the back door.

Jacob stood. "What can I do for you, my dear?" His brown shirt and trousers hung like sacks on his skinny six-foot body.

"I have a mystery for you." She pulled the leather square from her trouser pocket and opened it. "I found this in Hank's shop. I've never seen anything like it." She held out the scrap of paper.

He took it lightly in his hands and moved beneath the hanging lamp over the bargain books table. *The Weaver's Web* readers glanced at him and lowered their voices.

After a few minutes, Jacob turned to Annie with a scowl. "I thought I knew old books." He pulled a carved wood pen from behind his ear and tapped his remaining teeth with it. "No one knows how to make paper this smooth. I can't even feel the imprint of the letters."

She put her head next to his as he moved the paper every which way to bring out the words.

"I don't like defeat," he said. "This little paper will not get the best of me."

Annie smiled. "That's why I'm here."

He tapped his teeth some more. "We need Colorado Springs for this. Any history worth knowing is archived there. Leave it with me, Annie. I'll write to the historians tomorrow. I'll make them curious enough to send for it."

Annie touched his arm. "I just found it today, Jacob. Let me puzzle over it for awhile myself." She held out her hand for the paper.

"But, Annie—"

"It was Hank's, Jacob. I'm not ready to let it go just yet."

"All right." He returned the paper, defeat showing on his face. "I see you reopened today."

"There's no one else to do it but me." She tucked away the leather packet. "Besides, I'll have a baby to support soon."

Jacob squinted at her stomach. "Excellent, Annie. You need a new husband, then."

Annie bit her tongue. She liked Jacob, but what was it with everyone over forty nagging her about husbands?

"Not right away, Jacob. But if I need a matchmaker, I'll let you know."

Jacob's squint vanished. "Redeemers forbid it. Milly is the

marriage expert." He shuddered. "Last year, she came in here every week for six months pretending to want the newspaper."

Annie suppressed a smile. "And she really wanted you?"

"That was the worst spring and summer of my life." He walked Annie to the door. "If you need me to write those letters, all you have to do is ask."

"I'll let you know."

Cold, thick fog pulsed through the streets as she walked back to Sara's. Her teeth were chattering by the time she opened the house door.

The mingled aroma of carrot cake and baked ham reached her. Annie tossed her cloak at the nearest chair and ran into the kitchen. A moment later, she set the just-finished cake onto the counter and Sara appeared in the doorway.

"You beat me to it. What did Jacob say?"

"I'll tell you over supper. That ham smells done."

\* \* \*

Annie washed and Sara dried after supper while Max ate another piece of cake.

"I'm going home tonight, Sara." Annie handed her the last plate.

"Are you sure?" Sara set it in the sideboard. "You know you can stay here as long as you want."

"I know. But now's the time. We cleaned everything. It's as ready as it's going to be. The little guy and I need to make the place our home again." She patted her stomach. "Oh—little Hank kicked. I felt him."

Sara put her hand next to Annie's. "I don't feel anything."

"It was a flutter, kind of. Like baby bird wings." She held her breath. "There. He did it again."

Sara shook her head. "Still can't feel it. He must be too small yet." She squeezed Annie. "Go home if you need to, but be back here at eight for breakfast."

"Yes, missus." Annie looked over at Max. "Spice cookies for supper tomorrow?"

Max finished the last bite of cake. "Now I know why Harris Baker complained for weeks after you quit to be a leatherworker with Hank. Put raisins in them and you've got a deal."

Sara walked Annie to the door. "You still have a nightgown and toothbrush at home, right?"

Annie nodded. "I checked this afternoon." She put her hand on the latch.

Sara covered it with hers. "You know, about Hank's paper..."

Annie frowned. "Yes?"

"If you don't mind, I'd kind of like to read it again."

They'd left the lamp in the kitchen, so Annie couldn't see Sara's face. She wanted to. She'd never heard her sound shy before.

"Why?"

Sara shrugged. "It's interesting. It almost makes me want to dig out my mom's old poetry books."

"Your mom wrote poetry?"

"I found them after she died. So, anyway, can I borrow it for tonight?"

Annie reached into her pocket with her free hand. *Weird ending to a weird day. When Sara doesn't act like herself it's time to go to sleep so today becomes a nice, normal tomorrow.*

"Sure." She handed the calfskin packet to Sara. "See you at eight."

Sara clutched it. "Thanks. I'll take good care of it."

Annie paused on the step for a minute after Sara closed the door behind her. Fog poured down the empty street like dye into a vat. So much for spring: Her teeth chattered already. She ran across the street but stopped at her own front step. A bulky shadow crouched in the inn's vegetable gardens. She took a step toward it. Better make sure; she could always run back to Sara's.

The fog shifted and thickened. She stepped closer. Nothing there now. Spooked, she dropped her key on the first attempt to open the kitchen door. She looked over her shoulder. Still nothing. She unlocked it on the second try, jumped inside and slammed it shut.

*Hank would laugh at me. He loved telling ghost stories at Midsummer.*

She stood with a hand on the kitchen table, waiting for her breathing to slow. As her heart stopped galloping, the baby fluttered again.

"Don't worry, little guy. We're going to be okay."

The clock chimed eight-thirty. Her teeth started chattering again. *A cold breeze? The door must've slammed off the latch.*

She turned around.

Two shapes in brown hooded cloaks stood in the doorway.

Annie opened her mouth to say "Who are you?" as the nearest one glided toward her.

*Was he walking or floating? Don't be silly. You can't float on fog.*

He seized her arms and the second one moved forward until his face was inches from hers. She saw a grim, compressed mouth and blue eyes before his hand brought up a needle. Its end glistened.

She screamed as he stabbed it into her neck.

# Chapter Three

Annie touched her hands to the floor. Stone. Why was she lying on stone? She opened her eyes.

A small, dingy room: stone walls and floor, rotting wood ceiling. One narrow door with an iron grating in the top. What light there was came through the grate from a lamp hung outside on the opposite wall.

Her neck twinged when she turned her head. She lifted one hand to it and found a small, painful bump on the side.

She sat up with a gasp. The room spun. She put her head between her knees and took several deep breaths. When her head settled, she got to her feet and stumbled to the door. She pushed and pulled but it merely rattled.

"Hello? What's going on?"

Her voice echoed. She stood on tiptoe and pressed her face against the grating. The lamp revealed a narrow hall on the right and an open doorway at the edge of her sight on the left.

She sat down with her back to the door, knees to chin, and tried to cover her bare feet with the bottoms of her trouser legs.

"Wait a minute. Where did my shoes and socks go?" Her wobbly voice resonated in the stone room. She sneezed and the bump on her neck throbbed.

"They drugged me." The fear rushed back. She jumped up and pounded on the door. "Hey! Let me out! Hey! Hey!" After several minutes, her hands hurt too much to continue and she slid down against the door again. The chill gray walls closed in on her.

*They looked like Redeemers.*

She tried to stop the thought. Not Redeemers. Never Redeemers. They inspired awe and gratitude and respect. They weren't cheap thugs from a bad Last War novel.

Then who kidnapped her? What were they going to do to her? She began to shake.

* * *

*Water.*

*She dunks her face into her cleaning bucket and slurps.*

*The bottom vanishes and her entire head plunges in. Her throat floods. She chokes.*

* * *

Annie opened her eyes. She lay face down in a cold puddle in the middle of the cell. She coughed and sat up, spitting water and dirt. Several more drops splashed in her eyes and on her face. Thunder rumbled through the walls.

Rain. She moved out from underneath the leak in the ceiling. What building in Kansas City had a bad roof? If she was still in Kansas City.

*Don't think like that. Drink.*

She tried to catch the drops on her swollen tongue, but she was weak and shaky from lack of food and sleeping on the cold stone floor. Instead, she cupped her hands and caught a mouthful. Her nose wrinkled. It smelled like old stone. She touched her tongue to it. Tasted like old stone too. She drank it anyway.

She yawned and her lips cracked. How long had she been here? If she calculated it by hunger, it had to be two or three days. She wished there was a clock down that dark hall.

She pushed herself to her feet and pressed her face against the grille again. The lamp burned high and clear and it had a new wick. She wasn't alone, then, wherever she was. If her throat weren't so sore, she'd yell down the hall for a cup of coffee and a stack of pancakes.

*You're trying to distract yourself with food. Keep thinking about how to get out of here.*

A small flutter answered her.

"I know, little guy. I'm hungry too. I'm working on it." Her lips cracked and blood trickled down her chin. "We'll get both of us fed soon."

A breeze tickled her left ear.

Annie jerked around and the room spun. She fell back against the door until it settled right way up, then got on hands and knees. *Whatever it takes, no matter how weak I am.* She crawled along the wall in the direction of the breeze, gritting her teeth against every scrape of her knees along the grimy floor. At the first corner she felt a current of fresh air and her fingers probed the crumbling mortar between two stones.

A way out. She scoured the floor for something to chip away at the weak spot, but only a few shards of stone littered the empty floor. *Fine. Whatever I need to use.*

Annie licked more blood from her lip. "We're getting out, little Hank."

The room filled with small tapping sounds as fragments of mortar littered the floor at her knees. The breeze increased. She was sure of it. As she dug deeper with the thin piece of stone, it snapped into fragments.

The door rattled and swung open. Annie spun around and stood, swaying a moment, to face whatever was coming.

Five Redeemers entered the cell and stood in a row before her.

*No. Not Redeemers. They're only dressed like them.* The one on her right said, "Love your enemies, do good to them that hate you, bless them that curse you, and pray for them that calumniate you."

His voice chilled her more than the stone under her bare feet. No one moved. The breeze puffed against the backs of her knees.

Annie licked her lips. "Who are you? Do the Redeemers know you're imitating them? Why are you keeping me here?"

Two of them grabbed her arms and threw her to the floor.

"Help! Somebody help me—" She kicked the one at her feet before he clamped her ankles together and nodded to the rest. She spat at him, but nothing came out of her parched mouth.

Four of them hoisted her to their shoulders and sang, "De profundis clamavi ad te Domine."

"Let me go—" She thrashed and squirmed as the fifth one led them out of the windowless room. Her breaths came shorter and sharper. Cold sweat covered her forehead. Lamplight showed her only a termite-riddled ceiling.

*Don't show them you're afraid.* "Who are you? Where am I?"

"Quia apud te propitiation..." They carried her through a

doorway and she gagged at the stench of rotting meat. She jerked her head to the left and saw a row of lamps and statues of people on a long wall. A huge, dark, empty room opened on her right.

"People don't just disappear. My friends will be looking for me." They kept singing. Her throat clogged and tried to choke her. "So will Jacob. He wants that paper I found." The hands tightened their grip. Long fingernails dug into her arm.

*A woman? Who were these freaks?*

They stopped in front of a wide table. Two wooden boards shaped like a T lay on its mottled surface.

"Shut up." Annie tried to raise her voice above theirs. "Stop that sing-song and talk to me."

"...anima mea in verbum eius..."

They wrestled her down onto the boards. The song picked up sharps and flats as she clawed at their arms and hands and got in one good kick to someone's knee. Two of their hoods slipped backward in the scuffle, almost revealing their faces.

Splinters pricked the backs of Annie's hands and her heels as she bucked up and sideways. Maybe she could make them afraid. "The Redeemers will find out—you can't dress up like them and kidnap people—aargh—and get away with it." *Why wouldn't they stop singing?*

"...ex omnibus iniquitatibus eius." They paused. "Amen."

The leader moved to the end of the table and spoke. "The soldiers therefore took the garments, and they made four parts, to every soldier a part." Then he picked up a knife from the floor and slit her shirt up the middle.

*Oh no, oh no, oh no.*

He reached across her and cut open her sleeves. She kicked and jerked and squirmed, but that merely gave the others room to pull the ruined shirt away. The leader snagged the knife in each trouser leg and cut through them and her underwear. Despite her efforts he tugged everything out and dropped it.

"Please—" She tried to see the woman's eyes beneath the hood. "Don't let them do this." All four leaned forward and compressed her arms and legs onto the wood. She tried to shove herself off. "What's wrong with you? Please stop them."

The leader held up her shirt and sliced it into two pieces, then did the same to her trousers, folded each piece and set them on the floor. When he rose into her line of vision again, he held a battered mallet and four nails.

A new terror grabbed Annie. "Somebody help me!" Echoes garbled her words.

The woman twisted Annie's right hand palm up. The leader placed a nail at the base of her palm. Her head cleared when the point pierced her skin. He raised the mallet above his head.

Annie tried to scream 'Stop' but it stuck in her throat. She wrenched up her head but couldn't budge her shoulders or arms.

The mallet swung down in a quick arc and drove the nail through her wrist and into the wood.

She shrieked. White-hot flames blazed up her arm and into her head. The mallet *clanked* on the nail again as she screamed and writhed. Her squelching flesh muffled the third blow. Blood splattered her face and hair.

He pricked her left wrist with another nail. A brief rush of air touched her as the mallet descended and the nail pierced her with a *clang*.

Blood flew into her left eye and the world turned red. Her screams bounced off the ceiling and back at her. He pounded in that nail with two more strokes. Warmth bubbled into her throat and she vomited bile and blood over her face and chest.

Their hands bent her legs and placed her feet flat on the rough wood. Annie opened her eyes and saw a third nail, longer than the ones pinning her hands to the crossbeam, through a red mist. The leader positioned it where the top of her foot met her ankle.

Her shrieks smothered the ring of iron on iron. Her leg and arms felt like kindling in a bonfire. Her back arched and pulled on her hands and she collapsed, choking and sobbing.

"Help—someone help—"

Her rolling eyes followed a trail of her blood dripping down the leader's brown robe. Black fog crushed her. The lamps faded.

Her cheek stung. A slap. Her other cheek stung. Fire crackled up her leg and along her arms. She gasped and opened her eyes.

The woman's hand hovered over her face.

Annie moaned. The hand gestured toward her feet. She followed it through a reddish-gray haze. The leader raised the mallet.

"No—"

He nailed her right foot to the wood, splattering her blood and flesh with three final blows of the mallet. Her world shrank into those four cold wedges of iron.

The executioners lifted the wood and carried their handiwork to the wall. Pain like molten glass surged through Annie, flooding her head. More bile choked her as her body swayed and dipped.

She moaned and gasped as they heaved her against the wall just above four horizontal brackets. The leader nodded. They dropped the crossed planks into the brackets.

Annie's body jerked down and forward and thrust her feet and wrists against the nails. She choked on another scream and vomited blood on her legs. The shudders and heaves drove hundreds of knives into her.

*Stop. Stop moving.*

Her head cleared enough to hear her tormentors recite: "For those whom he did foreknow, he also did predestinate to be conformed to the image of his son."

*What does that...?* Her legs twitched and a cry turned into a hacking cough.

The leader turned away and gathered up the pieces of Annie's clothes. The others lifted lamps off their hooks. The leader stopped in front of her and said, "There was darkness."

Annie's head buzzed and throbbed and the four of them seemed to float through the shrinking and expanding doorway. When the leader entered it, she moaned. "No."

*They're leaving me alone. Alone in the dark to die.*

The light faded as he said, "And with a loud voice gave up the ghost."

He vanished and they began to sing again.

"Victimae paschali laudes immolent Christiani..." Their voices faded a moment later.

*They must've passed the cell door already.* Tears fell down Annie's cheeks onto her thighs. She sobbed once and her heart thudded. She couldn't breathe.

*Move.* Her lungs burned. *Move.*

She tried. The only option was to push upward against the nails in her feet. Her legs knotted with cramps, but the pressure on her chest eased. She breathed in the dense reek of rotting flesh and choked.

Her eyes opened. *I can still see.*

She leaned her head back against the wood. Sunlight angled through a crack in the distant ceiling. Her arms went numb and the rotting-meat stink faded. The board swayed behind her and dust motes swirled around her, dancing along her arms. Her head lolled onto her left shoulder to watch them — and looked straight into the liquefied eyes of a decaying body nailed to another T-shaped support. She gasped and her body sagged. The skin around the nails in her hands tore further and more of her blood spilled onto the floor. A harsh moan burst from her throat. Blood welled into her mouth. She spat. Her head cleared.

She had to look. She had to make sure she wasn't losing her mind. She struggled up again. A maggot burrowed through the corpse's face and dropped onto the floor. She gulped down bile and turned her head to the right.

A dried-out skull's empty eye sockets stared at her.

She jerked away from it and a scalding flood washed through her, starting at her nailed wrists. Her control broke and she slid downward.

*These people have strange tastes in wall decorations.* A bleak laugh from her own mouth surprised her. *Wonder who I'll scare when I'm rotting up here?*

Her choppy, gasping laugh ratcheted higher, louder. It didn't matter. The noise wouldn't bother her neighbors. She pushed up and for a moment laughed so hard the wood rattled and tears washed the blood from her eyes.

More melted-glass agony smothered her and she stopped laughing. "Help—me—"

# CHAPTER FOUR

Annie held herself up. *Need air.* In—out—feet throbbing—in—out. Blood streamed over her toes and stars sparkled before her eyes. She liked the stars. So pretty. Her legs bent. Splinters pierced her backside. Her shoulders and back cramped and shuddered, tugging her wrists against the nails. She coughed and spat frothy blood.

*How long have I been here?*

She pushed up. Three...four...five...six... Her ears filled with rushing wind and the shaft of sunlight at the edge of her vision faded. She sagged.

She blinked and saw sunlight on the floor again. And something else. Lots of somethings crawling over the shining, red floor.

*That's my blood.* Her stomach flopped. *It looks like gallons. Why aren't I dead already?*

The moving floor split into dozens of furry gray bodies. One reared up and put its paws on the wood. Its whiskers twitched. It licked her toe.

"Get away."

The rat splashed back into the puddle. The others snapped at it until it found its own territory and lapped with the rest.

Phantom knives sliced her arms and legs again. She turned her head to see that the skeleton had pulled out its nails. With a clattering laugh it leaned over and gouged her with them.

"Stop." Her voice grated in her throat. A wet chuckle made her turn to the left. Maggots fell from the corpse's grinning lips and its stinking breath fogged over her.

She coughed and retched, but nothing came up. "Shut—up. You're dead." Bloody saliva dribbled from the corners of her mouth. The laughter stopped.

If she looked again, would it talk to her?

*Annie.*

She jumped. This time the imaginary boiling glass swamped her arms and legs. Sledgehammers pounded her temples. She tried to push up and failed. Her lungs screamed at her.

*Breathe! Ignore the voice!* She pressed all her weight on her feet.

"Please—" She didn't know who she was pleading with. Her legs trembled and collapsed. "Please..." The room rushed away from her. The molten glass cooled and she floated away from the nails.

*Annie.*

She knew that voice.

It didn't matter. Nothing hurt anymore. The sparkles played glowing fiddles and danced a jig around her and she laughed and kicked her right leg across her left at the next measure.

Her body snapped back onto the wood. Her legs convulsed.

*Push!*

She managed it in between spasms. Cold, putrid air filled her nose and chest. She whimpered with relief and then moaned as the nails rasped her feet. Blood ran over her toes.

So tired.

Just slide down. Give up.

*Annie.*

She bent her knees a fraction, but braced her feet against the nails to keep breathing.

"I said—shut—up!" She opened her eyes.

A tall man with long black hair stood in front of her, awls in each hand, and wearing a familiar leather apron.

"Hank?" Her mouth hung open for a moment and her shoulders scraped down the wood. She hissed and pushed up a bit. "You're dead."

He grinned. *You can't breathe, can you? A good husband always helps.*

"What?"

He plunged the awls into her feet.

She shrieked and her back arched. Her right shoulder popped and she slewed to her left.

"Ha—Hank—" Blood gushed from her wrists. Her muscles blazed like a midsummer bonfire. She tried to say his name again, but only sobs came out. In a few seconds, she'd sobbed out all the air from her lungs.

She shoved against the nails, but her dislocated shoulder strained and crunched. She sobbed again. "Hank—"

A new pain ripped her stomach. Again, and her legs folded. She'd thought her voice was beyond screaming, but a crackling shriek echoed around her. Again—like a knife carving her. Her eyes saw only red haze and white bursts. Hot, slimy wetness glopped onto her heels.

*Redeemers help me, it hurts—*

Another long, twisting stab in her stomach while more hot, thick globs splattered her heels and plopped into the blood on the floor. Then the pain faded and her vision cleared.

Three black masks faced her.

She gasped and pushed back against the wood. "Get away."

Two hands reached out and gripped her right bicep. She wailed as her arm jerked. A hand gripped the wood near her right wrist. Another hand raised a pair of pliers to the nail and yanked.

She opened her mouth to shriek and the room vanished.

\* \* \*

Annie opened her eyes. She lay on her back. A low ceiling. Candlelight. She blinked a few times.

A face in a black mask leaned over her.

"No." She flung out her arms to push the face away, but the flames shot through her and she went limp.

"Stop moving. I won't hurt you." The mask muffled a feminine voice.

Annie opened her eyes again and raised her arms. Blood oozed through bandages around her wrists.

"They—nailed—me—to the wood." She stared at the green eyes within the mask. "Am I dead?"

"No. You're very much alive, and I've been up for two nights running to make sure you stayed that way." She unwrapped the bandages from Annie's right wrist, and wiped away the fresh blood.

*That burns...and it's cold...salve.* She stared at the ceiling. *I'm breathing.* Sweat dripped down her face and she clenched her teeth as the bandage came off her other wrist. *She held my arm... he swung the mallet...* Her arms and legs convulsed at the memory. She clamped her lips together, but the moans broke through.

Her hand dropped to the bed and the mask floated over her. "Drink this."

The woman held a glass to Annie's lips and she swallowed bitter water. A minute later the room blurred and began to sway.

*That was a drug... They still have me... Someone help...*

\* \* \*

"Wake up."

A hand slapped Annie's cheek. Her eyes opened and saw another mask.

"No! Let me go!" She tried to get up, but someone held her down. She started coughing.

"Quiet."

A man's hairy hand put a glass to her mouth and she swallowed plain water.

He still held her down with his other hand. "You were screaming. I had to stop you. Sorry I hit you."

A candle flickered wildly near her. His eyes gleamed. She tried to scoot backwards but collapsed with a moan.

"Listen. This room is below the vegetable garden so the plants can hide the air holes. I don't know how much the sound carries, but I heard you through the door. You have to be quiet."

"They were hammering – were nailing—" Her throat felt like a sanded board.

"A nightmare," he said. "You're safe. I'll leave the candle. Get some sleep."

"Who—"

He was already gone.

Everything was hazy around the edges from the drug, including the waves of melted glass flooding through her.

*They want to kill me... I have to get out...*

\* \* \*

The light looked different this time when she opened her eyes. She turned her head to the right and saw an oil lamp on a table next to the bed. The woman sat in a narrow chair reading a book.

She stared at the mask. It covered the entire head like an oversize winter hat with the brim unrolled down to the neck. It had to be thin cloth to let her breathe and talk without nose or mouth holes.

"You were out almost two days again," the woman said, closing the book. She put a hand on Annie's forehead. "Fever's finally down. I'll be right back."

Annie's throat still felt like someone had scraped matches inside it. Tiny somethings pricked her shoulder blades and butt, too. Then the familiar liquid agony swamped her arms and legs.

The door opened and the aroma of chicken soup distracted her for a moment.

"You need something in your system besides the painkiller," the woman said. She set down the bowl and moved Annie to a half-sitting position. The blanket slipped off Annie's bare chest and the woman tucked it around her again.

"Glass," Annie gasped through clenched teeth.

"What?"

"Furnace. Liquid glass—burning—" She moaned.

"Oh, the pain." The woman picked up the bowl and held a spoonful of soup to Annie's lips. "Swallow this. I'll give you more medicine as soon as you finish it all."

Annie gulped the soup. It soothed her throat, but she tasted her own tears with it after the fourth spoonful.

"Almost done," the woman said. "Two swallows to go."

She forced down the last of the soup. Her ears were playing tricks on her again—she could hear the molten iron hissing into her feet and wrists. The cupful of soup bubbled into her throat, but the woman had the glass ready. Annie drank, choked, and snorted some out her nose.

"It's valerian and dried poppy," the woman said, "with some other herbs to heal you up and keep the fever away. We're going to switch to chamomile, but not until you stop screaming." She laid her down on the pillow.

The room tilted. Annie gagged and pressed her hands on her stomach.

"Don't." The woman caught her arms and rubbed her stomach for her for a moment. "Okay now?"

"...think so."

"The drug will start working any minute."

"Where..."

"You're in a hidden room in our cellar."

She stared at the woman's eyes, then looked past them at the mask.

The woman nodded. "I'm sorry about the masks, but they're necessary. We need to keep ourselves secret from everyone."

Annie wanted to ask the woman her name, but the poppy got to her first.

# CHAPTER FIVE

"I'm awake," Annie said as the door opened.

"I have soup and tea and painkillers," the woman said as she closed the door.

Now that she wasn't drugged into oblivion, Annie realized she hadn't felt the baby kick. It didn't really worry her because every other part of her throbbed. Little Hank wasn't big enough yet to be felt over the rest of her shredded body.

Her feet pulsed and twitched and pulsed some more. She'd fingered one bandaged wrist with the other hand in the middle of the night and knives, hammers, and nails pounded and sliced both arms.

The last nightmare had circled over and over at the Hank hallucination. If the awls, somehow, some way, had actually stabbed her, how big would the holes be? Her imagination infested them with maggots. Sometimes the maggots laughed.

The woman rearranged the sheets around her chest and Annie clenched her legs. "I have a problem."

The woman showed the first emotion Annie had seen. She snickered. "Sorry." She put a hand over the bottom of the mask. "That just sounded funny."

Annie scrunched her forehead. "Oh. I'm one big problem from head to toe." She attempted a smile, but failed.

"So what's the trouble?"

"I need to pee." Her bladder ached worse as soon as she said it. What was she going to do? She couldn't get up. Would the woman put a—please, no—diaper on her?

"We're all prepared for that," the woman said. She knelt and took a shallow bowl from beneath the table. "I'll scoot this under you."

Annie wanted to dig a hole in the floor and disappear.

"Don't try to push with your heels," the woman said, folding back the blanket and sliding one hand under Annie's hips. "Just let me lift you up a bit. There."

Nothing in Annie's entire life had ever been this embarrassing. "Could you turn around?"

"You want me to hold this in place, I think." The woman put her arm between Annie's legs and held the bowl rim. "Go ahead."

Heat crept over Annie's cheeks, but she closed her eyes and used the bowl. The woman removed it, said, "This is cold," and cleaned her with a damp cloth. She opened the door and set the bowl and cloth outside.

When she returned to Annie's side, she looked down at her a moment. "Are you blushing?"

Annie tried for a smile and one side of her mouth inched upward. "I don't have enough blood left for that."

The mask over the mouth wrinkled. Was the woman smiling twice in one visit?

"That was almost a joke. Good for you." She lifted Annie by the armpits and sat her against the pillows. "How about some soup?"

She swallowed a spoonful. It slipped down her abraded throat and warmth blossomed in her stomach. She closed her eyes and sighed.

"Here, poppy now."

A few minutes later Annie drifted on a serene drug river. The knives and hammers, now locked behind fences, stomped and cursed her from distant banks.

The woman gave her tea. Its strength and sweetness brought her back. She splashed out of the river. She wanted a sense of time and place again.

"I have lots of questions."

The woman nodded.

"Where am I?"

The mask shook. "I can't tell you."

"Why not?" She pinched her lips together and counted to five.

"Am I still in Kansas City?"

"Yes."

"Is it still 2216?"

"Of course." She gave her more tea. "It's still June, too."

The calendar sloshed around her head. "Sara and I opened the shop... Monday the twenty-ninth." She squeezed her eyes shut. "We found that piece of paper that afternoon... I think..." She looked at the woman. "Tell me the date."

"It's the ninth."

Annie tried to calculate, but the numbers winked in and out like fireflies. "I lost so many days." She sipped tea. "Will you tell me your name?"

"No."

Annie started to clench her fist, but a knife leaped the fence and flew toward her. "I'm tired of thinking of you as 'the woman.'"

"Think of me as your nurse."

"Are you?"

Another shake. "That's cheating. Finish your tea."

She met the woman's eyes. "Not yet. Listen. They dressed like Redeemers." Once she said it the words wouldn't stop. "They wore warm brown hooded cloaks. The color of spice cake, you know? Comfort food. That's what I always think of when I see Redeemers. They stripped that comfort and tossed it on the floor with my shredded clothes." She coughed but waved away the glass. "The Redeemers are safety and peace and when they came into that little room dressed like them—"

"Wait. You lost me. They who? Which them?"

Another blaze up her legs. It would've been easier to sink down on the wood and suffocate. So easy. No blood. No nightmares. No hammers or bonfires or nails. No nails...

"Annie." The woman picked up the glass. "Drink."

She grimaced at the bitter, gritty liquid. "I mean the ones who tried to kill me. Two of them came into my house that night. They dressed like Redeemers. They didn't talk. One of them grabbed me and the other stuck a dripping needle into my neck."

"And that knocked you out? What about when you woke up?"

"That's not what's important. They pretended to be Redeemers. Don't you get it? Whoever they are, they can go anywhere and no one would think twice about them."

"But I'm sure the Redeemers—"

"The Redeemers are everyone's peace and safety and they're

destroying that. Someone has to tell them. But how? You can't just knock on the abbey door like you're coming for supper. They have to be stopped."

Annie took several deep breaths. The corners of the room were getting fuzzy. She tried to talk faster, but she couldn't feel her lips anymore. "If you knew where I was and how to sneak in and take me down before I died, then you have to know something about these imitation Redeemers." Her tongue grew thicker. "Who are you?"

"I can't tell you that."

"Why not?" Finally she couldn't feel her feet, thank the Redeemers.

"Because it's dangerous for you to know, and for us to tell." The woman picked up the tray. "Don't ask again. As far as everyone knows, you disappeared on the twenty-ninth and your friends are still wondering what happened to you. The current rumor is you couldn't handle the shop on your own and you either ran away to start over or you killed yourself. Anyway, it doesn't matter. No one you know will ever see you again."

The woman tucked the blanket around Annie. "Think of it this way: You're dead."

# CHAPTER SIX

"It's two weeks today," the woman said as she fed Annie buttered toast. "You're improving. The doctor will be pleased."

"I'd like to thank him," she said. "If I could stay awake long enough."

"I'll hold off on the medicine if you can handle it."

"I'll try." She ate the last of the toast. "It's not knocking me out like it used to."

"We cut back the dose. Too much of it is bad for you."

A knock at the door. The woman dusted off her hands and opened it. "She's finally awake at the right time."

"Good morning, Annie." The doctor doubled up his six-foot self to get through the door. His baritone was too big for the little room. His unmasked face beamed at her.

"Quiet," the woman said.

"Sorry," he stage-whispered. "I forgot." A wry smile wrinkled his freckled face and spread curly beard. He sat on the bed. "It's nice to see your eyes open."

"Daniel," she said. "It's really you. I mean, I can see your face."

"I'm the only doctor in Kansas City," he said. "And I refuse to hide my moustache." He twirled the meticulous sandy curl at one end.

Annie discovered she could still smile.

"I'm going to do a test," he said, picking up her right hand.

"What kind of test?"

"To make sure all the pieces and parts work." He unwrapped the bandages, and inspected both sides of her hand. "Very good." He handed the woman the discolored cloth. "Just a single strip to keep the salve on now."

Annie cleared her throat. "I want to see."

He looked at her. "Are you sure?"

"It can't be as bad as I've been imagining." She met his eyes. "Right?"

He shrugged and held up her arm.

A half-inch roundish dent pulsed at the heel of her hand. A sunburst of scabs circled its outer edges, but the entire wound glistened an angry red. She glanced at Daniel, and he turned her arm over. A large area on the perimeter of this wound was shredded and scabbed, but the whole of it also glared and throbbed.

Her hand trembled and her ears tried to trick her into hearing it rip as the wood dropped into the wall brackets. She squeezed her eyes shut but opened them at Daniel's brisk voice.

"Make a very loose fist. Nothing strenuous; I only want to watch your fingers move."

Slowly she curled her thumb inward. The fingers followed. A whisper of flame scampered up her arm. She pressed her lips together and breathed fast and deep.

"Close them completely."

Her fingernails touched her palm.

"Excellent. Now open your hand as far as you can."

She held her breath and stretched her protesting fingers. Ripples of pain danced from shoulder to fingertips.

At last he said, "Relax."

She moaned with the exhale.

"Five working fingers on that hand." He set that arm down and picked up the other. "Let's try the left."

She began to close the fingers on that hand. The ripples were different on this arm. She concentrated on Daniel's face. The ripples became waves and three fingernails touched her palm.

He stared at her hand, brows knit. "Open it," he said.

She looked at her hand. The thumb and first two fingers bent like they should. The last two sat in a half-curl, their tips toward the ceiling. She scowled at them and the first three creaked open. Not the last two. She closed them again. Opened them. The two fingers lay there like they belonged to another hand.

"Stop." He pushed gently on the fingers, bent them down to her palm, and moved them in circles. "Try again."

She stretched her hand to its limit. Waves of pain incinerated her muscles. The last two fingers still didn't move.

He sighed. "I'm sorry, Annie. I was afraid this would happen. The nail severed the tendons. The others work because the damage was able to reknit, but it was too severe for the last two fingers."

"You mean they'll stay like this for the rest of my life? What about my feet? What if I can't walk? How will—"

"We won't know until you try to move them," he said. "Here." He moved to the end of the cot, flipped up the blanket, and cupped her right heel in his hand. "Point your toes."

She jerked her foot forward and yelped. *Slower, idiot.* Bit by bit, she stretched the foot nearly straight.

"Now bend it back toward your head. Now wiggle all your toes." The waves turned into one long, screaming flood.

"All right; that foot works." He set it down and picked up her left. "Point your toes."

She repeated the same three actions. Short, sharp whimpers joined every breath. Tears dripped off her chin.

He set the left foot next to the right. "You will be on your feet in four weeks."

She was so relieved, she laughed. It came out as a croak.

He plucked the water glass from the table and stirred a spoonful of green and white powder into it. "Drink."

After she swallowed it all, he fluffed the pillow around her head.

"I'll be back in a few days," he said. "Remember: don't ask any questions, because you won't get any answers."

The woman took the lamp and went out with him.

For once, Annie didn't mind the dark. She wanted to use it like a blank piece of paper to plan.

She would walk again.

She'd figure out a way to earn a living using one and a half hands.

She would learn who tried to kill her and bring them to justice. Which meant somehow finding a way to speak to a Redeemer, even though she was dead.

Why should she be dead? Because the woman said so?

The woman.

Annie thought fast, before whatever Daniel had fed her turned her brain into sludge.

For these the last two weeks, Annie had used the hours in between nightmares for hard thinking. "The woman" so concerned with hiding her identity seemed to assume Annie was incoherent when awake and unconscious the rest of the time. Big mistake. She put it on in a hurry more than once allowing long blonde hair stuck out from underneath it. Annie put that together with the little the woman allowed herself to say, added in the masked man with hairy hands, and reached the only possible conclusion.

Her head was starting to fray from the drugs. She hooked her nails into the conclusion and breathed it in. Sara and Max. Her best friends since they'd all been in grade school.

And Sara thought if Annie knew it was her under the hood, Annie's knowledge would somehow, in some magical way, lead the hooded killers straight to their house.

So much for trust. So much for friendshop…friendshoop… friendship.

Annie's eyes closed. She dragged the lids open.

*Little Hank, it's you and me now. No one's worth trusting.*

She waited for the baby's answering flutter, but drugged sleep took her first.

# CHAPTER SEVEN

More than Annie wanted fresh air, she wanted out of this fruit cellar with its packed-dirt walls and shoring timbers. She was not a rabbit or mole. She needed sun and grass and the chance of getting either soon was less than zero.

So she worked on the cell she'd been building inside her head. It had grown since she created it one particularly long night after the lamp went out. Nights were just longer copies of the moments after they'd left her hanging and screaming and puking blood on the rats. Carved from a solid piece of stone, windowless, its stone door had no grate to let in any light. Last week she added locks along one side of the door. Even the handle doubled as a lock. When the memories clawed her down into their pit, she took one at a time and flung it into this room and slammed the door on it. Her hands turned the locks one by one, finishing with one deadbolt into the ceiling and one into the floor.

She'd just tossed in a forest's worth of planks shaped like Ts when Daniel bent his very tall self through the door. "The woman" followed him in with a filled lamp and snuffed the candle.

He sat on the side of Annie's narrow bed. "How's the pain?"

She stared at the blue diamond pattern on his shirt. "It's still there, but it's not taking over anymore. Does that make sense?"

"Good." He lifted her arms and checked under the wrist bandages, then folded back the blanket to check her feet.

"Daniel," Annie said when he finished, "all these drugs you've been giving me. They're okay for the baby, right?"

He didn't answer. Annie stopped breathing.

"Annie—"

*Little Hank?* She moved her hand toward her stomach.

The woman grabbed it. "Don't do that. You're not ready."

Daniel said, "Annie, you almost died. I'm sorry. You lost the baby before we could rescue you."

Annie turned her face away and wailed into the pillow. *Little Hank, little Hank, little Hank* rang in her head but no words came from her mouth. Without thinking, she pounded her fists on the mattress. The pain ripped up her arms before the woman stopped her, but it was nothing compared to the horrible emptiness behind her stomach.

*He's gone. He's dead. They killed him.* Her wails escalated into shrieks. Her body shuddered, the wooden bedframe creaking and popping. *Redeemers help me. Help me find them and kill them.*

The woman's voice penetrated her internal din. "Stop. Stop."

The doctor gripped her head with both hands and pushed his face against hers. "Annie. Stop. Now."

Annie gulped, coughed, gulped again, and heaved a deep breath. His face wavered through her tears, his moustache dancing. Above him, the woman held out the glass. He eyed the herbs in it and forced the dose into Annie's mouth.

She drank the bitter liquid in one long swallow. Bitter meant poppy, but she didn't care. She wanted oblivion.

"I'll be back tomorrow," he said as he rearranged the twisted blanket.

Annie didn't answer. After a moment they left her alone with the low flame from the lamp holding off the solid darkness of the room. But not her mind, not the dark memory of the huge space where they left her to die.

She took long, slow breaths, hearing her empty womb echo, willing the poppy to snuff her like a candle.

# Chapter Eight

Three steps across. Ten steps forward. Two steps to the bed. Seven steps along the bed. Repeat.

Ten weeks of this. She despised these walls. She despised this huge, patched red shirt. She'd been talking to herself like there were two Annies in this cold, narrow fruit cellar. Not that she would have begged Sara to talk to her. If Sara and her husband and their friends wanted to consider her dead, she was happy to help. Although why they bothered to rescue her was a riddle she still hadn't solved.

So she nursed her festering hate for the false Redeemers who killed her baby and piggybacked her former friends onto it. She had endless time in this prison beneath Sara's house.

Three steps across. Ten steps forward.

The door opened.

Annie stepped backwards as "the woman" closed it and unrolled a measuring tape with a flip of her wrist.

"Stretch out your arms." Sara wrote down that number and measured hip-to-ankle. "Sit down; I need your foot length."

"Seven and a half inches long, three wide," Annie said, but sat anyway.

The woman read the number by her right thumb. "Eight by three and a half."

"What? I have small feet."

"The nails changed their shape." She measured Annie's other foot. "The bones stretched around them."

After Sara left, Annie stared at the scars on her feet. *Listen to me, whoever you are, wherever you're hiding. I'm not dead and rotting on your wall. I'll find you. I'll even knock on the abbey door to tell the Redeemers where you are. I'll make you pay.*

She shook herself and stood.

Three steps across. Ten steps forward.

\* \* \*

When Sara brought lunch, Annie kept up her pretense of ignorance and said, "May I have a pen and some ink and paper? I need to practice writing."

Sara tilted her head.

"I thought you'd stop talking again." Annie sighed. "I'm going to need a job when I get out of here. I thought a bookseller would work. I don't want to go back to leatherwork or cooking for an inn."

Sara tilted her head the other way.

"I'd have to roll up my sleeves." Annie held out her arms and shook back the sleeves of Max's oversize shirt they'd given her. "See? How would I explain the scars? I can wear long sleeves at a bookseller's. It'll just be hot in the summer."

The woman held up her index finger and left the room. She returned with a stack of paper, a bottle of ink, and two pens, wide and narrow.

Annie steadied a piece of paper with her altered left hand, the last two fingers flopping and useless. She couldn't hide that with long sleeves. At least her right hand survived intact.

*Redeemers curse whoever mutilated me like this.*

She scowled at a page of wobbly letters and illegible words an hour later. She had a long way to go.

\* \* \*

Sara brought new clothes with supper a week later. Two shirts, one sage green, one dark blue; brown trousers, underwear, two pairs of socks, and ankle-high leather boots.

Annie took the blue shirt from her. "They're beautiful."

Sara turned her back while Annie dressed. "Turn around and see." Annie buttoned the sleeves and laced the boots. "The cuffs cover the scars and the trousers are just loose enough." She put a hand on Sara's arm. "Don't go away. I need to talk to you."

Before she finished the sentence, the door opened and Daniel grunted into the room. "I am fast losing patience with this child-size door," he said, stretching his back until it cracked. "All right, Annie, it's graduation time." He stood in the corner and crossed his arms. "Impress me."

Annie walked and then jogged from corner to corner. She pulled the sheets off the bed and remade it. She juggled three knitted exercise balls. Finally, she took Daniel's hands and squeezed with both of hers.

He smiled and nodded. "The scars will start to fade in a few months."

Annie crossed her arms and stood steady on both feet. "If they don't, I'll tell the Redeemers you should be replaced."

The doctor took a step back, but his voice stayed cheerful. "What on earth are you wasting my time for, Annie? I'm a doctor. I need to see sick people."

She grinned.

"It offends my professional pride that I can't parade my greatest medical success around town." He looked into her eyes. "And neither can you."

She nodded. "I know. I was never in this little room and you never helped heal me." She swallowed bitterness. "You couldn't have, because I'm dead."

"Good." He handed her a small green glass jar. "It's the ointment you've been rubbing into the scars. You'll need it for awhile yet. And I have to go."

She stood on tiptoes and kissed his cheek. "Thank you."

"Just doing my job." He crouched to open the door. "I won't miss this rabbit hole."

Annie put her hand on the Sara's arm again. "Wait. What can I do to thank all of you?"

Sara shook her head. "Nothing. You're dead."

Annie kicked the door after Sara closed it. So much for denying anger and her burgeoning hate to do the right thing. *You're lower than pig shit, all of you.*

\* \* \*

When Sara brought supper, she handed Annie a knapsack.

"You're leaving tonight. We'll take you to the outskirts of town. Head for Topeka or Falls City. Never forget they might be looking for you."

"What do you mean?"

"We don't know what they'll do, so don't take any chances. You look a little different, but you might want to change your name."

Annie began rubbing the left-hand scar.

"What are you doing?" Sara pointed to her hands.

She looked down. "I didn't know I was doing it."

"Don't get into that habit. It draws attention."

"Wait a minute. What do you mean, I look different?'

Sara went out and brought back a small, round mirror.

Annie glanced once and threw it face down on the bed. "I look like a moldy carrot. The curls don't hide all those white streaks." She picked up the mirror again. "I could be my own older cousin. A haggard cousin." *I used to be kind of cute. Perky.* "You're wrong. I don't need to change my name." She handed back the mirror and swallowed a sudden rock in her throat.

* * *

Getting kicked out of town. Just like that.

Annie stared at the dirt walls. Did they just inch closer?

*You can't close in on me. You're holding up the house. I'm not afraid of you.*

She set the exercise balls on the little table and picked up the pen and ink bottle.

'Thank you for rescuing me. I did not want to die and rot in that room.

'I've had a lot of time to think, and here's what I've come up with: Everything was normal until I found that page from an old book hidden in Hank's shop. When I brought it to Jacob's, one of the killers must've seen it and me as some kind of threat. So since I need to dig into old books, I'm heading to the Topeka bookseller's first. When I get the answer, I'll break 200 years of tradition and knock on the Redeemers' door with the news. The Redeemers will see that I get revenge for little Hank's death.'

She paused before dipping the pen again. Everything she'd written so far was the expected message of a grateful and compliant patient. Her mouth twisted as she wrote the rest.

'I saw through your disguises weeks ago. Thanks for the important lesson: Trust is for victims. Whoever these hooded killers are, if they track down you and your spineless friends, I leave you with one piece of advice: The only way to breathe when they hang you on the wall is to push up with your feet. It hurts like I guess childbirth might hurt, but I'll never know that for certain now. Enjoy the rest of your lives, Sara and Max.'

\* \* \*

"I have to cover your eyes," Annie's former best friend said.

Annie stared at the black hood in her hand.

"We're not going to hurt you."

*I believe that, if I believe nothing else.* Annie stood back to let Sara cover her head, trembling despite herself.

When it was secure, Sara rested one hand on Annie's back. "I've got the knapsack. Here's the door. Bend over."

Annie walked up twelve steps and through another door, where she smelled the beef stew and fresh bread she'd had for supper. A third door opened and Sara put a hand on her elbow to guide her through.

*Fresh air.*

Annie stopped and sucked in the biggest breath she could. The woman jogged her elbow and they walked. And walked. Annie tripped over something when they turned a corner and big hands caught her. That meant Max was here too. She heard frogs and a nightingale, and smelled the river.

Finally they stopped. Sara pulled off the cloth. They stood just inside the woods at the west end of town, next to the wheat fields. Sara gave her a walking stick and the knapsack.

Annie took one in each hand, reminding herself to be polite. "Thank you."

Max stepped toe-to-toe with Annie. "Listen to me. Never tell what happened. Never mention us. Some of us wanted to leave you up there to die. Don't forget that." He lowered his voice, which wasn't disguised by the mask one bit. "And don't draw attention to yourself or the Redeemers will find you."

"What?"

Sara pulled at him, but he shook her off.

"Don't be stupid. You know it was the Redeemers who took you. Stop lying to yourself."

Annie's head rang. *Not the Redeemers. They couldn't have tortured her. He was wrong.*

Max grabbed her shoulders. "Wake up. The world isn't the comfortable place you thought it was."

*I know that.* "Redeemers forbid the thought."

Sara said, "Yes. Keep using all the traditional sayings. Blend in."

"You lied to me."

Max raised a hand to slap her, but Annie blocked it. "I'm not helpless anymore. Keep your hands off."

His mask nodded. "Good. Fight. Just because we didn't say anything doesn't mean we lied. I wanted to tell you before Midsummer but it wasn't my decision."

Annie wanted to scream at both of them, but she wanted to get away even more. "Anything else?"

"The Redeemers aren't your only problem. Blend in. Be average. Don't give anyone a reason to hunt you." He pointed west. "Now leave."

Sara made a shooing motion at Annie.

She turned her back on them and walked into the trees, searching for an expression nasty enough to throw at them. They had lied. She didn't know. They should've told her. Redeemers curse them both.

She counted twenty trees and looked over her shoulder. The woods already hid Sara and Max, but she heard a few last footsteps. When they faded, she faced west without regret and listened to pine duff crunch under her feet.

She was free.

All she needed to do was find a job, unearth books she'd never heard of, and search them for certain clumsy, formal kinds of writing. Then assemble enough evidence to make it worthwhile to knock on an abbey door and request to speak to the Redeemers themselves.

Well, she had nothing better to do. She was dead.

An owl hooted.

The hooded killers must know she wasn't dead. If not yet, as soon as they took someone else. When they lit the lamps they would see no Annie dripping maggots on the floor.

Not "they." The Redeemers.

The world tilted under her feet when she thought it.

*It's not true. Think of something else. Like who are the other "they" Max meant. No, no, no. That's not a subject for a long night by myself in the woods. Find another topic.*

She clenched her fists, as much as they would clench. Thank the Redeemers she could still walk.

Unless she really did have the Redeemers to thank for using

her like a living piece of lumber. For killing little Hank.

*I'd better practice smiling, because it's my cover. I'll smile and sweet-talk myself into a job and my boss will never guess that I'm my own decoy. I'll find books with those weird-sounding words and draw out—the Redeemers?*

The world tilted again, but she kept walking.

# CHAPTER NINE

Five days later, Annie leaned on the front desk of Topeka's east side inn. She was grubby, her feet burned, and she would've fought wild foxes for a decent meal.

"How much for one room with meals, and please tell me I'm not too late for lunch."

"A dollar a day, and lunch ends in an hour," the innkeeper said.

Annie didn't like his narrow eyes or pinched mouth, but she wasn't about to trek across town to the west side inn. "Here's for the first week." She counted out seven one-dollar coins, a surprise from the bottom of the knapsack.

"Sign, please." He turned the book toward her and dipped the pen.

She wrote 'Annie Cook' and tried not to cringe. It wasn't really a lie—she had been a cook for years.

He brought the book to his nose and his straggly black hair fell onto the page. "Welcome to the East Topeka inn, uh, Missus Cook."

"Just Annie is fine."

"Annie. This way."

He led her up the wide central stairs to a long hall and opened the third door on the left. "Bathroom two doors down on the right."

She tossed her knapsack and stick on the narrow bed. "I'll just wash my hands and go straight down for lunch."

When she opened the bathroom door, he was tapping one foot

on the top step. "This way."

Most of the three dozen dining room tables were filled. Their bright checkered tablecloths and the sound of clinking plates and glasses gave Annie a pang of nostalgia for her old job.

"Fern," the innkeeper called at the doorway. "New table."

A pudgy brunette appeared at Annie's shoulder. "This way. I'm Fern. Chicken soup and sausage bread today. Beer or wine or cider?" She pulled out a chair at a table in the center row.

"Cider, please."

The man and woman at Annie's right looked over at her, and she re-braided her disheveled hair. Fern arrived in the middle of that and set down a tall glass, soup bowl, and plate of steaming bread. Annie's stomach growled.

Fern giggled. "Been traveling awhile?"

"Days. I've had it up to here with gutting fish."

Another giggle. "Roast deer and sweet potatoes tonight. You'll love it. Welcome to Topeka. I wish I had your hair. The white makes you look so mature. Call me if you want more of anything." She swept the plates and mugs from the table at Annie's left.

Annie grimaced. *Mature.* She took a huge bite of sausage bread and concentrated on filling her stomach.

She got her bath after supper and rubbed Daniel's ointment into her scars before she collapsed on the bed. Pillow and sheets never felt so good.

\* \* \*

She woke screaming in the dark, hands and feet throbbing.

*I'm bleeding. Can't breathe—*

She pushed herself upright. A moment later it hit her. She'd just used her hands. Moonlight filled the room because she'd forgotten to close the curtains.

*I'm in Topeka. That's right. Calm down. Breathe.*

She untangled the covers and went over to the window. Like a child playing hide-and-seek, Annie hid behind the curtains and looked up and down the empty street.

*Don't be ridiculous. They're not sneaking into the backyard or climbing up the wall after you.*

She peeked over the sill anyway.

*You're useless. You can't even get a decent night's sleep. No wonder you have circles the size of dinner plates around your eyes. Go to bed.*

\* \* \*

The clang of the breakfast bell woke her a few hours later. She was first into the bathroom to splash cold water on her face. When she finger-combed her hair, she cringed at her reflection: The circles under her eyes were darker than they had been last night. She fluffed her still-red curls over the white streaks, but it didn't help. No wonder Fern called her mature.

Back in her room, she made the bed and did a final check. Cuffs fastened. Boots tied. Not a thing different from anyone else at the inn. She followed the aroma of pancakes downstairs.

She sat at the same table as the evening before, like all the other guests. Fern brought pancakes. Annie spread raspberry jam on the top one and had already taken a bite before Fern returned with the coffeepot.

Twenty minutes later, Fern tilted the pot over Annie's empty cup. "Refill number three?"

"Thanks; no," Annie said. "Can you tell me how to get to the bookseller's? I need a job."

The coffeepot hit the table. "Not with him. His last secretary quit two months ago because he groped her."

Annie made a gagging noise. "Is he so strong she couldn't get away?"

"He doesn't look it. Besides, she gave him a black eye that lasted for a week."

"I can take care of myself, too. I'm going to risk it, unless you need another waitress."

Fern crossed her arms. "Nope. There's me in the morning and Howard at night. We take care of everything."

"Then the bookseller it is." Annie pushed back her chair.

"Your choice. He hasn't found anybody else who'll work for him. Turn left when you go out and keep going for two blocks. It's on the corner. Button your shirt higher."

Annie basked in the mid-September sunshine as she walked and rehearsed her interview speech. Topeka wasn't that much different from Kansas City. That was good on two levels, she supposed. First for the familiarity of living and working. Second for the ease of remembering how everything familiar turned to shit in her scarred hands.

Down the street, dairy farmers delivered milk and cheese to the grocer. At the first corner, the postman watched the blacksmith re-shoe her horse. Annie smiled at her. All the postmen she'd ever seen were women. Probably another pre-Last War leftover. The postman smiled back just as a heavy, wide cart passed between them, leaving parallel ruts in the packed-dirt street.

Annie eyed its load of rectangular gray blocks. Only one place those could've been quarried from—the pre-war ruins to the north. Brave of them, unless old Topeka wasn't hit by one of the bombs that made rocks glow. She didn't remember. It had been a long time since Last War history class.

She reached the second corner, took a deep breath on the bookseller's stoop and opened the door. A stack of newspapers toppled over with a *whump* and a dust explosion. Annie blinked several times to get accustomed to the dim light from the dirt-covered windows. Grime coated the tables and shelves as well.

"Hello?" She stepped over three piles of books and dodged another newspaper tower.

"One moment." The crotchety voice came from under her feet. A minute later, a bald head appeared through a trapdoor at the opposite end of the room. A hunched body followed, its wrinkled trousers and ink-stained shirt covered in dust.

"What may I do for you?" the bookseller asked.

"It's more a case of what I can do for you." Annie smiled. "You need an assistant. I write clearly, I can organize supplies, and I even clean floors and windows. Hire me."

His thin-lipped mouth hung open. "You certainly are not timid."

"I need work. I just arrived in town and I like to eat daily. Let me show you what I can do and we can discuss wages this afternoon."

He waved a hand at the mess. "You may try."

"Where are the cleaning supplies?"

He had already turned his attention to the current week's newspaper. "In the back room under the sink. My last secretary kept them there."

Annie tripped over the corner of a hidden box on her way to the back.

*He doesn't look strong enough to lift one of those stacks of newspapers. Maybe he caught his last secretary by surprise.*

The back room wasn't any brighter. Annie groped under the sink among cobwebs and beetle shells. *Dead beetles are still better than live silverfish.*

She picked up something that might be a jar of vinegar. When she blew on the lid, a cloud of dust covered her head, making her sneeze. She waved away the cloud and opened the jar—yes, vinegar. Her eyes smarted and she coughed so hard the lid rattled. *It has to go uphill from here.*

She primed the pump, filled a bucket with water, and mixed in a cup of the vinegar. Enough light leaked into the little room for her to see a pile of wrinkled rags on a shelf above the sink. She picked up several and carried everything into the shop. There were no customers.

An hour later she had cleaned all four windows and both doors inside and out. The rags were soaked and the smell of vinegar filled the air. The bookseller looked up from the shelf he was searching.

"That is an improvement," he said, no approval in his voice.

She hid a smile as she gathered up the used papers. "I can't do a decent job on the floor until it's cleared off. I can start with the tables or the shelves, whichever you prefer."

"The tables."

For the rest of the morning she sorted, stacked, and dusted. A few customers entered and bought paper or looked through the old newspapers. She ended the afternoon by drawing up a plan for organizing the shelves. He tilted back his chair as she spread out her sketch on his desk.

"Nothing is alphabetized," she said. "The best way to tackle it is to empty things out one bookcase at a time, using the tables to hold stacks. When I get the first case cleared out I'll start re-shelving, beginning with the *A*s. That way I'll gain room on the tables as I refill the shelves. The newspapers are a whole 'nother issue. I'll work on that."

He rolled up the sketch. "Two dollars a day. You are staying at the inn? Be here after breakfast. I close at sunset during the summer. I am also closed every Monday." He looked her up and down.

He paused a shade too long at her cleavage, but Annie let it slide. *Get hired first, then slap his lecherous face the first time he tries to do anything more than look.*

"You are too dirty to give me a sample of your writing. I will assess that tomorrow. You would only ruin good paper today." He slid the sketch into the long center drawer. "I like to know the names of my employees."

Annie held out her hand. "Annie Cook." It came easier this time.

"Zachary."

They shook on it and he walked to the front door. "It is closing time."

* * *

Annie danced a victory jig in her room after supper and sponged off her clothes. When the bathroom emptied she dashed in for a quick bath and hair wash. After she shrugged into the patched red shirt she used for sleeping, she got comfortably cross-legged on the bed and unscrewed the green glass jar's lid. The small, square room filled with the pungent odors of peppermint and black cohosh. She scooped up a fingertip's worth and began massaging it into her right-hand scar.

* * *

She woke up just in time to swallow a scream. In the dark the headboard looked like the wall they'd hung her on. She leapt out of bed and yanked open the curtains. For the rest of the night she stood at her window, trembling and staring at nothing.

* * *

After breakfast, Annie waited for the bookseller on his doorstep. The hammers and nails inside her imaginary stone prison room clanked and rattled and even called her name. She kept a calm face, but her hand trembled when she covered a yawn.

*Forget the nightmare. Focus on today. You need this job.*

The butcher's shop was directly across the street, and Annie missed Sara. The old Sara. Not the deceptive coward beneath the friendship mask. It didn't matter that Annie was eighteen, already married once, and had been earning her living since she graduated school at fourteen. She was alone in a new town, afraid to go to sleep, afraid of starving, afraid of how she'd react if she ever saw a Redeemer in the street. Just in case Max and Sara hadn't lied about that one thing.

Her throat closed and her eyes teared up. What a wilted dandelion she was. She bit the inside of her cheek took several deep breaths.

Zachary unlocked the door and glowered at her. "If this is going to be a pattern, I will have to get a key made for you."

She hadn't heard his feet on the stairs or the floor. Creepy. As soon as he turned his back, she checked his feet. Leather slippers. No wonder.

She opened two shutters and he pulled out his desk chair. "Sit there. I will get paper and ink."

She unstoppered the ink bottle with the first three fingers of her left hand, the only working ones.

"Is that a recent injury?" he said.

"No. You'll see that it doesn't affect my work."

As soon as she dipped the pen he began dictating a letter. He hovered a bit too close and she shifted away more than once. If he always moved this silently she'd have to watch her back. When he finished speaking, she blotted the letter and handed it to him for inspection.

"Acceptable. As you are right-handed, I agree with your evaluation of your abilities. Plan on Tuesday and Thursday mornings for secretarial duties."

Friday, Saturday, and Sunday she worked to exhaustion and felt she was barely making a dent in the accumulated mess. She dusted each book as she stacked it, read the title, checked for worm and water damage, rifled the pages and shook it over her lap.

Nothing hidden in any of them. Well, what did she expect from the very first row of books? Pages sprinkled with 'thee' and 'ye' and that other word... 'God.' Whatever that meant.

She reached the bottom shelf on Sunday. It was stuffed with sections and loose pages of books that had fallen apart. *Oh, yes, come to Annie.* The dozens of unknown treasures took her all day to wade through.

The end of the shelf appeared way too soon. But she glanced at the next case and saw that the bottom also held the same mishmash of paper. Satisfied, she dusted off her hands and sneezed twice.

That evening he counted six dollars into her hand. "Remember, I am closed on Mondays."

# CHAPTER TEN

"Fern, what's there to do on a day off?" Annie said the next morning as the waitress poured more coffee.

"Ooh. The stonemasons are making bricks for the baker's new oven. They take off their shirts before noon, it gets so hot," she said with a giggle. "A bunch of us go there after breakfast to watch them."

Annie laughed with her. "Maybe later. I was thinking of a play, unless your museum has something good."

"The theater's doing a weird drama this month. All in poetry. My boyfriend fell asleep when we saw it."

When Annie grimaced, Fern said, "Skip it. Trust me. If you're into museums, ours has this "School for Adults" exhibit right now. All kinds of pre-Last War stuff dug up a few years ago out west Colorado Springs or someplace like that."

"Perfect. How do I get there?"

"Go out the door and turn right. Then go straight for three blocks and turn left at the corner where the cat lady lives."

Annie raised one eyebrow.

Fern snickered. "It's a small house with about fifty cats in the yard. She had her son make a couple dozen scratching posts and climbing contraptions for all of them. You can't miss it. The museum is halfway down that street. It has a neat sign that looks like a broken pot hanging over the door."

A short time later, Annie craned her neck to study the sign. It wasn't just a pot. She'd seen drawings of those. It was an ancient wine jar.

She pushed open the door and inhaled the mingled aroma of old books and furniture polish.

A prim woman with thick glasses and graying hair pulled into a bun sat at a desk facing the door. "One dollar admission, please."

Annie paid the exorbitant price and the woman began to recite.

"Archaeologists in Colorado Springs unearthed these artifacts three years ago." She handed Annie a four-page brochure. "Local glassblowers found a deposit of old, broken glass. As they were digging it up for reuse they saw that what appeared to be solid ground was actually the roof of an enormous building."

She opened one of the brochures to a floor plan and pointed to it.

"The central room in our museum is a reconstruction of the largest area of that building. The east room shows several unusual styles of clothing. The west room holds books and the south room is the mystery room. Research continues into possible uses for the objects in there." She nodded at the open double doors behind her. "Except for the clothes, everyone is encouraged to touch and explore these pieces of the past. We close at four. Enjoy the exhibit."

The main room looked like several shops all in one place. Chairs in one corner, candles to the left, pots and pans on a table next to dented gray cups. No, not cups. She picked one up. Sealed top and bottom. How could anyone open it? She set it down and squinted at a crinkled bag made of some unknown shiny material.

*"Onion Rolls." Bread in a bag? Interesting. Did it mean chopped onions in the bread itself? I'd like to try baking that.*

Cooking hadn't changed much otherwise. That dented pot looked like one she'd got as a wedding present.

"So one person used to sell everything. What would they do with all that money?"

An old man studying the "Rolls" bag scowled at her. "Shh."

She escaped into the clothing room. A long white dress covered in yellowed lace and discolored glass beads hung on a dressmaker's dummy in the center of the room. Pinned to the wall behind it was a beige garment so short and narrow that it looked like a cut-off trouser leg. Seventeen different styles of dresses, trousers, and shoes covered the other walls.

Annie stepped over to the stand next to the white dress. It held a sheet of paper covered with guesses about its purpose. Above the paper a small card listed the archaeologists' tentative dates: 2009-2011. She scanned the entries: Costume. Party dress. Weaver's showpiece. The pencil-thin item's card on the wall read '2011,' but its suggestion sheet was blank. She scribbled, 'Underwear for the fancy dress.'

Annie wasn't as interested in old clothes as she was in old books. She wanted to leap into the book room, lock the door, and paw through every page there. But nine schoolkids—sixth-graders, maybe—and a teacher monopolized it at the moment, so she went into the mystery room.

Five tables supported rows of outlandish objects. She stopped in front of a two-foot high clear cone supported by a square black base. She tapped the cone and heard a dull *thunk*. It looked like glass, but it wasn't.

Three of the tarnished buttons on the base still had partial labels: "Puls," "Hi," and "Of," which she assumed was "Off." A black cord with a frayed end extended from the back.

Interested in spite of the books calling to her, she opened the brochure. "The purpose of every object in the Mystery Room is still unknown. They are alike only in the attached cords at their bases, some of which retain a hard cube with one, two, or three metal prongs. The prevailing theory is that these are all some kind of machine, and the cord is a crank. However, no one has yet succeeded in making the crank start any of the machines."

Annie wandered among the tables, touching and shaking things. When she picked up a rusted round item to inspect its two thin cords with discs on each end, it fell open like a mouth. She held up one of the discs. It had dozens of small holes on one side. So did the other one.

Perhaps they filled the mouth with water and it came out the little holes like rainfall. She checked the card beneath the raining mouth. 2004-2005. The current guesses were "Air Blower" and "Toss-and-Catch Toy." She wrote "Watering Can" underneath them.

She turned back to the not-glass machine. Its paper read: "Fish or Flower Holder." "Water heater."

An intent pre-teen boy stopped next to her and inspected a square mouth-like device. The top half had an inset of something else that looked like glass but wasn't. The bottom had all the letters of the alphabet on buttons, completely out of order.

*What was the fascination with mouths back then?*

"Wonder what they'll make of our tools two hundred years from now?" she said to the boy.

He pushed up his glasses and squinted at her. "They'll stare at it in museums just like we are."

Annie smiled at him. "The Redeemers keep records of everything now." *How normal I sound when I say "Redeemers." Practice is everything.*

He shrugged. "They couldn't stop the Last War. Bet there'll be another."

"Why?" Her smile faded. This kid needed a lesson in "happy."

"Come on, missus. My brother and I fight all the time. My dad argues with the sheep farmer because his sheep eat our hay." He looked toward the book room door and lowered his voice. "I bet you in a hundred years the Redeemers won't be in charge anymore and some archaeologist will dig up the instruction book on how to make a bomb."

This kid needed a lesson in 'Redeemer respect' too. "Won't happen." Annie lowered her voice to match his. "Even if someone found a bomb shop—and they wouldn't—"

"They're finding stuff every year."

"They wouldn't," Annie said in her best teacher-like voice, "because all the bombs blew up all the other bombs. And even if such a book existed, the Redeemers would know what to do with it."

The kid looked over his glasses at her. "And what would that be, missus?"

*Brat.* "They'd destroy it."

His glasses slipped farther. "No one destroys a book."

Annie planted her hands on her hips. "Not a schoolbook or a play or even a romance novel, no. But what's useful about a bomb?"

"Well, it could, maybe—"

"Alexander Farmer." The teacher stared pointedly at Annie's companion. His class now clustered around the table nearest the book room doorway.

The kid said under his breath. "Sheep shit."

Annie stepped around Alexander. "I beg your pardon, Master Teacher. Alex and I were discussing Last War History."

The teacher unbent. "Not at all, missus. I'm glad to see Alexander listen to someone's opinions besides his own."

Annie leaned into the boy's ear. "Learn to respect the Redeemers before you end up in Colorado Springs prison, Alexander."

He frowned at her, but whispered, "Thanks."

She left him with his class as they discussed possible uses for a chipped white box with two oblong holes in the top and levers on one side.

Ten seconds later, Annie stood in the middle of eight packed bookcases. Life didn't get any better than this. She bee-lined for a table beneath the west window displaying three of the best-preserved specimens.

A glass box protected the central book. It was open to a page covered with tiny print and detailed ink illustrations. The pages were crumbling at the edges but the top of each clearly read, *Grimm's Fairy Tales.*

To its left was a nearly perfect *The Complete Tales of Edgar Allan Poe.* On its right, *Shakespeare's Tragedies.* She opened that one.

A' would have clapped i' the

clout at twelve score; and carried you a fore—

hand shaft a fourteen and fourteen and a half...

*Huh.* She thought she understood English. Maybe this was more than two hundred years old.

Page v—*since when was that a page number?*—listed three dates: 1956, 1984, and 2001. Annie gave up.

She turned to the shelf closest to the door. Just at her eye level the top row of books began with *Grey's Anatomy, The Count of Monte Cristo,* and *Huckleberry Finn.* She quickly returned the first and third to their places. The middle one engrossed her for a few minutes, but the type was small and muddy and made her eyes hurt.

People browsed around her all day and stepped over her when she sat on the floor to get to the bottom rows. Annie went from shelf to shelf like she did at work, searching every single book. The fourth bookcase held the shabbiest of the lot: Romances with browned paper covers and faded paintings. Cover after cover came loose in her hand as dried brown glue crumbled to the floor.

*Why didn't they print them to last? Everyone loved romances.*

The bottom shelf of the fifth bookcase was an embarrassment to those long-dead booksellers. Every book had water damage and whole sections had vanished from most of them. A fairly legible *A Tale of Two Cities* stuck to the back of a worm-eaten *Gone with the Wind.* They both looked hopeless, but what else was she here for? The *Wind* book really was unreadable, but she flipped through what remained of the other. A few lines of type set off from the rest of the text toward the end caught her eye.

*That's it. That's the same style.* 'Saith'—whoever heard a word like that? Carton—was he the hero? Would he quote these weird words? Did he have the book it came from? Would someone kidnap him and nail him—

*Stop it. Get it out of your head for five minutes.*

Annie glanced around the empty room. She couldn't take the whole book; that'd be stealing ancient history. But she could take a little piece as a souvenir. She fanned the pages. Chapters three and four and half of five were missing. Most of the last several chapters, too. She only wanted this one page. No one would miss it.

With a quick *rip* the paper disappeared into her pocket.

# CHAPTER ELEVEN

Annie opened her eyes onto a faceful of pillow, pulled up her head, and sucked in a huge breath. Her heart pounded. This time the nightmare had stuck at the bottom of the wood, looping over and over at the point where she tried to push herself up.

The room stopped spinning after several more gasps. She threw off the covers and stared, shivering, out the window at the pumpkin vines rustling in the warm breeze. Finally the nightmare relaxed its grip.

This windowsill was becoming her second home. She hated it and her obsessed brain's nightly Halloween theater performance.

For the umpteenth time she picked up her trousers from the dresser and felt the back pocket. The piece of paper didn't even make a bump. She reached in and fingered it to make sure it was still there. Tomorrow—no, it was today now—she'd find a scrap of leather to protect it.

\* \* \*

"There has been a definite increase in customers," Zachary said to Annie's breasts after a rush before the lunch break. "Cleaning the windows was advantageous."

She crossed her arm high to the right and snapped her fingers. His head jerked up. "Thank you." She went back to the sink to wash her hands. "Which way the leatherworker's from here?"

"It is four blocks to the north and two blocks to the west."

She rolled her eyes. *Only a man would give directions like that.* "North is to the left?"

"Certainly."

She ran all the way. The smells of dye and new leather hit her as she opened the leatherworker's shop door. For a moment, she heard her husband's voice again. He laughed as she struggled with her first hide, spilling dye all over the floor and her shoes. She'd laughed with him and wiped her green-stained hands on his shirt.

An old woman with a face like a walnut pushed back a chair and stood up. "What may I get for you?"

Annie blinked away the memory and smiled. "Do you sell scraps? I'm looking for a piece about eight inches by six."

When the woman returned the smile, her face crinkled up and her eyes nearly disappeared. "The box is just under the table behind you. Let me get it."

It was large and packed to the brim. Annie took it from the knotted hands and lifted it onto the counter.

"Thank you. Some days I'm just too old to pick that up." The old woman smiled wider, revealing the gaps between her teeth.

They searched the box. Annie found a piece slightly larger than she wanted, dyed a rich blue. The old woman found a red and black striped piece exactly the requested size.

"I have to have this blue one," Annie said.

"I don't blame you." The old woman rolled it up and tied a string around the center. "Ten cents, please."

That night Annie took her pocketknife to the scrap and trimmed it a half-inch larger all around than the page from the book. She drilled a hole in the middle of one narrow side and inserted the string. Then she smoothed the page out on top of the leather. She worked with care: The paper's discolored edges looked ready to crumble every time she touched them. Starting at the new bottom end, she rolled them up together, wound the string twice around the thin cylinder, and tied a bow.

*Now for a permanent hiding place.*

She bit off a length of the brown darning thread she'd borrowed from Fern and threaded a new needle. She took off her trousers, pinched together the inner side of the left-hand pocket, and sewed it into a second, narrow compartment. The leather roll slipped right in. Finally she pulled the needle off the thread and tied those ends in a bow.

She inspected her work inside and out before putting the

trousers back on. It looked smooth enough. When she climbed on top of the dresser and angled her hips in front of the small oval mirror, the bulge was nearly invisible.

Annie removed the roll and picked up her ointment jar on her way down. In her usual position on the bed, she untied her secret and spread out the page. With a shoe at the top and the jar at the bottom to keep it from rolling back up, she studied the text as she massaged ointment into her scars.

* * *

Zachary made good on his promise of a key. When the nightmares woke Annie close to dawn, she would grab a quick breakfast, open the shop, and plunge into work to douse the memories.

Wherever he slept, cellar or attic, she never knew he was lurking behind her until she heard his precise, "Good morning." That and the odor of roasted garlic. Annie used the garlic as her "Zachary in heat" alarm. So far all he'd managed to do was stare into her cleavage like he'd lost a coin in there.

Tuesday after her trip to the museum she heaved an overflowing box onto his desk.

"I've cleaned out the loose pieces of books from two shelves on the back wall. What are we going to do with them?"

"You have already examined them. What is able to be salvaged?"

Her mouth opened, but nothing came out.

"If I objected to it, I would have said something earlier."

"I like books."

"A useful attribute for this job. Stop looking guilty. Put together the books that can be rebound. I will show you how to do that next month. When you finish all the bookshelves I will hire a cart and you may take the boxes to the paper shop for recycling."

Annie spent the rest of the day refilling the alphabetized books into the first shelf along the back.

Around suppertime Zachary said, "To where did you move the first-grade arithmetic textbooks?"

She looked up from the corner where she was kneeling. "Second pile on that table." She gestured behind her.

He folded the newspaper he was reading and walked over. "Show me, please."

"Oh. Sure." She stood and pushed two stacks apart. "Right under these A-B-C books."

As she lifted several thin volumes off the top of one pile, he reached from behind her and squeezed her right breast.

She dropped the books, whipped around, and slapped him across the face. He grabbed her forearm. They held that awkward pose for several seconds, her face mere inches from his, and his hand clutching her arm halfway between wrist and elbow.

"Don't ever try that again," she said with a pointed glance at her boot poised over his instep in those soft slippers.

He followed her gaze and jerked his foot backwards. "You have made yourself clear."

"Remove your hand."

He looked away from her foot to his hand and her arm, blinked, and released her.

Annie sidestepped out of his reach. "I'm leaving."

"You will be here tomorrow morning?" he said.

"I'll think about it."

Instead of returning to the inn, she marched through town to the river and sat on its banks. Her eyes stared at the water for a long time. Tough as shoe leather? Guess so. The question was, should she go back? Of course she needed the money, but she needed access to all those old books even more.

At the price of looking over her shoulder every five minutes? She couldn't take on more worry—all the sleepless nights were dragging her down as it was.

*Plip* A trout broke the water. More *plips*. Evening feeding time for everyone; secretaries included. She dusted the back of her trousers. Supper first. Decisions in the morning when she cooled off.

# CHAPTER TWELVE

*The Redeemers pick her up and sing a Midsummer drinking song. Even as she struggles she knows that's not what happened. They carry her down the hall and into the putrid darkness.*

Annie woke up and looked out the window. It was well past midnight; the moon was high. She punched the pillow into a new shape and turned over.

*The leader rips off her clothes and gropes her naked breasts. She yells and tries to slap him, but the others hold her down. He brings out the hammer and nails.*

She woke again. This time she got out of bed and opened the window wider. She took several deep breaths of muggy air before trying to sleep again.

*Her heart pounds in her ears. Blood pumps out around the nails in the same rhythm.*

*She blinks and the nails disappear. She lifts her arms and studies the open wounds. Blood dribbles onto her face.*

*The leader catches her blood and wipes it over her body: Face, breasts, stomach, thighs. Deep inside her, little Hank cries out to be fed. The bloody hands hold a nail over her womb and raise the hammer.*

Annie flung off the sheet and stuck her head out the window. Thunderclouds covered the sky but roosters crowed on the outlying farms. *Dawn. Redeemers be thanked.*

She unlocked the door and used the bathroom. The aroma of brewing coffee worked its way upstairs by the time she was dressed.

Fern was just filling Annie's cup when Annie fell into her dining room chair. "Please tell me the coffee will bite back this morning."

"I'll dump in extra grounds just for you."

Annie yawned into her napkin. Three cups and an omelet later, she'd shoved all the nightmares into her mind's locked room.

The thunderstorm broke during her last cup. She went out to the front steps and held up her face to let the water wash the remnants of last night out of her. A spectacular bolt of lightning hit on the other side of the river, and the next thunderclap shook the ground beneath the steps.

Time to decide: Forfeit yesterday's pay and look for another job? Go back and let him think she was desperate enough to put up with anything?

"Missus Cook."

Zachary stood on the sidewalk below her, rain pouring off his wide-brimmed hat.

Annie swallowed. "Yes?"

"I have come to ask you to return to work." He paused. "Please."

"Why?"

He appeared to gather himself. "I require your services. You are an asset to the shop."

She waited.

"I assure you that the incident of yesterday will not be repeated."

*He wasn't groveling, but he looked cowed.* She bit her bottom lip. Now that they were face to face, she knew: The job wasn't worth it.

"Only until Sunday, Master Bookseller. Then I'll be moving on."

His shoulders sagged, but after a moment, he nodded. "Very well. I will expect you at nine."

When she arrived, the shutters were open and his desk was cleared of everything but two stacks of paper, one clean, the other covered with words and numbers in several shades of ink.

Zachary indicated his desk. "I have something of more importance today than the shelves. These are the running accounts. Please make up bills listing any outstanding charges and total the current balance."

He stationed himself at the opposite end of the shop while she sifted through his center desk drawer until she found ink and the swirled glass pen she preferred.

Just before sunset, she shook out her hand for the dozenth time. Ink smeared her floppy fingers, and freckled both hands. When he lit the lamps, she wiped the pen and stretched. Her back cracked like popcorn popping.

"We're not closing?"

"I am, but I would like you to stay and assist me in packing away the newspapers. We require the floor space."

Two hours later, he poked his head through the cellar trapdoor. "There are four additional stacks. How many boxes remain?"

She leaned on the box she had just closed. "Two."

"We will manage."

She pushed herself and lugged everything up the rickety steps in three trips. In another half-hour he had labeled all the boxes and she had them stacked against the far wall in the back room. Her dark blue shirt was gray with dust.

"Thank you for staying." He opened the door for her.

"Warn me next time so I can pack a sandwich," she said, beating dust from her sleeves.

Haze obscured the half-moon and darkened the streets. Her stomach grumbled louder than the crickets and frogs. At the corner, a second-floor overhang shadowed two tall figures. She crossed the street to take a different route.

They blocked her way. She looked up and saw hooded cloaks— no faces—as a harsh female voice said, "Heretic, you belong to us."

The woman grabbed her arm. Annie turned into the hold and smacked the heel of her right hand where the assailant's nose should be. A popping noise and a gasp rewarded her as a man's hand gripped her shoulder. She ducked and twisted and kicked upward. His breath went out with a *whoof* and she ran.

Footsteps echoed behind her. Her fatigue vanished. *Not again. Not again. I can't let them get me.*

Every slap of her boots on the road sounded like hammers on nails.

The night and her dark clothes shielded her as she zigzagged through the streets. The sound of her pursuers grew fainter. She headed northwest to the river, her mind peopling the empty streets with cloaked Redeemers who snatched at her from every doorway.

The scents of water and wet rocks grew stronger. She heard

rustling leaves. *Willows. Cover.*

She zigzagged among the waving, leafy branches until she reached the west end of Topeka. The last tree before the outlying farms sheltered her as she waited for her heart to stop galloping. She looked back toward the town. No running feet. No concealed men or women dashing around the corners of the last houses.

*What gave me away? Was someone at the inn spying on me? The museum. Was someone behind a bookshelf?*

And worse than all those unanswerable questions, the realization: *I admit it. The Redeemers tried to kill me. Not four people in Redeemer costumes. Redeemers help me, nothing in the world is safe anymore.*

For the rest of the night she headed west, using the tallest rows of corn and sesame as cover. At sunrise, exhausted and asleep on her feet, she simply walked into the river. The shock of the cold water cleared her head. Her loud gasp caused a group of frogs to dive into the water in a series of scattered *plops.*

"Sorry." Annie took a deep breath and submerged to untangle her hair.

*The secret paper is still in my pocket.*

She splashed out and fumbled the saturated pocket out of her trousers, yanked at the thread, and pulled out the blue leather roll.

"Don't be soaked. Don't dissolve."

The outside of the leather was splotched an even darker blue, but it had shielded the paper from damage. She let out a relieved sigh and set it on the grass in the sun. The early morning was already hotter than yesterday at noon. The warmth and a nearby beehive lulled her, even as she tried to listen for sounds of a chase. She fell asleep as her clothes and the leather steamed in the sun.

A sheepdog barked in the distance and she jerked upright. *What— Where—* The world fell into place a minute later. Topeka. Ambush. Killers in the street.

She stretched, squinted at the early afternoon sun, and slid the little packet into its hiding place. She was dry and hungry and hot.

"And my fishing pole and knapsack are at the inn." She shook her head. "If you're hungry, you're alive, idiot. You can buy more supplies when you find another job."

She scooped several mouthfuls of cool water from the river, then continued west. All afternoon she peered into the trees for lurking brown robes and looked around at every loud rustle. The gorgeous fall day would've been perfect for fishing or reading or herb-gathering. That is, if every fish splashing didn't sound like her blood hitting the floor in that dark, echoing room in Kansas City.

She tried several times that afternoon to stab a fish with a broken branch.

"Talk about hopeless. Shut up, stomach. I'm not a Redeemer to charm fish into my hands. Besides, my matches are back at the inn, so I couldn't cook a fish even if I caught one. It won't kill you to go hungry for a day or two."

She realized what she said, and kicked herself. There was a fine line between blending in and remembering exactly who wanted to finish what they started. She looked down to see her left hand rubbing the right-hand scar.

*I'm going to have to face what the Redeemers really are. I can't beat them if I'm afraid to get inside their heads.*

The idea turned her colder than the snow she'd seen only twice in her life.

Once she saw the afternoon sun glint on something in Old Topeka to the north, across the river. She shaded her eyes with one hand. There might be a ruin worth seeing at this distance; the river was barely a hundred feet wide here. A man's deep voice, faint and far behind her, called something and another deep voice answered. Annie stood completely still.

*Forget history. Look behind. Are they following? No. But these cattails only reach as high as my forehead. Cattails aren't topped with curly red and white hair. Hide, idiot.*

She dropped to the ground and crawled out of the cattails on the riverbank and up into the reeds. They overhung the cattails by at least a foot. Sometimes it was good to be short. She stood and kept walking. A fox leaped in front of her and she squealed. A deer or two crackled through the cattails later, but she clapped her hands over her mouth before she gave herself away. The voices earlier had probably been shepherds or farmers, but the Redeemers had already tracked her to Topeka; only Redeemers knew how.

*I'm thinking in circles. Sara and Max were right. I'm never safe. Never.*

Just before the moon set she came upon an extensive apple orchard. Long rows of laden trees stretched in front of her, and her mouth watered at the scent of hundreds of ripe apples. She scooted around a prop and under the branches of the nearest tree.

Her feet hurt. Her back hurt. She was so tired the rough bark on the tree limbs looked comfortable. She could take a quick nap and be out of here right after sunrise.

She climbed into the crotch, shaking a few apples loose. She caught two. They were perfect—just at the tart-but-ripe point. Her empty stomach roared at her. She resisted as long as she could.

Juice ran down her chin at the first bite. Luscious.

# CHAPTER THIRTEEN

*Thunder crashes overhead. Rain pelts her. A flash of lightning illuminates the plain stone abbey in the distance.*

*An old man rises up out of the mud at her feet. "Your husband is dead," he says, his voice too loud. "But he sends you this." Two awls slide out of his coat sleeves into his hands. He plunges them into her hands.*

*Sara, masked, appears next to her and pours bitter water down her throat, choking off her screams. The old man pulls her hands to his mouth and licks her blood.*

*He changes into a Redeemer holding a hammer and four nails. The Redeemer laughs. Short, sharp laughs. Like a dog barking.*

\* \* \*

"Scrap! Heel!"

Annie's tree shook and several apples hit the ground. A sheepdog barked below her, front paws on the trunk. She tilted up and her unstable balance gave way. With a yelp she crashed into a lower branch and landed on her rump in another shower of apples.

"Good boy. Good protector." A wrinkled hand caught the dog's collar.

Annie grasped the other hand a sturdy woman held out to her, and pulled herself up. Then she gasped and snatched her hand away, backpedaling into the tree trunk.

"Are you ill?" the woman said. "Shush, Scrap."

"No. No, I'm fine." Annie walked around the woman and the growling dog. "I'm sorry I trespassed on your orchard." She tripped and caught herself on another tree.

"You look like you could use some breakfast."

Annie insides melted. She didn't think a disguised Redeemer would offer her breakfast.

Food. Apples. She'd better come clean. "I ate two of your apples last night. I don't have any money to pay you."

"You can help work the farm then. There's plenty to do."

"I—sure." Stupid guilty conscience. Why didn't she say no? She could keep her mouth shut other times.

Annie stared sideways at the woman. *She might be bait for a trap. She might be just what she appears to be. What if she isn't?* As Annie tried to calculate whether or not she could outrun the dog, she tripped on another tree root. *Can't think straight. Too tired.*

The scent of apples warming in the sunrise surrounded Annie as they walked through the orchard. The dog sniffed trees and barked at mourning doves. Annie's stomach growled nonstop by the time they reached a sprawling farmhouse. She stopped on the porch as the older woman went inside.

"Good morning, Nora," a very pregnant woman said, slicing bread at a counter.

"I've brought a guest for breakfast, Laura."

The two bustled about the kitchen, making coffee, frying eggs, toasting bread.

*They're distracted. I can still run.* Her foot touched the top step.

Nora looked out at her at that moment. "Come in and sit down for a bit."

Laura pushed dark brown hair away from her face. "There's soap and a towel at the sink for washing up."

Annie became acutely conscious of spending the night in an apple tree. She smelled coffee. *It's worth the risk. A decent meal will give me the strength to escape if they're not what they seem.* She came inside and scrubbed away thirty-six hours of running and hiding.

"What can I do?" she said to Nora as she handed the towel to Laura.

"The table needs setting." Nora brought out plates and utensils for six and piled them at an oblong table under a wide window.

Laura went to the back door and called, "Eamon! Padraig! Siobhan! Breakfast!"

A black-haired man strongly resembling Nora appeared a few minutes later. He brushed hay off his pants and paused to kiss Laura as he headed for the sink. A younger man and woman followed, who also shared Nora's black hair and eyes. Nora grinned at the three of them and nodded at Annie as they all took seats. Annie chose the chair next to the open door.

Nora said to her, "Coffee and pancakes?"

"Thank you."

The young man poured coffee for her. Her hands shook when she lifted the cup. Everyone looked at something else and she drank. Laura handed Eamon the pancakes and the table filled with movement.

Annie passed cherry preserves and apple butter and forced herself not to gulp a large bite of warm, fluffy pancake. The preserves tasted like her own. Hank used to slather her apple butter on slice after slice of bread all through the winter.

The family sorted out the day's work while they ate: pasture the sheep, make cheese, spin wool, and continue the apple harvest. Annie said nothing, one eye on the open door, the other catching someone looking at her every time she turned back to the table.

When business was settled, Nora said, "But we haven't introduced ourselves."

Five faces turned toward Annie, and she jumped.

"My name is Nora, and this is my eldest son, Eamon." She laid a hand on his shoulder. "His wife, Laura, is expecting their first in about a month." Laura smiled, a hand on her moving belly.

"Next to you are Padraig and Siobhan." She smiled and paused.

"My name is Annie." *I won't be jealous of her baby. I'm better than that.* When the polite silence became an obvious request for more, she added, "I was working for the bookseller in Topeka."

"And now?"

"It was time to move on." She bit into another pancake. "Your preserves are very good. I used to make a good cherry pie. Hank would tease me for days to get me to make one."

Her teeth shut with a click. *Watch your mouth. You're too tired. Don't tell them anything else.*

"You can make pie crust?" Siobhan said. "Mine either crumble to bits or turn into mud."

"Don't we know it," Padraig said, and Siobhan punched him. "If Mom talked you into working here for awhile, could you teach Siobhan? We'd all be grateful."

"That would be fine with me," Nora said.

Annie gripped her hands together under the table. If she pushed the chair to the left, she could make one smooth jump for the porch.

Eamon said, "You don't have to worry—mom's always taking in strays. There's a constant procession of lost dogs and motherless calves—Ow!" He looked at Laura. "Why'd you kick me?"

"I'm sorry, Annie," she said. "He still doesn't have his mother's manners."

"What's wrong with my manners?" Eamon leaned down to rub his shin. "I was only trying to show her we're friendly people who have a home open to travelers."

"You were comparing Annie to a stray cow, dear. That's not the way to welcome a guest."

For the first time since Annie escaped from Topeka, she smiled. These were regular people. Safe people. "I can stay for today."

The men downed coffee, gathered plates, and headed out. Laura packed up bread, cheese, and two apples and followed them. Siobhan pumped water into the sink and washed while Annie dried. Nora brought aprons from behind the pantry door and began to make bread.

When the dishes were put away, Siobhan handed Annie an apron and said, "I'll get the lard from the cellar. The bowls are in the cupboard right next to you."

Annie and Siobhan measured, mixed, and rolled out all morning. Nora finished kneading a half-dozen loaves and left them to rise. By lunchtime they had four flaky crusts, enough for all the apples in the window baskets.

How she missed this. Cooking, chatting, anticipating a leisurely supper; so satisfying. Like the smile on Hank's face as he took the first bite of her first cherry pie of the season. His cherry-sticky kisses. Or Sara sending Max over with a dinner bribe—she'd roast ham and potatoes if Annie would bring a pie.

Annie punched down the memories with the rising loaves of bread. After lunch, they set the pies in the oven and Siobhan brought out a basketful of mending. Annie followed her to the rocking chairs on the porch. "I can help you make a dent in that."

As she rocked, the soft noises of the sheep and the rustling apple leaves soothed the remains of her raw nerves.

Later, Siobhan rang the dinner bell on the porch while Annie carved up a chicken; Nora came in to slice the cooled bread. Laura trudged over to the corner and put her swollen feet up on a spare chair. Eamon brought her a cold cloth and a full dish.

Annie wanted this peace. She wanted to stop running.

When only chicken bones remained on the plates, she stood. "It's time for Siobhan's pies."

She sliced and Siobhan served. Eamon looked around the table, closed his eyes, and took the first bite. His eyes opened, his eyebrows arched, and he swallowed. "Siobhan made this?"

Annie laughed along with them. Afterwards, Siobhan washed and she dried again. Eamon and Padraig went out to check the sheepfold for the night and Nora lit the kitchen lamps. The room glowed with warm light.

Fatigue hit Annie like a rock. She stumbled and clutched at the table.

"Annie!" Siobhan shoved a chair beneath her.

"Are you all right, my dear?" Nora bent over her.

"Yes," she said, holding her head up with her hands. "I'm just tired." She lifted her head, which weighed about forty pounds, and smiled at Nora. "It's time for me to leave. I need to keep going tonight."

"Can't you stay a few days?" Siobhan said.

"I'm sorry." Annie pushed back the chair and stood. "Thank you for your hospitality."

"We'd love to have you stay on. No—" Nora put up a hand—"I won't press you. But if you'll wait a minute I'll pack you a few supplies."

"Thank you. I'd be very grateful." She pumped water into the sink and splashed her face.

Nora came up from the cellar with an armful of provisions and dumped them on the counter. "Siobhan, would you get that spare knapsack from the closet?"

Siobhan loosened the drawstring as she came back into the room and filled the patched blue knapsack one item at a time. "Apples, cheese, dried mutton, nuts, raisins, salt. They should last 'til you get to your next job." She opened the front pocket for the salt packet. "I thought this was empty." She took out a piece of paper and handed it to Annie. "See what this is, would you?"

Annie unfolded it and read: He that eateth my flesh and drinketh my blood, dwelleth in me, and I in him.

The kitchen faded. Darkness and the stench of rotting corpses filled her head. Five voices spoke in unison. She'd forgotten the exact words. Something about an image.

The memory receded. No one in the kitchen spoke. Annie saw the yellowed paper in her hand again and set it down.

*Idiot. You dropped your guard. They made it as sweet as the apple pies and you gobbled it up.*

Her heart rattled into her throat, choking her. She glanced obliquely to the right—the door was shut.

Nora put a hand on her shoulder and she jumped for the door anyway.

"Annie, wait!" Siobhan said.

Annie wrenched up the latch, leaped over the two porch steps, and hit the ground running. Eamon came out of the barn.

"Stop her!" Nora called.

Eamon stepped in front of her as she tried to dodge him. His wide arms swallowed her as he swung her around to face the house. She writhed and kicked and tried to bite his arms.

"Quick, bring her back inside," Nora said, holding open the door.

Padraig ran over and helped Eamon wrestle Annie up the steps and into the kitchen. Before anyone said a word, she stomped on Eamon's left foot.

"Ow!" He released her.

Her right elbow found Padraig's diaphragm and he sat down abruptly. "Oof!"

She spun in a circle. They surrounded her. *Think.*

Laura would be the slowest. She could get past her. She cut left, but Eamon tackled her at the table. They crashed to the floor and her head hit with a *crack*.

"What are you doing?" Siobhan's voice dwindled in Annie's ears and the bright, warm room went black.

# CHAPTER FOURTEEN

"Ohh…" Annie moved her head and the headache exploded. Her arms had fallen asleep, her butt was numb, and her face rested on something cold and earthy. She pried open her eyes—and saw nothing.

*Don't panic. I can't be dead. My head hurts too much.*

She blinked several times, but there wasn't a glimmer of light anywhere. If she could only feel her hands. She tried moving her arms and legs, and her boots scraped the floor. At least her legs worked.

*I can't get up. This headache will make me puke.*

She inhaled. The air smelled like dirt and apples and cheese. Apples… pies… Nora's house.

Her heart stuttered and the headache sent sparkles across her useless eyes. The paper in the knapsack. Eamon tackling her.

The sound of a key in a lock reached through her pounding head. Light shone around the outline of a door and Eamon walked in. The bright lamp he held blinded Annie. When her vision cleared, it confirmed her guess: She was sitting in the corner of a large fruit cellar. Its packed dirt walls and floor deadened his footsteps as he walked over to Annie and held the lamp in her face. She turned away her head and saw that her numb arms were tied behind her with twine.

He set the lamp on a barrel and stood over her. If he meant to intimidate her, it was working. She looked up, way up into his hate-filled face and stopped breathing for a moment.

"Why didn't those idiots wait for someone who deserved rescuing?" He crouched in front of her, breathing whiskey with every word. "Every minute you're alive is dangerous. To my family, to my wife, to my unborn baby. If I could get them in the kitchen to shut up and listen, I'd kill you now."

"Don't tell me about unborn babies, you piece of pig shit."

Without warning, he hauled her up by her chin. The toes of her boots barely scraped the ground. With a little effort he could snap her neck. She felt the strength in his grip.

"Are you listening, sheep shit?"

She couldn't fight with her arms tied, but she could pretend she wasn't afraid. She spat in his face.

He cracked her across the mouth with one hand. Stars blinded her. Her boots hit the floor and without another word, he tightened his grip. Annie couldn't breathe, couldn't speak, and fog crept across her vision.

"Eamon!"

A ringing, rushing noise in Annie's head muddled the voice. Her legs wouldn't hold her upright.

"Eamon, let her go."

"Get your hands off me, Siobhan."

Annie flopped like a caught fish as his arms were pulled to the left and he pulled back, left and back.

"Laura's in labor. Get upstairs now!"

Eamon dropped Annie in a boneless heap on the dirt. His footsteps thudded on the ground, then the stairs. She hardly heard them over her deep, desperate gasps for air.

Hands lifted Annie and propped her against corner shelves. Fingers pulled open her eyelids. The fog cleared and she began coughing.

"Are you all right? Can you talk? I'll get you some water." Siobhan, pale and looking frightened, ran up the stairs.

Annie took another shuddering breath. *Not dead yet.* The buzzing in her ears diminished. Another breath, and the coughing returned. Then Siobhan appeared and held a glass of water to Annie's lips. Annie spilled much of it down her shirt, but her throat cleared.

"Redeemers save us, your hands are turning blue. I'll be right back."

Annie leaned her head against the wooden shelf and listened to the beautiful sound of her own breathing. She tasted blood on her mouth from Eamon's punch, but when she ran her tongue over her teeth, all were intact.

Siobhan returned with a bread knife and sawed through the twine around Annie's wrists. Her arms dropped to her sides, useless.

"I've gotta go help Laura, but I'll be back later. Don't worry about Eamon. Mom will keep him in line."

She locked the door behind her, leaving Eamon's lamp on the barrel. Annie wondered if she'd really forgot it or if leaving a light was a ploy to make her think Siobhan was on her side. Annie chuckled, then coughed some more, discovering how sore her throat was.

That was when her numbed arms started tingling. It wasn't bad for the first minute. Then every nerve ending from her fingertips to her shoulders woke up at once. She couldn't rub feeling back into either arm because they both felt like she'd rolled in a patch of red-hot needles.

She pushed her face into her knees to muffle the tiny screams. *Don't make noise. Don't let them think you're weak. Redeemers help me, I'm on fire.*

When time started ticking for her again, her face was tear-stained and she had to force herself to breathe normally.

"Well, I've survived worse." She was proud of her steady voice. When she held her hands to the lamp, her fingernails looked normal. Her hands hardly shook when she unbuttoned her sleeves and pushed them up. Deep, thin red lines circled her arms from her wrists halfway to her elbows. No blood, though. Perhaps her shirt protected her skin.

"But did they see the scars? More important, how did they know about me?" Annie paced the square room like she used to pace her recovery cell. "They have to be Redeemers without the brown robes. Of course, stupid. They're in disguise." She rubbed her still-sore arms. "Redeemers curse them."

She stopped.

Nothing to distract herself with down here. No place to run. Too easy to think only about the Redeemers. The eerie, awe-inspiring leaders who descended the Colorado Springs mountains after the Last War and saved the survivors from terror, and death. Everyone trusted them. Everyone venerated them. Annie even knew of a cousin of a friend who claimed his great-aunt married a Redeemer. No one was sure what to think of that, even though Redeemers had to have sex and babies like everyone else.

Babies. Shouldn't think about them.

*Yes, I should. The Redeemers murdered my baby. The Redeemers tried to murder me. They're still trying to murder me.*

But Redeemers were the source of everything good in the world today.

Hammers knocked on the door of the cell in her head. The nails rattled. The *t*-shaped boards called her to come embrace them. Annie pounded both fists on the packed dirt wall above the barrels.

*Redeemers are also rabid-dog crazy killers.*

She sat down hard on the nearest barrel before her legs gave out again.

"It's simple. Everything in the world has turned to shit."

# CHAPTER FIFTEEN

Annie pasted her ear to the cellar door and held her breath. Nora's family was arguing so loudly in the kitchen, Annie could identify individual voices.

"I say we do it tonight." Eamon's voice. Annie wondered where funny, self-deprecating Eamon disappeared to.

"And I say you're not the head of this house, Eamon." Nora's voice: hard; cold. So different from the comforting, helpful woman in the orchard.

"Laura wouldn't be upstairs having our baby three weeks early without that little bitch's performance after supper." Footsteps paced toward, then away from Annie's listening perch. Eamon passing and repassing the open cellar door. "Forget turning her in. I want—"

A muffled *bang.* "I want you to be quiet and listen." Nora's hand had hit the table. "Laura is not having the baby yet. The pains have already stopped."

"I told you, Eamon." Soibhan's voice, annoyed.

"And put down the whiskey. You're useless when you drink." A new voice. The other brother... Padraig.

"Shove it, Padraig."

"Oh, go upstairs and check on Laura."

"Don't tell me how to take care of my wife."

Scuffles, grunts, and Nora shouting, "Stop." Different footsteps nearing the stairs.

"Mom, she can't get out of the cellar." Siobhan. "We shouldn't do anything 'til we all calm down."

"I'm perfectly calm, thank you, Siobhan." Nora, colder than before. "We all agreed to the plan. I will see that we carry it out. Eamon, go up to your wife. Padraig, get everything together in the barn. Siobhan, don't think about bringing anything to her. I want her hungry and disoriented as well as frightened."

"Mom—"

"Siobhan, not even the Redeemers waste food and water on the ones they choose. Learn from them." Several different footsteps passing the stairs this time. "We will solve this problem tomorrow night, and that is final."

Annie backed away from the door, her fists stuffed in her mouth to keep herself quiet. Out. How to get out?

Footsteps on the stairs now. Eamon must be coming to kill her despite Nora's orders. Annie's heart stuttered even as she looked for something—anything—to bash in his head and escape.

The cellar held only barrels of apples and shelves stacked with cheese wheels. Nothing weapon-like. The lock turned. The door opened. Annie took a quick breath and stood her ground in the middle of the room.

Siobhan slipped in, a finger on her lips and a glass in her other hand. Annie breathed again. She could get by too tall, too skinny Siobhan. She flexed, ready to kick Siobhan's legs out from under her and jump for the stairs.

Siobhan set the glass near one of the cheese wheels. "You must be thirsty. I'll bring you more water when Mom's asleep. The barrels behind you have apples in them, if you're hungry."

Annie hoped her voice didn't shake. "Why do you care?"

"Huh? Look, I'll be back later. Don't worry." She locked Annie in again.

Annie's mouth dried out further just looking at the full glass of clear, cool water sparkling in the lamplight.

*It'll be drugged. Don't touch it. The apples might be okay. They'd be here for the family to use.* She hooked two fingers through the hole in the cover of one barrel and hefted it. The scent of apples flooded the room. The next minute two plump, red ones were clutched in her other hand and she dropped the cover.

They were just as succulent as the apples in in the orchard and she ate every bit of the first one except the seeds and stem.

She was halfway through the second when she remembered dirt plus water equaled mud.

"The doorsill. If I create enough mud under the door I can dig a big enough hole to squeeze through."

*No, I can't. I'm dead for real this time.*

"No, it only sounds impossible."

*It is impossible. They'll come for me tomorrow night and rip my clothes off and drag me to the barn and nail me to the wall and no masked strangers will hear my screams and rescue me.*

"Shut up, shut up, shut up." She grabbed the glass and poured half of it across the doorsill. It sat for a minute before the dirt absorbed it. She poked the spot. Iffy. She poured the rest. It absorbed faster this time and her fingers sank in a bit when she pressed it.

She tossed away the glass and clawed at the wettest spot. Claylike dirt caked under her fingernails as she stripped shallow rows across and over and across.

Too little. The sill was probably the hardest-packed dirt in the entire fruit cellar. When she scooped out the last of the damp soil, the oval dent was only a few inches deep.

Annie worked up a mouthful of saliva and spit into the hole. "Idiot. What good is that going to do? You need another cup at the very least."

Or maybe not.

Annie stared at the ridged gap for a long moment. Then she unbuttoned her trousers, pulled down her underpants, and aimed a pungent stream of urine into the gap. She grimaced at the smell, but the rapid splashes sounded as beautiful as Midsummer dancing music.

Before she thought about it too long, she yanked up her clothes and plunged her hands into the wet earth. At least the dirt absorbed the odor.

Good thing her nails were already stuffed with clean dirt. Another inch gone from under the door, but the dirt was getting hard again. The skin ripped away from the fingernails on the three working fingers of her left hand. Pigs on stage. It wasn't deep enough yet. She needed at least ten inches, possibly more.

"Ignore it. You know what's waiting for you if you quit." She needed a tool; something hard and flat, like a spatula. She kept digging, her ripped fingers making no useful impression now.

*Give up. I'm dead. That little bit of blood from my fingernails isn't all I'm about to lose.*

"Stop it." The shallow depression beneath the door was about five inches on the right side, but only half that on the left. She clawed harder. Her fingers cringed as she hit something solid.

"What?" She scrambled to her feet and brought over the lamp. A tree root. "My secret cherry pie recipe in exchange for a shovel. Any takers? Anyone?"

Annie sat on her heels. No one would believe a ghost story where the cause of death was a tree root.

*I'm dead. I'll never beat the Redeemers.*

Inside her head, the locked room rattled and shook, every piece of wood, nail, hammer, and bucket of blood threatening to spew out and overwhelm her.

"No. I am not giving up. Whoever comes through that door tomorrow won't expect the hole in the sill. They'll stumble and I'll slam my good fist in that weak spot on everyone's jaw. My brothers didn't teach me to fight for nothing."

# CHAPTER SIXTEEN

Fear kept Annie awake, even though sleep would've been preferable to the voice in her head telling she should give up and accept the nails. She had no choice. She was dead. As Annie turned down the wick yet again to try and make the oil last, she decided she'd rather skin and cook a nest of snakes than listen to another minute of it. And she hated fried snake.

The alternatives her panicky brain offered weren't much better. How did the Redeemers know she'd stop at this particular farm? Max and wouldn't have contacted Redeemers. Could bubbly Fern in Topeka be a Redeemer spy? The museum where she'd stolen the page from the old book had been crowded all day. It must have been someone in there who got a message to the Redeemers.

Another illustration of her new life truth: Everything and everyone was shit.

Hours after she'd quit digging at the tree root, the lock turned. Annie clambered on top of the barrel next to the door and raised both clenched fists. Eamon was at least a foot taller than she was.

The door opened. In the lamp's dimming light, Annie saw straight black hair and cracked her fists on Siobhan's neck.

Siobhan grunted and fell. Her lamp rolled into the room, looping a trail of oil. Annie jumped down and righted the lamp before it emptied.

*Luck, stay with me.* Annie snatched the pieces of twine from the nearest shelf and tied Siobhan's hands and feet. Siobhan would yell herself hoarse when she woke up, but if it was still night outside, Annie would to be miles away by the time Nora and the others came after her.

"Not this time, Redeemer," she whispered. She closed and locked the door and crept upstairs to the kitchen.

The kitchen was one shade lighter than pitch black. Not even the moon shone through the windows. Annie boots made only small *tick-tacks* on the wood floor as she tiptoed to the front door and turned the handle.

Nothing.

*Stupid. Of course it's locked.*

No way she'd find the key without a light. The window, then.

She felt to her right, bumped a chair but caught it—*Quiet*—and climbed onto the wide, solid kitchen table. Her fingers felt around the window frame and found the latch. A bit at a time, she slid it up until it clicked free. Well-oiled. *Didn't expect that to work against you, did you, Nora?* The left-hand pane swung free and Annie leaned over the sill.

Clouds must have been covering the visible sky, because Annie couldn't see more than a foot in front of her. The sill was about two feet above the porch... the darker shadow to her right was a rocking chair... that meant the other chair was even farther right.

The table creaked once as she shifted onto the windowsill, but the only sounds that followed were the hall clock ringing the half-hour. Annie had no idea which half-hour, and the sky wasn't helping. With a light hop, her boots hit the porch. The chair next to her started to rock and she stopped it with her hand. She pushed the window closed with her other hand, but the latch wouldn't fall into place from the outside.

*Nora will figure it out as soon as she comes down to start breakfast, but I'll be miles away.*

She crept off the porch and down the steps she'd leaped over the night before. Left turn around the house, through more rows of apple trees, into harvested wheat fields, and then the woods. To her right, the river bubbled around its rocks. She was headed west again at last, away from another cache of Redeemers.

*And then what? If all I do is keep running west, eventually I'll fall into... what is it called? The ocean.*

"I have a plan." The trees above and the thick pine duff deadened her voice as well as her footsteps. "I'm going to find out why the Redeemers did this to me. Then I'm going to tell…"

*I can't tell the Redeemers. That's like a mouse escaping a cat one day and knocking on its door the next.*

"All the Redeemers can't be like the ones in Kansas City."

*Or like the ones on Nora's oh-so-welcoming farm.*

"The world is bigger than those two places. Jefferson City. Plainville. Liberty. Big Piney. Fountain. Grand Junction." She breathed a little freer with each name. "Colorado Springs. Redeemers aren't bees or ants. They're individuals who think for themselves."

*Proof of that idea would make me sleep better.*

"It's like playing cards. What if the Redeemers in Kansas City really are rabid-dog crazy and trying to bluff their way through, thinking that no one would report them to Colorado Springs?"

She veered toward the river and walked forever. At least that's what her feet thought. When her mouth felt like she'd been eating newspaper, she stretched out on the bank. Her arms were just long enough to scoop several handfuls of water into her dry mouth.

"I'm the player with the best hand. I'm going to knock on the door of the abbey in Colorado Springs, find out, somehow, what makes Redeemers tick, and stop them from killing anyone ever again."

The sound of water gurgling over the rocks soothed her as much as her plan did. The grass underneath her was as thick as a cushion and her eyes closed for just a minute. Fish *plipped* to the surface. Crickets and robins sang.

\* \* \*

*Ribbit.*

Annie's eyes opened. A bullfrog was staring at her like she'd squashed his personal blackfly collection.

The sun slanted through the overhanging reeds; it had to be near noon.

"Stupid. Do you have a death wish? You don't have time to sleep. Move."

The front of her clothes was soaked from shirt collar to boots. At least her back was warm and dry. She splashed her face, creaked upright, and stretched.

Annie started jogging to wake herself up. *Pigs on stage, I'm hungry. Why didn't I take some apples and cheese before I escaped?*

Something moved in the pines.

Annie increased her pace. *They caught me. What made me*

*think I could escape Redeemers?*

"I'm not caught yet," she whispered as she angled into the reeds. They covered her, but were so thick she had to push them apart with her arms to make any progress.

Behind her came the sound of something big shoving itself through the reeds. The thick stems snapped and cracked like wooden boards breaking. Annie plowed a narrow path through to the riverbank. Fear pumped her heart faster.

*Rock. Find a rock.*

She slid down the foot of bank into the shallows. No more noises came from the reeds.

*They're waiting to hear you move.*

Nothing but pebbles at her feet.

*There. To the right. Two rocks in the mud.*

She splashed once. *Reedemers hiding in the reeds, please think that was a fish.* The bigger rock fought her. She clawed under it. Too big. Buried too deep. *Pigs on stage!* There. It came free in her hand.

Weapon ready, she turned around and saw Siobhan on the bank above her. Annie's thoughts froze for a moment. Then she chucked the rock at Siobhan's knee.

"Hey!" Siobhan clutched her leg and went down on that knee.

Annie leaped up the bank and ran. A moment later, Siobhan's feet pounded behind her, limping at first, but gaining strength with each step.

"Stop, you idiot! I'm on your side."

Annie kept running. The grassy edge of the bank curved left ahead of her. The trees appeared closer there for her to use as cover.

Siobhan's footsteps still followed her, no closer but no farther away. Annie speeded up as she reached the curve. She'd been correct. Pines and chestnuts and maples with thick, wide branches.

Something hard struck her left shoulder blade and she hit the grass face first. A second later, Siobhan hauled her up by one arm and showed her the still-wet rock in her other hand.

"Don't fight me or this'll give you a two-day headache."

Annie forced herself to stay still. Siobhan would relax her hold sooner or later.

"That's the first smart thing you've done since last night." Siobhan pulled Annie to her feet and shoved a knapsack into her arms. "We have to keep moving. I don't trust Eamon not to follow us. Laura's labor was a false alarm."

The threat of Eamon following them was the correct carrot

to dangle in front of Annie's nose. She gestured over her shoulder. "Deeper into the trees."

Siobhan shouldered her own knapsack. "Good."

They pushed through the reeds and weaved between the sparser trees near the river until they reached the dense mix of older trees.

"You're fast," Siobhan said, falling into step with Annie. "It's a good thing I know the woods between home and Abilene. If you hadn't tied me up, this whole chase could've been avoided."

Annie said nothing. If she had to put up with Siobhan all day, she needed to decide how to play her end of the game.

"I'm starving, too. It took me hours to untie myself." Siobhan opened her knapsack and rummaged inside. "If there were such things as curses, like I read about in an old book once, you'd be warty and bald right now."

Annie didn't return her grin. *The best place to watch an enemy is right at your side. At least 'til the enemy falls asleep, and then watch the magic, kids: One disappearing Annie.*

"Would you please get that fence post out of your butt and say something? Aha, here it is. I brought apple bread." She unfolded a napkin and handed it to Annie: Two pieces of apple-nut bread lay on it. "You must be hungry too. Before the lamp gave out, I saw only two apple cores on the cellar floor. That was lots of fun, by the way, feeling in the dark for the knots you tied." She brought out a second napkin-wrapped package. "Come on. Eat."

The bread smelled sweet and spicy. Annie wanted it. Nora might be evil, but she was a good cook. Nora might be good at adding poppy or some other herb to the bread to make the Redeemers' victims compliant or helpless.

Siobhan stared at her, mouth full. "What's the matter?"

With a pointed look at the bread, then at Siobhan, Annie handed back the full napkin.

Siobhan laughed. "Matthew's hairy ass, you think it's drugged." She took the slices from Annie and ate a bite from each piece. "Ffhare," she said, mouth full. "Ffee? It's fine." She shoved them back at her.

Annie grabbed the napkin and took a huge bite from the top piece. Allspice, apples, walnuts, honey—as good as New Year's.

The sun angled into their eyes when it found a way through the long-needle pines that had taken over the woods.

When Annie finished the first piece of bread, she said,

"Matthew's hairy ass?"

"You haven't heard that one before? I thought everyone knew that expression."

Annie swallowed a bite from the second piece. "I'm sure the Redeemers have lots of private sayings the rest of us don't know."

Siobhan coughed, tried to swallow, coughed again. "What?"

*Oh, please.* Annie kept walking.

Siobhan jogged a few steps until she stood in front of Annie. "Did you mean that? You think I'm a Redeemer? Mom too, and the rest of us?"

Annie sighed. "What's the point of this game? You had the strange words on an old page from a book. You used it to set a trap. Your family was more subtle than the Redeemers in Kansas City, but the result was almost the same." She finished the rest of the bread. "You tried to kill me again."

Siobhan's shocked face seemed genuine. "No, no, no. Where did you get that idea? We're Readers, same as the ones who rescued you in Kansas City."

*Readers? How stupid did the Redeemers think she was? Everyone knew how to read.* "And I'm the Queen of America, still alive two hundred years after the Last War."

Siobhan snorted. "Seriously. Readers. We rescued you."

Annie stopped. "You did? You were in Kansas City?" A second later she started walking again. "Never mind. You're good, Redeemer. I believed you for a minute."

Siobhan grabbed Annie's arm. "What are you talking about? Redeemers tried to kill you. We're the good guys who saved you. Well, not we, as in my family in person, but Readers just the same."

Every muscle in Annie's body tensed, ready to fight her off. "That's why Eamon tried to strangle me in your fruit cellar. And why Nora wanted me too scared and weak to fight when you came to nail me to your barn wall." She broke Siobhan's hold on her. "I know what Padraig had to get ready while I was locked up. I heard you arguing in the kitchen. I'm not stupid, Redeemer. Just trapped—at the moment."

# CHAPTER SEVENTEEN

Siobhan was too fast for Annie this time. She clamped down on Annie's shoulders before Annie could dive deeper into the woods.

"Listen. I ran away, too. If you heard the argument, you know I didn't agree with them."

Annie raised one eyebrow. And I should believe you because?"

"Because Readers weren't meant to be like that."

Annie wanted to scream. "Who?"

"Readers. Us. For the third time, the people who pulled you off the cross before you died."

"Cross?"

Siobhan said, "I knew the masks were a bad idea. You can tell me later why the Redeemers targeted you. Just trust me, please. Mom and Eamon and Padraig and Laura are wrong."

Short, fat spruces crowded the long-needle pines now. Before nightfall Annie could lose herself. Siobhan might know these woods, but Annie knew more about covering her tracks.

"Annie, pay attention." Siobhan waited until Annie returned her gaze. "All us Readers know about you. We got word of the rescue from Kansas City, and that you weren't one of us. That's when the fighting started. Meetings in every town, letters between important Readers, lots of shouting. Should we leave you alone, should Kansas City have let you die, should we set the Redeemers on your trail."

Annie turned her face away. If only Siobhan would shut up and leave.

*Hank. The baby. Me. If I was dead, I wouldn't have to feel this pain.*

If only she wasn't such a good swimmer she could wade into the deepest part of the river, lie face down, and let herself sink.

"No."

"What?" Siobhan said.

Annie shook her head. *No, I won't. I am not giving up.* She pinched the ridge of her nose and stuffed the seductive voice into the locked room with the hammers and nails.

When she started walking again, Siobhan kept at her side, worry and eagerness in her face.

Annie played Siobhan's game. "You want me to believe you're not Redeemers in disguise."

Siobhan dodged several bulging tree roots. "Yes. Of course. I don't know where you got that idea. Redeemers always look like Redeemers."

"Not in my experience." Annie caught her left thumb worrying at the right-hand scar and stilled herself.

Siobhan's eyes flicked down at Annie's hands, but she only said, "I suppose, yeah, all this is new to you. Look, it'll take awhile to explain, but there are two main points. One—"

"Redeemers slaughter people like farmers slaughter cows." Annie welcomed the hate in her own voice. Hate kept her on her guard.

"Almost. Redeemers kill Readers. Nobody else."

"What in Matthew's name is a Reader?"

"We're, that is, well," Siobhan trailed off. "It's complicated. Here's the important part: We're not all doing it right."

Annie slapped away a spider. "Only some of you kill people?"

"Sheep on toast, no." Siobhan turned a full circle. "We need to head back to the river. Eamon and Padraig use this area to hunt deer sometimes. They won't fish today because mom said yesterday she wanted to make deer jerky."

Annie shrugged. "Fine." She let Siobhan lead. Maybe that would lull her into thinking Annie's directional skills and woodcraft weren't all that good.

They drank, then hiked along the river for an hour. Without warning, Siobhan stopped Annie and pointed to a hummock on the riverbank.

"That's a rabbit warren. I'll set a snare for when they come out to feed at dusk."

Siobhan didn't bring up the subjects of Readers or Redeemers while they waited. Annie wondered if Eamon and Padraig were tracking them or if Siobhan had invented the pursuit to keep Annie tied to her. Siobhan seemed earnest and sweet now, but so did the rest of her family at first.

Half an hour later a skinny brown rabbit dangled from the snare. Siobhan loosed and gutted it. "Might as well camp here."

Annie leaned against a pine, watching her. "We're far enough away for your brothers to stop following us?"

Siobhan buried the entrails and wiped her hands on the grass. "You've been gone something like eighteen hours. Eamon won't leave Laura that long, and Padraig's more likely to take the cart to Abilene and tell them to look out for you there."

"I'll get firewood, then." Twenty feet into the trees Annie gathered enough twigs and branches to keep a cooking-sized fire lit for several hours.

*Run now? She's occupied with skinning the rabbit.*

No. Annie needed what Siobhan knew. She was as strong or stronger than Siobhan. She didn't have to worry about fighting her. She would pump her dry and leave her behind.

She carried the wood to their chosen spot by the river and dumped it. "Do you have matches?"

Siobhan pulled a box from her knapsack. "I left home prepared. Yours has the same supplies."

"Why did you bring it?" Annie built the fire, found a knife in her knapsack, and stripped a sturdy twig to use for a spit.

"We can't live on air and river water all the way to Abilene. I also packed blankets, fruit, salt, nuts, jerky, and fishing string,"

Annie skewered the rabbit, set it in two Y-shaped forked branches, and gave it a test turn. *Don't feel guilty about the knapsack. Her brother tried to strangle you and her family was preparing to kill you.* She turned the rabbit slowly. "If only we had some basil and thyme."

Siobhan said, "I never thought of that. Mom and Laura are the cooks."

"It doesn't matter." Fat began to drop and sizzle in the fire. "Siobhan, why are you here?"

Siobhan became very busy finding plates, knives, and forks in both knapsacks. Annie waited. And waited. She turned the rabbit twenty times before saying, "Have you even asked yourself that question?"

The utensils rattled on the plates. "I'll get some water." She produced two cups and filled them at the river. When she handed Annie a full cup, she said in a deliberate tone of voice, ""I didn't agree with the deal my family struck."

Annie kept turning the rabbit with the same smooth motion. "What deal?"

Siobhan muttered, "Shoulda brought whiskey."

"Do you react to it like Eamon?"

Siobhan's head jerked up. "No. Eamon's always been an ugly drunk. The rest of us just get stupid. What I meant was, sometimes a gulp gives you temporary courage."

Annie said nothing.

"Sheep shit." Siobhan straightened her spine. "The deal to turn you over to the Abilene Readers. If anyone gets out of line, they get sent to Abilene. I've heard stories of Readers too scared to come to another meeting, of giving their Pages to relatives." She shook her head. "I can't imagine what would make someone give up their Page."

Annie started to ask, "What are you talking about?" but it was late and she was tired. Instead, she stuck her fork in the rabbit and tasted the juices. "This guy is so skinny, he's almost done. Let me have a little salt."

\* \* \*

Because of Siobhan's hints and teases, Annie stuck to Siobhan until they reached Abilene. She'd been to Abilene twice with Hank. She could lose herself there. Forget this Reader/Redeemer nonsense Siobhan kept trying to shove down her throat. If Siobhan opened her mouth, it meant a lie was about to come out.

"Look." Annie pointed southwest that evening as they looked for a secluded flat place to sleep. "Do you know what city that used to be?"

Skeletons of tall buildings caught the setting sun. Shiny bits glinted here and there as they continued walking. Hills covered most of the ruins from the river view.

Siobhan looked and turned her head away. "I hate those old cities. The empty windows look like dead eyes."

"You have a strange imagination. I think they look like caves waiting to be explored or big boxes hiding all kinds of surprises."

Siobhan shuddered. "Like a city full of ghosts."

Annie snorted. "Our first-grade teacher told us that one too. I think our parents told him to say that so we'd all stay away." She squinted at a larger flicker. A mirror? An ancient machine? "I'd love to explore one of the old cities."

"Are you crazy?" Siobhan said. "They're dangerous. Never mind the ghosts."

"I know, I know. Because of those special bombs that made some cities glow at night for decades. It's so annoying. No one knows which cities glowed and which didn't, so we have to avoid them all."

"Exactly. You want to start glowing yourself and die young?"

"I'm already dead. Nothing worse can happen to me."

Siobhan opened her mouth, glanced at Annie's covered wrists, and apparently changed what she'd been about to say. "Count me out. Nothing will get me into those piles of rock. Especially the southern ruins. They're supposed to be more dangerous than the northern ones."

"It'd be more interesting than herding sheep, wouldn't it?"

"Not if I end up turning into my own lantern."

That night, Annie showed Siobhan her trick to string a fishing pole and how to skin a trout without slicing her fingers.

Siobhan snapped off the fish head and cringed. "I hate that sound."

"But you like how the skin pulls right off with it." Annie slit the bottom of her own fish and broke off its head. "Doesn't bother me."

In the afternoon of the fourth day after Annie escaped from Siobhan's cellar, they reached the first of the outlying farms around Abilene.

"How much farther to the inn?" Annie said, walking faster.

"A couple miles," Siobhan said.

"Coffee."

"Fish I don't have to gut."

The hall clock at the inn struck five-thirty when she opened the front door.

Siobhan paid a week's room and board for both of them.

The bald innkeeper pasted a smile on his harassed face. "Up the stairs, third door on the left. Bathroom just opposite. Supper at six."

They washed the dust from their faces and hands and dropped their packs on the small blue dresser at the far end of their room. It wasn't much. A two-drawer dresser and two narrow beds pushed against plain wooden walls. One bed had the window at its foot and the other had a chair.

"Window or wall?" Siobhan said.

"Window, if you don't mind. I like to look out when I can't sleep."

A bell rang at the foot of the stairs. The aroma of baked ham and potatoes made their mouths water as soon as they opened the door.

The conversation in the packed dining room nearly deafened Annie after four days of woods and silence. They dug into full plates. Siobhan took seconds. The graying waitress brought coffee and cake after a freckled boy cleared their dishes.

"Do you know if the bookseller or the weaver is open late tonight?" Annie asked her after her first, wonderful sip of coffee.

"Weaver's at the table in the corner." She pointed. "Bookseller should be open. You need jobs?"

"Yes. How do I get to the bookseller's?"

"Left out the door, then left again. First shop past the market square." She hefted the coffeepot and went to the next table.

"Want me to walk you there?" Siobhan said.

Annie's eyebrows came together. "Why?"

"Moral support? Strange town?"

"It's light out. I don't need a babysitter." *She can stick to me like pine sap if she wants, but she is one Redeemer whose plan will fail.*

"That's not what I meant."

"Right." Annie hurried through her cake and left.

Unlike Topeka's, this bookshop was clean and well lit. Several people were still there reading or discussing the newspaper. She hovered near the bookseller as he made change for an old man.

"Excuse me," she said.

"Yes?" He was younger than Zachary in Topeka, but he already had the same squint from stooping over printed pages six days a week. Nice hair, though. Blond and curly.

"I write clearly and take dictation well. I can organize, alphabetize, and I'm not afraid of hard work or long days. I'm sure I can be of use to you." She gave him a smile that said "hire me."

He raised an eyebrow. "You sound quite competent. However, I already have an excellent secretary. Perhaps the innkeeper? I believe his second daughter was his bookkeeper, and she recently married the doctor's younger son."

Annie reappeared at the inn as the late diners were finishing dessert. She knocked on the innkeeper's office door, kitty-corner to the front desk.

"What?"

She opened the door and his scowl gyrated into an attempt at a smile. "How can I help you?"

Annie modified her "hire me" speech and his smile became genuine.

"You're serious?" He gestured at the papers covering his desk. "Harold didn't send you here as a practical joke?"

Annie grinned. "I don't know Harold and I really just got into town today."

"Missus, you are a better sight than a full house—almost." He came around and shook her hand. "Can you start tomorrow? Nine dollars a week and payday is Sunday. My name's Albert. Yours?"

"Annie Cook."

"Cook? You're not trying to get employed here just to turn into the apprentice cook?"

"If I never peel and chop another onion, I'll die happy."

"This job does smell better. Great. Right after breakfast then."

Siobhan wasn't in their room when Annie went up, so she stretched out on her bed and made plans for the money she'd soon be earning. After indulging in visions of new socks and a spare shirt, she speculated about the bookshelf in the living room downstairs. The bottom shelf looked like a book graveyard, almost as tempting as a new recipe used to be.

She woke when the door slammed.

"Slug," Siobhan said. "Did he hire you?"

"No, but the innkeeper did. He needed a bookkeeper." She sat up. "What about the weaver?"

"Carding wool. Boring, but it's a job. I'm beat. Just going to brush my teeth." She stopped with her hand on the door. "How long did it take them to find you in Topeka?"

"About a week."

"Any ideas on how?"

"No."

"Was it right after you ripped the page from the book in the museum?"

"Yes."

"Did someone follow you or anything?"

"What's your point?"

"There must be something that gives you away."

Annie ticked the points off on her fingers. "It wasn't my job. All the booksellers have employees. It's not my looks. They're average. It's not my hair. I'm not the only redhead in the world. Even if they were on the lookout for my hair, I look older now with the white streaks." She thought a moment. "It might be how I looked through all the books."

"Who noticed?"

"Zachary called me on it after I filled a box with pieces and parts."

Siobhan pounced. "Did he have a lot of customers? Did people watch you?"

"He watched me. He liked to grope." Annie faked a yawn. "I'll use the bathroom as soon as you're done."

\* \* \*

*Hank's naked body drips with blood. His hands, knotted around nothing, looked like they were trying to reach the spikes in his wrists. His nailed feet twitched. His legs trembled. His long black hair shadowed his face.*

*She tries to pull out the nails with her bare hands. They pass through her husband as though she was the ghost, not him.*

*His eyes open. "You lost my Page."*

*She kneels in the pool of blood at the bottom of his* t-shaped *boards. Her fingernails try to hook around the nail heads in his feet. He screams. She splashes backwards through the blood.*

*"You lost our baby," he says.*

*She clutches her stomach with both hands. When she removes them, they leave a bloody imprint of a newborn baby.*

*"You should be dead, too," he says. The nails pull themselves out of his wrists and feet. They impale her on the floor. She screams. He falls. His body crushes her. He opens his mouth and she thinks he's going to kiss her.*

*He vomits blood into her eyes, nose, mouth.*

# CHAPTER EIGHTEEN

"Annie, there's two brand-new dollars in my pocket," Siobhan said Sunday morning at breakfast.

"And?" Annie said through a mouthful of buttered biscuit. The Hank nightmare still clung to her like spider web. She'd dreamed it for three nights running. She would've traded her week's wages for six hours of sleep.

"I saw these gorgeous bead earrings in the glassblower's window. Come tell me why I absolutely have to buy them"

Annie smiled. "I used to have a pair of silver filigree earrings with a green glass drop bead at the bottom. Hank bought them for our wedding."

"I'd love to find a romantic husband. I swear time's running out and I'm getting too old to have babies. I mean, I'll be eighteen next March. The farm is killing my prospects."

Annie turned hard as a clay pot at the mention of babies. "I'll go with you after lunch. I have to get to work now."

* * *

Even at noon, the late October sun was too weak to warm them, so they hurried. Annie turned her attention inward to her feet, but they didn't even twinge. The air smelt of falling leaves and cut hay. A horse and cart clopped past them and she smelled fish.

"Here's the window," Siobhan said, puffing a little.

"That pale green vase is beautiful," she said. "Look at the

delicate loops on the top edge, like leaves."

"Where's the earrings I saw?" Siobhan said. "Ooh, look at the sets of buttons."

Annie pressed her nose to the window. "Wow. How does he do this? Daisies, poppies—look at that shade of red. Hey, Siobhan. There you go—sheep."

"Cute."

"Wine bottles, suns, moons... Here they are. The ones in the corner with the triple strands of red, orange, and yellow. Come in with me."

"Only if you stop me from buying the ones like them in the shades of green."

Heat and light hit Annie like twin sledgehammers when they opened the door. Squinting against the glare, she saw two figures holding long pipettes with globules of soft glass at the ends before a blazing furnace. A larger figure gave rapid instructions.

"Roll the pipes in your hands as you blow," a deep, feminine voice said. "Gently. Now blow harder—not too hard. Watch the glass take shape with your breath. Yes—yes—oh—" the shape at the end of the left pipette burst with a loud *pop*.

"Put it back in the cauldron, Hunter. Olive," to the other figure, "blow gently. That's it—slow down the rotation—right—now."

The instructor jumped to the end of the successful pipette and removed it from Olive's hands. With a deft twist, she freed the newly formed glass and molded the edges smooth.

"That's a good start. Both of you come to the crucible to try again."

Annie coughed. "Excuse us." All three figures turned toward her. "We'd like to buy some earrings."

The instructor stepped forward and pulled off thick leather gloves.

"Take a break, kids. I'll call you in a few minutes."

Olive and Hunter set down their pipettes and ran through a far door.

Annie's eyes adjusted to the glowing furnaces and she saw the instructor smile as they left.

"My children," the glassblower said. "They're just learning this step of the process." She pulled a cloth from beneath her leather apron and wiped her hands. "How may I help you?"

"We'd like to see the triple-strand earrings from the window."

"Certainly." She opened the wood shutters that covered the back of the display window and stretched a long arm over a vase and around a lamp. "Which ones?"

"Flame-colored and green."

"Here you are."

Siobhan and Annie turned the boxes to let the jewelry catch the light from the furnaces.

"They're perfect," Siobhan said. "Nearly an inch long, too. Did I see a mirror?" She half-turned toward the window. "Thought so." She picked up a small round mirror from behind the shutters and held one against her earlobe. "What do you think, Annie?"

"The colors are just right. Buy them. Now tell me these are all wrong for me."

Siobhan tipped her head to one side, then the other. "No, those beads don't go with your hair or set off the hazel in your eyes. They won't help you attract a new husband at all."

Annie replaced the earring in its box and handed the box to the glassblower. "Thank you anyway."

Siobhan closed her own box. "Always go with your gut, I say. I'm buying these. How much?"

"A dollar twenty-five."

Siobhan handed her exact change and the mirror.

Annie said, "I'm heading back to the inn, Siobhan."

She shivered s soon as she reached the sidewalk—the sun was nothing compared to those furnaces. She jogged the long way around the block to get her circulation going, and ended up at the theater. A gaudy orange and purple poster covered the top half of the door.

*Double Trouble.* "You'll split your sides laughing!" "The funniest show ever written!" "See it twice! You'll laugh so hard he first time you won't hear every joke!"

She grinned at the exaggerated drawing of a surprised man tripping over a ridiculously high threshold.

The wind blew leaves and dust into her hair. *Brr.* She needed a fire.

She ran back to the inn and pulled a shabby but comfortable armchair right up against the living room fireplace. The box with information about all the yearly customers needed organizing; she could easily do that in front of the fire.

A bucket clanged down the stairs and boots rat-tatted through the hall. The housekeeper came in, added a log to the fire, and tied back the curtains on all three windows.

*Get up, slug.* Annie smiled at the housekeeper and fetched the box form the office. Three hours, several thick pieces of paper, and half a bottle of ink later, every page was updated and in alphabetical order.

"Free." Annie set the box next to the chair and squatted in front of the bottom bookshelf. "Where did they dredge these up?"

Something called *Carlyle's French Revolution* wasn't written entirely in English. Were those squiggles supposed to be a language? Some sentences used the right letters, but none of those made sense either.

She re-shelved it and tried *King Solomon's Mines*. Yellowed, brittle paper; small type. Useless. Then her luck improved and for the next hour she read chapters in *Kim*, *Moby-Dick*, and *The War of the Worlds*. The first two were kind of interesting, but wow did they need some romance. The last one merely frustrated her. War books always seemed to be full of words that made no sense.

Next came a group of children's books. *Hop on Pop* made her giggle. *Charlie and the Chocolate Factory* made her hungry and she checked the clock: Twenty minutes until supper. She pulled out *The Secret Garden* and *A Little Princess*.

*Yes.* A rhyming—what did Siobhan call it—Page in *The Secret Garden*. It didn't sound anything like the words in her hidden pocket, and the word "ghost" made her wonder if it qualified. Perhaps it did, because it had a capital 'G' like someone's name.

"Let's test Siobhan's story. She should be back from her day off by now." Annie returned the other books and took the Page book to their room. Siobhan was already there, mending a hole in her backpack.

"You found what?" Siobhan locked the door.

"What you call a Page, I think. Here." Annie opened the book to the rhyme and handed it to her.

Siobhan read it to herself, then read it aloud. "Maybe. It doesn't sound quite like the other ones I've seen." She looked at the book's cover. "Where'd you find this?"

"On the living room bookshelf. There's a whole row of mostly ancient books on the bottom."

Siobhan slammed the book closed. "Out in the open? Was anyone else in the room when you found it? Did anyone see you read it?"

Annie plucked the book from Siobhan's hands. "Don't treat it like that. It's delicate." She waved away the lingering dust cloud from Siobhan's violence. "I don't know if anyone saw me. I was on the floor for an hour or so. Anyone could've come in or out. The housekeeper did once, early on."

"Sheep on toast, Annie, Redeemers plant Pages to trap us."

*Here it comes again, the claim that Siobhan is different than her family. She's the "good" Redeemer, or Reader, or whatever name she wants to use to get me to trust her.*

Annie laughed. "Who do you personally know that's actually happened to?"

"Well, nobody. But I heard of—"

"A cousin of a friend whose great aunt found one and—what?"

"Disappeared, moron. Like you did. Redeemers make Readers disappear. I told you."

"I think you're a lying sack of shit, Siobhan Farmer. I don't believe a word of this 'Reader' garbage you've been shoveling."

Siobhan's fists clenched. "Do you have rocks for brains? Why would I make up a story like that? Even a first-grader could see I'm telling the truth."

"I stopped believing fairy stories when I was five, sorry."

"But the Redeemers are—"

"You. The Redeemers are you and your drunk, heartless family. Find another cow to slaughter. It won't be me."

*Am I sure? Am I seeing Redeemers everywhere, no matter who I'm talking to? Am I throwing away my only chance to learn secrets I started this revenge journey to find out?*

Siobhan was talking fast, trying not to yell. The walls of the narrow room started to close in on Annie like the ones in the hidden cellar in Kansas City. *Out. Now. I don't care what she's trying to say.*

"I'm going around the block, Siobhan. Don't feel the need to be here when I get back."

\* \* \*

When Annie closed the door and stood on the back doorstep, she breathed long and deep. Sky. Fresh air. Freedom. It was cold outside, but not enough to ask the innkeeper for a spare coat. Besides, a fire and mulled wine waited by the living room fire.

Annie wandered among the pumpkins, orange in the moonlight and still warm from the sun. 'Bruiser,' the inn's contender for the blue ribbon in the Halloween biggest pumpkin contest, reclined in state on a hump of straw inside its own fence. She could make a hundred pies from it. A smile flashed over her face. The gardener would tear out his hair in clumps if he knew what she was thinking.

A less-wicked thought seized her. The pumpkin glowed as though it had been polished. The next minute, she stepped over the two-foot high fence and calculated her chances. Bruiser was at least four feet high and wide, its sides smooth at glass. She put one foot on the straw and grasped the stem. It was a good six inches around. She hooked her other leg over the pumpkin's top curve and heaved herself up. A scramble, a grunt, and there she was, eye level with the first-floor roof. She wedged between two ridges, straddled the stem, and whispered, "Giddy-up, Bruiser, or you'll be tomorrow's dessert!"

There wasn't enough laughter in her life anymore. *Face it. There's no laughter at all anymore.* The truth of it closed down on her like winter fog.

The noise of a horse and cart sounded around the corner. She slid off the pumpkin and jumped its fence. In a moment she was walking along the outside of the garden, just another inn guest taking an evening stroll.

The horse entered the square, pulling a small cart with a covered load. A Redeemer held the reins. *Hide. Now.* Her head swiveled right, left, right again—yes, he was still coming this way. Was the big pumpkin too obvious a hiding place? The horse clopped nearer. If he saw her dive behind the tomato plants it'd be like waving a "Notice me" sign.

Her legs kept walking at the same relaxed pace.

The cart drew level with her. Her hands shook like leaves in a wind; her knees clacked. Where was the river from here? South— straight ahead. That meant the woods were ahead and to the left. She could run faster than the horse could pull the cart.

What if he jumped off to chase her?

The driver's head turned toward her. She watched from the corners of her eyes. The hood was too deep to see a face. She put one hand on the garden fence, ready to push off it and run.

The cart continued up the street. The hood turned away from her and the Redeemer slapped the reins lightly on the horse's back.

If the horse picked up its pace, she didn't notice. As soon as the Redeemer took his eyes off her, she vaulted the fence, barged through the tomatoes, and shoved open the garden door.

*Slow down. Breathe. Close the door. Breathe.* Annie pushed damp hair off her face and tucked in her shirt. A voice finished speaking in the living room and laughter and applause followed. She used the noise as cover to run upstairs.

*Pack.* Where was her nightshirt? Middle drawer; got it. Her cup and pocketknife clanked at the bottom of her knapsack and she clutched them. *Quiet.* She had to get out without anyone seeing or hearing her. Should she leave Siobhan a note? No paper or anything in here. She wasn't about to light the lamp, either. She wrapped the cup, plate, and knife in the nightshirt. The blanket went in next; she had nothing else.

The door opened.

"'Night," Siobhan said to someone in the hall.

Annie dived in front of her and locked the door.

"Hey!" Siobhan tripped over her in the dark room.

"It's me. Don't light anything."

Siobhan lit the lamp and looked at the rumpled bed and lumpy knapsack. "What's going on?"

Annie put out the lamp. "I have to leave."

"What? Why?"

"There was a Redeemer driving a horse and cart." She talked so fast she barely understood herself. "He looked at me. I couldn't see his face. He flicked the reins to make the horse go faster. He could be telling them where I am. They could be halfway here by now. I have to go, Siobhan. I have to go right now."

She pulled open the top drawer and tossed Siobhan's nightshirt and spare socks on her bed.

"Annie, what are you doing?"

"If you're not a Redeemer, if you still want to come with me, you have to pack." When Siobhan didn't move, she stuffed the clothes into her knapsack for her.

"Slow down," Siobhan said.

"They could be at the back door!" Her voice cracked and she shoved Siobhan's knapsack into her arms.

"Stop it." Siobhan tossed it back into the corner. "You're overreacting. He didn't jump out of the cart and grab you like you said they did in Topeka, right?"

Annie shouldered her own knapsack and grabbed her fishing pole. "No. So what? If you're not coming, goodbye." She unlocked the door.

"Wait." Siobhan elbowed her aside and slammed shut the

opening door. "This is ridiculous. Think for a minute. The time they kidnapped you and the other time you stopped them, they went for you as soon as they saw you, right? Right?"

"Yes." Annie turned the doorknob.

Siobhan put her back against the door. "But this one didn't. What does that tell you?"

She tried to force open the door. "He's going for help. Let me out."

"No. Will you stop for a minute and use your head? Whenever you've seen a Redeemer, do they take any real notice of us?"

Annie tried to think over the blood pounding in her ears. "I don't... no. No, they don't. They only glance at people like they're making sure we're staying out of their way."

"See? What did you just tell me the one outside did?"

Annie stopped yanking the doorknob. "He glanced at me and then looked forward again."

"Did he slow down?"

She closed her eyes and pictured it. "No." *If Siobhan relaxes her shoulders one inch, I can pull open the door.*

"Did he look back?"

"No."

"See? You just proved it. He didn't come after you, therefore he didn't recognize you."

Annie opened her eyes and looked down at her throbbing fingers. They were white and scarlet from her death-grip on the doorknob. She relaxed one finger at a time, the blood rushing back into them with a final series of throbs. Siobhan stepped away from the door.

Annie yanked it open and ran down the back stairs. Siobhan's footsteps hit each stair a second behind hers.

She inched open the garden door and put one eye to the crack. No one. She opened it a smidgen wider. Tomatoes and pumpkins and moonlight. She took a deep breath and opened the door all the way, legs poised to run. No one in the garden, on the road, or lurking beneath the windows.

"I told you," Siobhan whispered in her ear. "Come back inside. Sheesh. You really do need me around. One of us has to keep a clear head."

*Did I overreact? Crickets are singing in the garden. That means no one's disturbed them. Maybe he didn't see me. Maybe Siobhan's telling the truth.*

Annie stepped back inside and closed the door. She climbed the stairs first, trying to hide her trembling leg muscles. When Siobhan put a hand on her elbow, she knew she wasn't succeeding.

"It's just the reaction," Siobhan said. "You'll be fine in a minute."

Siobhan steered her into their room and locked the door. Annie slipped off her knapsack and huddled on her bed, shaking so much the frame rattled.

"I'm going down to get you some hot wine," Siobhan said. "Don't run away, please."

When the doorknob turned a few minutes later, Annie leaped to the window and flipped up the latch.

Siobhan came in. "It's just me. Don't jump out the window, either. You'll squash the mums." She held out a steaming cup. "Here. You need this."

Annie took it with trembling fingers, but managed not to spill any. With a shiver she traced the wine's warmth down her throat, past her stomach and into her toes. "This is good."

Arms crossed and one toe tapping, Siobhan watched her finish. "I'll take it to the kitchen."

Annie drew the curtains and changed into her nightshirt, but didn't unpack anything else.

Siobhan rattled the doorknob a few minutes later. Her voice hissed through the keyhole. "Come on, Annie. It's me."

She didn't flinch away from Siobhan's rolling eyes. "Look, Siobhan-maybe-Redeemer, if I always assume they're after me I won't be caught by surprise again."

"For the last time, I am not a Redeemer. Sleep on it and maybe your brain will wake up amazed by the truth."

Annie didn't bother to reply. She wrapped the blanket around her shoulders and sat on her bed beneath the window all night, falling asleep and jerking awake to Siobhan's snores. Every time, she lifted one edge of the curtain and checked the gardens and street.

# CHAPTER NINETEEN

What a miserable job," Siobhan said over supper the next night. She rubbed bloodshot eyes. "And I thought herding the stupid animals was hard."

Annie set down her soup spoon. "We need theater."

"You're kidding."

"I'm tired of looking over my shoulder every time I go out after dark. You're tired of picking straw out of wool. Break time." She waved at the waitress. "Angie, is *Double Trouble* as funny as the poster says it is?"

"You haven't seen it?"

Annie shook her head. "Should we have?"

"You two been living in a cave?"

Annie smiled at Angie's amazed face. "So it is that good."

"It's the funniest show I've ever seen. Hey, Marvin," she caught the arm of the waiter as he passed, "they've never seen *Double Trouble*. Should they go?"

"Are you kidding? You haven't lived 'til you've seen it," he said. "I laughed so hard the second time I had hiccups for hours."

"Told you," Angie said. "It plays every fall. Everyone in town has seen it at least twice. Didn't you hear about it last year when they traveled with it? Where are you from?"

"Kansas City."

"Outside Topeka."

"That explains it. They went west last time. They're going east with it in the spring." She picked up their plates and glasses. "I'll bring dessert. It's six-thirty now. Shovel it in and run."

They ran.

\* \* \*

"Oh, my. Oh, my." Annie searched for a dry spot on her handkerchief as they huddled into a corner, away from thirsty intermission wine-seekers.

"Mine is soaked too," Siobhan said. "How will we get through the second half?"

"'Madelyn, don't open that door!'"

Siobhan punched her. "Stop!"

They went into another laughing fit.

\* \* \*

"How many times can one actor trip over the same threshold?" Annie said when they reached the street after the play finished. She tucked the sodden handkerchief into her pocket and wiped her eyes on her sleeve.

Siobhan flapped her arm. "My sleeve is soaked."

"Mine, too. And why is it even funnier the twentieth time?"

"I have the worst stitch in my side."

Annie slowed her steps to let Siobhan walk it out. The rest of the exiting audience flowed around them toward the inn and down the side streets.

"At least we don't have the hiccups."

Siobhan straightened and took her hand off her ribcage. "How did it go? Steal a kiss—"

"Feel the bliss—"

"Close the bedroom door now." They finished the verse together.

Annie coughed on the river-damp night air. "The rest of those lyrics aren't fit for the ears of anyone under fourteen."

A straggling group of twelve—and thirteen-year-olds walked around them, and the last one turned and stuck out his tongue. They ran out of sight around the post office, singing the same song.

Siobhan inhaled ostentatiously. "'Through the keyhole—'"

"We—" A cloth bag came down over Annie's head. She breathed in flour and coughed.

"What the—" Siobhan's voice was muffled.

Two pairs of hands grabbed Annie and pushed her forward.

"Quiet!" a voice said at her ear.

Annie stumbled over a threshold. The hands pulled her up. Her head snapped back and her brain shook off the surprise. She dug in her heels. The hands gripped harder. Stairs appeared under her feet and the hands dragged her faster. She tripped and slid. They yanked her forward and her shoulders nearly wrenched out of their sockets.

The stairs ended in a smooth floor. The hands turned her around and shoved her onto a hard seat. She heard scuffling and whatever she was sitting on bounced. The cover was yanked from her head and a lamp thrust in her face.

Annie flinched and turned her head to the left. Two flour sacks lay next to her on a wood bench. Siobhan sat on the other side of the sacks, her black hair speckled with flour.

*Don't give in. Don't show fear. Defy them.* Annie shoved her hands into her trouser pockets to hide their trembling and looked up.

Half a dozen people stood over her, their faces hidden by black masks.

A memory superimposed onto the masks—a row of hooded killers. They picked her up and carried her to a wide table that held two crossed wood beams. They threw her onto the wood.

She shook her head and the memory dissolved.

"Annie Cook."

She remained silent.

"Siobhan Farmer."

Siobhan brushed flour from her eyelashes and sat straighter. "Who are you?"

"You will do as we say."

"Why?" Annie said. *Two men and a woman. They sound like muscle.*

"You will stop looking for the Pages."

"What?"

"You will stop looking for the Pages."

"What do you know about it?" *Two more men. The skinny one has a deep voice but sounds younger. A weak link?*

"You are putting all our lives in danger."

*The last one is another woman. Sounds nervous. Doesn't like the plan?*

Siobhan sneezed. "We're strangers. How could anything we do affect you?"

"We are in every town. We protect our own."

*The first one again, farthest to my right. Were they hiding nails and a hammer? Did one of them have a knife to slice off my clothes?*

"What is this, a bad play rehearsal?" Siobhan said. "Let me guess: You speak next." She pointed to the one next to the lamp holder.

"Wait a minute. Who's 'we'? You six or are there more of you cowering outside?" Annie said.

The one Siobhan had pointed to said, "You do not need to know."

"This is ridiculous." Siobhan started to get up, but the one in front of her pushed her back down.

The lamp holder said, "Do you think you're simply indulging in an interesting bit of historical research?"

Annie seethed. These weren't Redeemers. Redeemers wouldn't waste time on word games. They'd either lock her up for days or start the torture right away. She had no time to waste on blustering masked Readers, assuming only readers played this game.

"We protect our own," the first woman said. "When we see a stranger poking around shelves of old books, we find out about her."

"You're itinerant workers, here to make some quick cash and waste your time at the theater," The lamp holder said. "You're trouble. You will stop looking for Pages." He stepped closer to Annie.

"At least you've stopped speaking like first-graders reciting a lesson," Siobhan said.

"First-graders know enough to pay attention when authority speaks," the woman said.

Annie made herself look bored. "Who died and made you the King of Abilene? Let's go, Siobhan. We don't have to listen to this." She stood and pushed between the lamp holder and the man next to him. That man and the woman beside him caught her arms and threw her against the wall next to the stairs.

*They both have muscles like blacksmiths. Redeemers help me— they really are going to kill me. And Siobhan. I was wrong about Siobhan.*

"Shut up and listen," said the lamp holder, his face only an inch from hers. "We will do whatever it takes to stop you. We can get you fired. We can toss you and your belongings into the fields outside of town like the garbage you are."

*Get them angry. Get them to let go, even if it means a slap in the face. Then grab Siobhan and up the stairs to freedom.*

"You're pretty brave, threatening two women in a dark cellar with all your pals for support. Do you kick puppies for fun?"

The hands tightened on her arms and shoulders. The man set down the lamp.

Annie wished he hadn't. When the masks were lit from below they looked like threats rather than shields.

"I can make you so scared of what we could do to you that you'll never go into a bookseller's again." He grabbed her hair and wrenched her head back.

"I can tell you more about fear than you want to know." Her heart pounded, but her voice remained steady. "I've been terrorized by the best."

"I wonder," he said, and took a thick piece of metal from his pocket. With a flick of his wrist, the metal opened into a knife. He held it up to her eyes. "If you can't see, you're no longer a threat to us." He touched the point to her cheek.

"Stop."

Annie didn't move. Neither did he. The others looked at Siobhan.

"Read this." Siobhan took a letter from her trouser pocket and handed it to the young man on her left. He brought it to the lamp and opened it.

"Walt, you'd better see this," he said.

"Read it to me," Walt said. "I'm busy."

"It says: Watch for a short woman with red hair. She's young, but her hair has white streaks. Her wrists and feet will always be covered, no matter what the weather is like. Her name is Annie, but she may change it. Expect her to use several different last names as well, and she may be working at a bookseller's. Important: she is looking for Pages. You must stop her. She is not one of us. They are hunting her. If they catch her in your town, all of you will be in danger. Copy this letter and send it to the group in the next town west along the river or north toward the hills."

*The letter Sara and Max wrote about me. The Readers are keeping ahead of me. Waiting to pounce. Waiting to finish what the Redeemers started.*

Walt released her hair but kept the knife open. "Let me see that." He read it and looked at Siobhan. "How did you get this?"

"Someone passed it to us last month in Topeka. I passed the glassblower a copy yesterday."

*I take it back. I was right about Siobhan. If only I'd ditched her one day earlier.*

"She showed up at our farm two weeks ago. They almost caught her in Topeka, but she ended up with us. We trapped her and then allowed her to escape. I attached myself to her as a minder. She didn't know that, of course. She hasn't found anything yet. If she does, I'll handle it."

*You liar. You snake. You Readers are nothing but apprentice Redeemers, learning terror and torture from your elders like I learned cooking from my grandmother.*

The woman holding Annie looked sideways at Siobhan. "How will you handle it if they catch her when she's with you?"

"She can defend herself. So can I. I think they're expecting her to be alone. We'll use me as an element of surprise."

"Or you could leave her and get away yourself."

"Or I could do that." Siobhan paused. "It's safe to let her go now."

Walt looked at Siobhan and then at Annie. He nodded. "Let her go."

The hands released Annie.

"When are you leaving town?" Walt said.

*I'd snatch your knife and slice off your mask if I thought it would do any good to know what you look like.* "In other words, leave town as soon as you get packed."

"Exactly."

*Drop dead.* "Siobhan gets paid tomorrow. Is it all right with you if we both have money to travel on before we go?"

"Don't be surprised if a few extra people hang around the inn tomorrow." He flipped the knife closed.

"Come on, Annie," Siobhan said.

As they passed Walt and the young man with the deep voice, Annie could've sworn their hot breath tingled her neck. Her legs begged to leap the stairs three at a time, but she forced them to walk at Siobhan's steady pace.

The streets were empty. The inn was dark. They took turns in the second-floor bathroom and went to bed. Neither spoke.

# CHAPTER TWENTY

Annie lay awake listening to Siobhan's snores and the clock in the dining room bong three times.

*Siobhan's been snoring for two hours. Now or never.*

Annie folded back the covers and stuffed her nightshirt into her knapsack. The first few inches of dresser drawer slid open without a creak. She pulled out her clothes.

*I didn't even get a chance to darn my socks. I'll have to get my new shirt in Plainville now.*

She ran her hands along the door. She'd heard squeaks and clinks around it soon after she pretended to be asleep. Siobhan's booby trap should be attached to the doorknob. There. A knotted string.

She leaned her knee against the string. *Have to maintain the tension. What an easy knot. Guess Siobhan had trouble in the dark.* She coiled the string around her fingers, once, twice—ten times, until she reached the empty candlestick balanced on top of Siobhan's boot.

Good trap. If Annie tried to leave, the falling candlestick would make just enough noise to wake up Siobhan. She set the string and candlestick on the floor next to the boot.

*Sleep tight, babysitter. You're out of a job now.*

She eased open the door and tiptoed out. The back stairs didn't creak. She opened the garden door with the same stealth. Not even a cricket chirping at this hour. She put on her boots in the doorway, settled her knapsack on her shoulders, picked up her fishing pole, and headed to the river.

The stars had faded and the sky was gray instead of black when she stopped at a low spot in the riverbank. Those humps to the south were old city ruins.

Siobhan said she'd never go into ruins, particularly southern ones.

Annie knelt and dipped her hand into the water. This section undulated and the current wasn't too strong. It was cold, though.

*Since when do I flinch at cold water? The river's not even a hundred feet wide here.*

She sat in the grass, took off her boots and socks, and rolled up her pants to her knees. Then she took the blue leather roll from her inner pocket, pushed it into the toe of one boot, and piled both socks on top of it. The little paper couldn't help her, but it was the symbol of her first success in clue hunting. Untying her knapsack, she stuffed the boots on top of everything and slid the fishing pole through the laces.

*Cowardly snake will never find me now.*

She waded into the water and gasped. Her whole body erupted in goosebumps. She splashed farther. The water reached her knees, her thighs. The weak current pushed her. She wobbled on the smooth, uneven rocks and dug her toes into the mud.

*Hope no catfish are up this early.* "Listen, fish, my toes are not on the breakfast menu."

Halfway across, the water sloshed over her waist and she slipped the knapsack off her shoulders. Holding it above her head like a trophy helped her balance.

The sky turned pale blue, the clouds pink. Her teeth chattered. The opposite bank came nearer and the water fell to her knees, then her ankles, and she squished up onto the grassy bank.

She needed a fire, but there were no woods on this side. The reeds and cattails could be dry enough to take the worst of the cold away. She untied her knapsack and dumped everything onto the grass to get to the pocketknife which always fell to the bottom. Shivering, she sawed through a wide swath of reeds. She piled them in an open spot and touched a match to the feathers on a reed. They burned down to the stem in a flash.

Maybe a cattail. She tried a new match on one. Pungent, but it burned longer than a reed.

She made a cattail pyramid, filled the inside with broken reeds and more cattails, and lit it.

This makeshift fire wasn't going to last. She pulled off her trousers and underpants and wrung them out. Since no one lived on this side of the river, she turned her bare bottom to the flames and the goosebumps faded.

The grass rustled to the south. She yelped and covered herself with her cold, wet clothes. When she looked up, two deer sprinted away from her. She laughed and got dressed.

The fire collapsed in on itself. *Well, it had been better than nothing. At least my feet are dry.* She swung her knapsack over one shoulder and her stomach growled.

"Wait a bit. I want to be out of sight of the river before I feed you."

The sun shone on the tops of the humps, changing them into crumbling walls and chimneys. Freedom. Siobhan the snake wasn't going to follow her into here. Annie hadn't planned to explore a ruined city, but it was the perfect way to uproot that particular clinging vine.

Maybe there'd be an ancient book or two in an old cellar. She stepped onto the cracked gray surface of a pre-Last War road.

Ten minutes later, she was thinking uncomplimentary thoughts about this particular pre-Last War invention. "If these roads weren't so wide, I'd never get through them." She picked her way over another pile of heaved-up road and looked around. "This could be the town square with all these wide buildings. Wonder how tall they used to be?"

Her voice echoed when she passed taller stacks of rubble. The sun shone directly overhead. Her stomach bunched itself into fists and pounded her spine.

Where were the robins? The squirrels? Did they keep away because this was one of the cities that used to glow? She was not hungry enough to catch and cook a glowing squirrel.

She picked her way along a sort-of path that ended at a pile of pebbled gray stone. It was low enough to straddle and get to the 'inside' of the building. The small piles of weed-covered stone told her nothing, though. She poked around the floor to see if this building had a cellar.

The broken stones hid nothing but dirt. No worms in the dirt, either. Annie kicked at a smaller pile and it fragmented beneath her boot heel.

*Last War glow poison can't kill me. I'm dead.* "There's plenty more to explore and the longer I stay here the farther away Siobhan the snake will wander. A perfect plan." She hitched her knapsack higher on her shoulders and climbed out the other side.

After several more low piles of broken rock, the wide road turned to the right and a dozen huge building shells confronted her. Two piles of reddish-gray stone ahead of her were hopeless, but the third had steps. She used hands and feet to get closer to part of a name carved in stone. "Kind of intact, too. What sort of building were you?" She knelt on a wide piece of horizontal rubble and tilted her head to the angle of the stone and read "Salina Public Lib."

"Salina must be the city. What's a Lib?" She looked at the surrounding stone for the rest of the word. "Oh, well. Let's see if I can get in here. Then I'll find something to feed you, stomach. Promise."

She shaded her eyes and looked across the eroded stones. A dark patch several yards beyond the sign could be an opening. She climbed and scrambled and when she reached it, she had to toss aside more pieces of old road and rock. A test sniff indicated nothing rotting down there. She stuck her face in the hole and wrapped her arms around her head to block the sunlight. That didn't work; the sun shone through a multitude of holes in the roof. No way to tell if anything glowed.

"I'm dead. I don't care." She stepped down onto narrow stairs. After the first seven or eight they were less obstructed. Ankle-deep dust and dirt covered the floor. Perhaps this had been the town storage center; rows of ceiling-high shelves had toppled like a giant deck of cards. Grimacing at the state of her clothes, she shuffled through the dust. When she brushed off the first shelf and touched a shape on it, whatever it was crumbled to powder.

She sneezed. "That looked like paper. Books. Ancient books. Am I the luckiest woman on the river, or what?" She covered her nose and mouth with her sleeve and stopped under the last hole in the roof. One set of shelves leaned over a shorter set, protecting it. She crawled into the narrow space and touched a thin rectangle.

"Come on, book. You need someone to read you after all these years." The outside disintegrated, but the center stayed together. More filled the lower shelf. In the middle of those, she touched one that poofed dust at her but didn't crumble.

"At last." She inhaled and coughed. With great care she pulled it out. *The Wind in the Willows.* Her luck ended when she opened it.

The pages were brown and the type illegible. "Blast." She tried the bottom shelf. Something had eaten through these.

"I did not find a pre-war bookseller's just to watch the books fall apart." Her voice fell flat; no echoes. Too much dust.

She stomped to the farthest corner of the room. No light reached here and shelves leapt out at her shins. "Ouch." She stretched out her arms so they would hit a wall before her nose did, and touched more books. Heavy covers this time, none of that flimsy paper. She held her breath and opened one. The pages broke off into her hand. She threw it onto the floor. "Come on."

She groped to her left and tripped. Inching forward on hands and knees, she found a wall with built-in shelves. This could have protected the books better. Her fingers bumped into something flat and smooth. Not a book cover. Nothing she'd ever touched had been this smooth. She lifted it. Wrong. It was a book. When she tested a page, it bent but stayed in one piece.

"Oh, yes, oh, yes. Come to Annie."

The book stuck to another book beneath it. She took them both. Giggling, heart racing, she banged her shins against more shelves getting back to the light. She sneezed again and again as she kicked up two hundred years' worth of dust.

Sunlight and fresh air, that's what she needed. She ran to the stairs and climbed them using her right hand, clutching her prize against her with the three working fingers of her left.

Wind blew through the ruins, raising funnels of dirt. Grass and trees and water called her name. All this dead rock gave her goosebumps. Humans needed the earth under their feet. She took the quickest route out, zigzagging to her left through crumbled streets. As soon as she reached the edge she ran across the tall grass, whooping and laughing, until she was surrounded by green again.

She unlaced her boots and kicked them off, then removed her socks and dug her toes into the cool ground. When her world was normal again, she dared to look at her only shirt and trousers. Random streaks and blotches of dust covered her, but nothing disastrous. She set the books on her lap and caressed the top one. She'd seen that clear covering somewhere. Right. The museum in Topeka. The bag that said "rolls" of some kind. Whatever that smooth material was, it was nothing if not versatile. She slid her thumbnail between the stuck covers. They cracked and fell apart.

"Oh, no, I wrecked the covers." The shards fell to her lap

when she took her hands off the books. But the book, *Superman, a Cinematic Retrospective,* had another, paper cover. It showed a man in a tight blue shirt punching the air in front of him. She looked closer. How could anyone paint this kind of detail? She could see individual strands of hair in the curl on his forehead. Two smaller paintings inset below the man were also detailed enough for her to count the blades of grass in one.

She set down that book and brushed away the broken pieces from the second book. *America's Favorite Desserts.* This artist used the same detailed painting technique. Rows of faded strawberries and blueberries striped the whipped cream on top of a cake. Next to the cake, a plate with cherry pie slice and a mound of something white on top of it.

Her stomach pointed out that she hadn't eaten anything since supper before *Double Trouble.*

The sun was near setting. The fish would bite now, if she could build a fire that would last long enough to cook one. Wait: She'd tripped over broken chairs in the Lib's cellar. She slipped on her socks and boots and was back at the cellar doorway in a few minutes. The angle of the sun made it darker down there. What if it glowed? *Glowing doesn't matter. I. Am. Dead. It'll take me five minutes to reach the back corner, pick up the wood, and get back out. Nothing can happen to me in that time. Besides, I spent at least half an hour in there earlier and I feel fine.*

The wood in the back definitely felt like pieces of a chair. She felt to her right and found more. It was on the brittle side but she wasn't about to nitpick.

Before the sun set, she caught two trout and built a small fire with half the wood and as many cattails as she could carry. The trout could've used some basil and onion. She read the recipe book while she ate.

*A cookbook is fascinating, but if luck had appeared the way I needed, one of these books would have Page words in it. The Superman book is nothing but painting after painting.*

When it grew too dark to read, she put her back to the fire to study the city. The humps looked as innocent as hills or tree stumps. Nothing winked or glowed, not even fireflies. Salina was a safe ancient city, then.

She fed the fire and pulled out the blanket. If she stayed on this side of the river, maybe she could find another town and maybe it would have a Lib with books too. Since it was one hundred percent certain Siobhan was hunting this stray sheep, looking for another non-glowing city

*What an idiot I've been. So sure I had my escape under control I ignored the danger signals pouring out of Siobhan's glib mouth. So full of my own ingenuity I allowed Siobhan to convince me to stay after the Redeemer drove by, all so her friends could try to intimidate me.*

Annie jabbed a piece of wood into the fire so hard it snapped and sparks flew.

First thing in the morning she explored the city a little longer. The streets she chose were lined with collapsed shapes of rust, metal showing beneath them here and there when she scraped with her fingernails. Nothing indicated what they used to be, and only a few of the houses had even a piece of wall standing. She left Salina behind at noon.

The weather changed that night and she shivered, fireless, among a group of shriveled birches. Chickadees burst into song as soon as the sun rose. She threw a clump of grass at them.

"Miserable birds. Who told you to be so cheerful in the morning?" She refused to think that traveling with Siobhan the snake made mornings less cold and lonely. Squinting through the stingy birch branches as she combed through her tangled curls, she changed her plans. The woods on the north side of the river never looked better. If she didn't find another ruined city by sunset, she'd cross back over the river. A warm night's sleep called to her almost as much as the books in her backpack.

No more cities loomed ahead of her, and the trees remained sparse and stunted. Deer clung to what shelter they gave, but she saw no squirrels or foxes. She looked in vain for apple or pear trees, or even wild onions or carrots. No wonder there were so few animals on this side. Nothing grew for them to eat.

She couldn't read and walk at the same time, so she weighed her chances of finding a job in Plainville, the next town along the river. Booksellers or innkeepers or...

How would she avoid the Redeemers or another gang of Reader cowards with knives if they came after her?

'Or you could leave her and get away yourself.'

'Or I could do that.'

"Get out of my head!" Annie banged her good fist into her right temple until she felt a bruise beginning. "Focus. What about doing laundry or waitressing at the inn?"

Waitressing conjured up thoughts of pancakes and coffee. She gave in to the distraction.

The excuses for trees increased all day. By early evening Annie was walking through apprentice woods. In twenty years, maybe, they'd be worth the name. The river ran wide, shallow, and rocky again, bordered by scrawny willows. She could use the rocks to cross and be dry in twenty minutes with a real fire.

She'd secured her boots and socks in the knapsack and was rolling up her trousers when the trees rustled behind her. She turned her head to see how many deer were investigating her this time and Siobhan plopped down next to her.

"Finally."

# CHAPTER TWENTY-ONE

Annie leaped to her feet. Her knapsack tipped over. Siobhan reached out for it and looked up in time for Annie to land a punch to her jaw. Siobhan fell backward. Annie snatched her knapsack and ran into the river. She fell halfway across, but kept her knapsack above her head and splashed upright again.

"Wait!" Siobhan called.

Annie reached the northern bank and pulled herself up on protruding tree roots. Her body shook from the cold water and she stumbled over rocks and more tree roots on her way into the woods. She didn't hear footsteps behind her until Siobhan's hands came down on her shoulders. Annie spun and cocked her fist.

"Wait." Siobhan put up her hands to block the punch. "Let me explain."

"You explained everything in the Abilene cellar."

"I have to talk to you."

"No. And don't follow me. I got away from you before. I'll do it again."

Annie made it to a cluster of massive yews, but Siobhan caught up to her and yanked her backwards by her collar. When she fell onto her back, Siobhan sat on her legs.

"Now you have to listen. I'll let you up after you hear me out."

Annie squirmed and grunted beneath her. "Get off me. I'll clock you with a rock if I have to." Her hand touched her fishing pole and she swung it.

Siobhan caught it and tossed it into the woods. "Five minutes. That's all I want."

Annie bucked her hips but couldn't dislodge Siobhan's weight. She stopped fighting. "Fine." *If she talks, she'll get distracted. All I need is leverage.*

Now that she had permission to speak, Siobhan couldn't seem to find the right words. Crickets and cicadas started a chirping contest.

"Your five minutes are running out."

"I'm not what you think."

"Right."

"Yes, I came with you as a watchdog. We got the letter a week before you showed up. Mom thought she recognized you from the description. You fell asleep on the porch in the afternoon, remember? Mom and I planned a final test then."

"A trap." Annie wasn't ready to push her off yet; her legs tingled.

"Okay, okay, a trap. We didn't expect you to panic like that, but it sure proved we were right."

If Annie could've worked up a wad of spit, she would've hawked it into Siobhan's lying face. "Get off my legs; they're numb."

Siobhan hesitated.

"I can't move them until I get the feeling back. You get five more minutes."

Siobhan hopped off and sat back on her heels next to Annie. "When I got Eamon off you, I dragged Mom away from Laura and got us all in the kitchen." She knotted and unknotted her fingers. "That fight wasn't a fight. We stood by the door to make sure you'd hear us. Eamon all drunk and worried made it sound more like we were arguing for real."

Annie rubbed her legs to get rid of the pins and needles. "It worked."

"I'm sorry."

"Go swallow some of the shit you're shoveling."

Siobhan flinched. "I know you're angry. But you don't have to do this on your own anymore. I'll help you."

"Like you helped in Abilene? You made sure they didn't waste any time. Attack Annie before she gets spooked and runs again."

"I didn't tell them to grab you off the street. They grabbed me, too, remember?" She pitched a pine cone toward the river. "All I did was my job, passing the letter to the glassblower. You know, when I bought the earrings."

"With a few suggestions of your own thrown in? Telling your charming friend with the knife how to intimidate me?" The pins and needles in her legs faded. She'd be able to run in a minute.

"He's not my friend. I had no idea they'd react like that. I thought they'd hover around the inn and slip you a note to get out of town. You know, just menacing enough to get you scared and clingy."

"After all you told me about the Abilene Readers bullying other Readers into doing what they said or else?" Annie laughed. "You're as bad as Eamon. Rather than dirty your own hands you threw me to Walt's gang. Why did you bother to interfere in Abilene? If he'd done what he wanted, I'd be blind or dead in some alley and you'd be on your way home."

"I did not throw you to them."

"What would you call it, then?" Annie could just make out Siobhan's face in the twilight. "I'm the cow you led to the slaughterhouse?"

She stood and Siobhan groped for her hands. "Please. Please." Tears clogged her voice. "Let me explain."

"Forget it. You've explained enough." She tried to pull out of Siobhan's hold, but her hands gripped tighter.

"I can help you. I know more about the Redeemers."

"Another carrot to lure the cow?"

"Please stop." Siobhan retrieved one hand and wiped her nose on her sleeve. "It's cold. Let's go make a fire and get dry and I'll tell you."

Now that Siobhan had said it, Annie remembered she was cold and wet and hungry. More than that, she was sick of this conversation. Her legs were fine, her knapsack within reach.

"Let go, Siobhan."

"You trusted me before. Please give me another chance."

"Wrong. I never trusted you. I have enemies chasing me from town to town. I don't need one at my side anymore."

Siobhan released her. Annie expected another argument, but Siobhan huddled into a ball instead.

Annie hefted her knapsack, turned away, and started another long, cold night's walk. The cricket-cicada concert had stopped sometime during their argument and she heard with perfect clarity the moment Siobhan started to sob.

*Don't fall for it. Look how she lulled you into complacency between her farm and Abilene. She'll throw you to the Redeemers. She said so. Keep walking.*

A deep voice said, "Stop!"

# CHAPTER TWENTY-TWO

A brown and red scarecrow sprang onto Annie and they crashed to the ground. Pine needles poked her arms and back and she rolled to one side. Her knapsack slipped off one shoulder when she clambered up. There wasn't a lot of moonlight, but she saw the scarecrow's silhouette get to its feet. She started to run, but the off-balance knapsack hampered her and he caught her. His breathing rustled her hair; he was at least a foot taller than her five-foot-nothing. She didn't bother to look down at his legs. He could outrun her.

Siobhan ran up next to them. "Who are you?"

"Jack Chandler."

Annie struggled in his arms. "Let go of me."

"Sorry." His hands popped up like she was on fire. "Siobhan, don't let her leave."

"How do you know my name?" Siobhan said.

"I was in the cellar with Walt on Monday."

Siobhan snapped her fingers. "You read the letter out loud."

Annie edged away. "I left town. You're all safe. Why are you following me?"

"I'm not following you. Not for them, if that's what you mean. I need to talk to you."

"Walt already got your message across." Annie took another step.

"Wait," Siobhan and Jack said.

"What is with you people? I'm not your sheep," she said to Siobhan. "Or your hunting prize," to Jack. She flicked the loose strap over her shoulder and kept walking.

Siobhan fell into step with her. "You don't understand."

Jack plowed through the yews to Annie's other side. "I've been looking for you since Tuesday morning. I tried the inn first. Was Albert furious! He'd just sent one of the waiters to your room to look for you, and you were gone. A bunch of people wanted to pay their bills and he didn't have anything ready. He put a good face on it but after they were all gone he sat down with his cronies and called you a few choice names."

*One foot in front of the other. The riverbank's only a few yards away. You could try to trip this guy into the river.*

"I liked him. Thanks for wrecking any chances of me getting a job with him again."

Siobhan sneezed. "Can we sort this out over a fire? I'm cold and starving."

"Please, Annie." Jack put a hand on her arm. "I have to talk to you."

Annie stopped walking and tried to see his face in the useless moonlight. *Redeemers preserve us.* He looked barely fifteen. His eager-puppy expression made Annie feel thirty-eight years old instead of eighteen. She couldn't leave him with Siobhan the snake. At least not until she made sure he wasn't another snake.

"I was going to catch some supper," she said to Siobhan. "I don't know if any fish will be in this section of the river since we chased each other through it."

"I have enough cheese and jerky for all three of us," Siobhan said.

"All right." *No big risk, even if Jack is another Siobhan, which I'm certain he is. We will eat and talk as though we all trust each other and as soon as the snoring starts, I'll vanish into the woods. These two have no idea how quiet I can be.*

Annie kicked something and looked down at a fallen apple. She looked up into a wild apple tree at last. She picked as many as she could reach.

"Where did you learn to hit like that?" Siobhan said, rubbing her jaw.

"I grew up with two older brothers. They taught me how to take care of myself."

The three of them gathered every fallen branch and twig between the pines and the river. Annie built a fire twice as big as usual and Siobhan bent two of the greenest branches in half. She planted the ends on the opposite side of the fire, took off her trousers, and draped them over the arches.

"Drying grid for wet pants," she said. "Jack, I hope you're not squeamish about seeing strangers in their underwear."

Jack hunched his shoulders. "I, uh, I guess not."

Annie inspected the apples. "I'll roast some of these."

"I'll get rocks to bank the fire," Siobhan said.

Jack set aside a trussed-up bundle of kindling, knapsack and quiver. Annie divided half a dozen small apples between three sticks and held the speared fruit over the fire. Its light gave her a better look at Jack. He needed a few extra meals and pieces of reeds stuck out of his thick, twisted rolls of hair.

*He really does look like a scarecrow.*

Jack rummaged in his oversized knapsack and handed Annie a leather bag.

"Deer jerky," he said. "Made it myself. It's not bad." He unhooked a wineskin from the pack and gave it to Siobhan. "The wine's from last year's really good grapes."

Annie chewed. "You have a good hand with spices." She traded Siobhan the jerky bag for the wineskin.

He beamed. "I didn't make the wine, so it's safe to drink. I'm lousy at fermenting."

Annie swallowed a mouthful and turned the apples. "These are almost done." She returned his jerky bag. "Thanks. Tell me what's so important you had to follow me for two days."

He talked through a huge bite of jerky. "Walt's been the head of the Abilene Readers for donkey's years. I dye candle wax for him six days a week. I was there when Gail the glassblower brought him the letter about you. Walt said he'd seen you at the inn. He and Gail made a plan to catch you one night and get you so scared you'd leave town. All they care about is keeping themselves safe." Another bite. "Walt made his wife snoop around the inn until she could sneak a look at the register for your names. Tuesday night Gail came running in after she saw the two of you go into the theater. Walt corralled me and his other apprentice and Gail got her husband and sister."

Annie hated these people almost as much as she hated Redeemers. *Another thought I never in a thousand years pictured myself thinking.* "Why did you grab Siobhan? She's one of you Readers."

"The glassblower didn't know who I was," Siobhan said.

Annie looked from Jack to Siobhan. Siobhan dropped her eyes to the jerky bag and muttered, "I know what it looks like."

"Yeah, Gail didn't know who stuck the letter to her try-on mirror," Jack said. "She had a lot of customers Sunday. Walt figured Siobhan was helping you search, and getting two people to bully made him even happier. He never expected you to stand up to him, Annie. Especially when he brought out that creepy knife he made."

Annie had to squelch his hero-worshipping gaze. "The apples should be ready." She blew on one, bit, and nodded. When all their mouths hung open, panting to cool the scalding fruit, Annie said to Siobhan, "How did you find me?"

Siobhan started, swallowed, and coughed. "It's October. The reeds stayed bent when you walked through them."

Annie punched the ground. "I thought they were still green enough."

"Most of them were. I was persistent."

"Didn't expect your sheep to jump the fence?"

Siobhan flinched. "That's not it."

"Whatever you say." She blew on her apple.

"You left a butt print on the riverbank, too."

*Idiot.* "I'll remember that next time."

"There doesn't have to be a next time."

*That's what she thought.* "You said you'd never cross the river."

"I had to find you."

*What was it with her?* "Is there a prize for making it to some finish line with me?"

"I had to explain."

"Explain about crossing the river." Annie pointed her stick at Siobhan.

Siobhan blew on her second apple. "I realized you went south because I said I never would. I stayed all day at the spot where you crossed. You picked an easy place, and besides, I can swim. I could've crossed in five minutes."

"What stopped you?"

Silence. Siobhan bit into the apple. "I was scared."

Annie said, "Nothing glowed."

Siobhan didn't smile. "I saw you in the grass when you came out of those thin woods. You were hidden pretty good 'til then." She brushed off her bare legs and checked the trousers. As she pulled them on own, she said, "Who were you hiding from? There weren't any people in the ruins, were there?"

"No." The idea gave her a chill. "People couldn't live in the ruins. Even if nothing glows there now, it could've glowed a hundred years ago."

"The old cities aren't as dangerous as our teachers told us," Jack said. "My dad and I spent most of our lives on the edges of ruins. He liked the dyes he could make from flowers and trees that don't grow anyplace else but there. I never saw anyone, alive or dead."

"Redeemers be thanked," Annie said.

They looked at her.

Annie made a frustrated noise. "Everyone says it. I heard you say it, Siobhan. Max told me to fit in, and he was right."

"Max?" Jack said.

"Long story."

"We've got time," Siobhan said. "You haven't told me your whole story yet, even though we've been together for days."

Jack sat forward. "Please tell us. I'm dying to know how you spooked the Redeemers."

Annie laughed. "You think I've spooked them? You've got it backwards."

"Sure you have. Whatever you did, it's different from other Readers. They want to stop you." The lovesick look intensified. "I want to help you."

"Why?" *Here it comes. The sincere-sounding lie, just like Siobhan's.*

"I've read more of the Pages than lots of Readers. My father sold dyes to every chandler up and down the river. When I turned fourteen and graduated school, he said I was man enough to carry on the most important tradition he had. Then he took me into the cellar and showed me his collection of Pages."

"Collection?" Siobhan said.

"Nine."

"What?"

Jack nodded. "Honest. Dad said it took him thirty years of digging in the ruins to find that many." He finished his last apple and tossed the core into the fire. "Abilene's Readers all have angry or scary or sneaky Pages. Walt's Page has someone telling off people who are cheating and lying, and Gail's talks about people trying to kill some guy by throwing rocks at him. So the group is mean and doesn't trust anyone, including each other. They don't listen to me because I'm still an apprentice, and Dad told me to keep the collection to myself. My Pages are mostly about ideas or events I don't really understand. They're as fascinating, as wandering the ruins."

*These Readers are loopier than drunks at a Midsummer wedding.* "Just tell me why you're here."

"You know something. Walt doesn't. I don't. I know lots of Reader stuff but it didn't stop me from being afraid of Walt. What do you know? What does your Page say that makes you not afraid?"

*Was this all these Readers thought about?* "Look, all I know about Readers and Pages is what Siobhan told me. I'd never heard any of it before her family locked me in their cellar."

Jack stared at Annie like she'd stopped speaking English. "But—why—" He shook himself. "Wait. I know what the letter said, but how can you not be a Reader if the Redeemers—"

"Back in May, I found a strange piece of paper my husband used to own. Apparently it was what you call a Page. Then the Redeemers tried to kill me. The Kansas City Readers rescued me. That would be my best friends, who wore those black masks and never told me who they were, as though I was too stupid to figure it out." Her voice took on the gravelly layer of hate she'd become too familiar with. "They wrote the original letter you al have been passing around. They told you all to watch me and hound me and use whatever ways necessary to make sure I didn't endanger your precious little groups of word-hoarders."

"Oh, wow."

An involuntary smile cut through Annie's black mood. She'd never been tempted to laugh at her troubles before. Too bad she'd leave Jack behind tomorrow. She liked his theatrical reactions to everything.

"After what the Redeemers and then you Readers did to me, everything, including Walt, is small potatoes when it comes to fear." She jammed sticks into the fire. "There it is. I don't have any magic Reader secrets. You Readers wouldn't spit on me if I caught fire. The feeling is mutual."

"But—"

"Annie—"

"Stop hounding me." Annie stabbed another stick in the ground so she wouldn't break it over their heads. "I'm getting some sleep.

I've been walking night and day." She pulled out her blanket from her knapsack and curled under it with her back to them.

Siobhan and Jack kept up a whispered conversation until Annie took her nightshirt from her knapsack and wrapped it around her ears.

Sometime after moonrise Annie woke to Jack's snoring.

*Now.* She folded her blanket and stood. A branch in the dying fire popped and broke. She picked up her knapsack and took a first step.

A hand closed around her ankle. She gasped and looked down.

"Will you stop it?" Siobhan's froggy voice belied her wide-awake eyes. "I'll stay up all night if I have to. You need to trust me."

She yanked her leg several times. Siobhan wouldn't let go. She debated another fight, but Jack would most likely get involved. After her time in Siobhan's storage cellar, she didn't want to tempt her into tying up her sheep to keep it nearby. Annie had enough of being tied and helpless. It was not the smartest way to go on the run. *Curse all Readers to death in some glowing pre-Last War city.* In the end she curled up on the ground and fell asleep with Siobhan's hand on her ankle like a leash.

* * *

"Wake up," Siobhan said.

Annie flung her arm over her face. "Why?"

"Because cold fish is nasty and we cooked the last of your apples."

Annie moved her arm and the morning sun slapped light directly into her eyes. With a groan, she sat up and wadded the nightshirt into her pack.

"Do I smell coffee?"

"Jack has a small pot and a jar of ground beans."

She bowed. "I kiss your feet."

He blushed so deeply she could see it beneath his dark skin. Pine needles still speckled his hair, but he'd brushed off his trousers and shirt.

"I only have one cup. We'll have to share."

"Anything for coffee." *How quickly they believed her funny comments. As though last night had never happened.* Annie sipped the rest of the coffee in the cup and blinked. "You could stand a spoon up in this."

"Is that good?"

"Perfect."

He grinned and watched her finish.

After breakfast, Annie washed everything in the river.

*Nice kid, for a Reader. Wish he wouldn't keep those deep, dark eyes on me every minute. He's not really a kid anyway. What's two or three years' age difference? It's just that he's so eager and enthusiastic about everything. And I'm suspicious and angry and old. At least I feel old.*

She shook excess water off the plates and utensils onto the grass.

*Better get back. They're probably hatching three different plots to keep me caged.*

When Annie handed around the clean dishes, they wouldn't meet her eyes. "Say it."

Siobhan set down her plate. "Don't go."

"We've been through all this. There's no argument that'll erase Monday night."

Jack looked blank. "What about Monday night?"

"That wasn't my fault. I told you."

Annie nodded once, twice, three times—slowly. "Right. I'm supposed to believe you now because you've proved how honest you've been all along."

Siobhan fiddled with her wet knife and fork. "There's something else I didn't tell you."

"But I'm not interested in any words coming out of your mouth." Annie stood over both of them, arms crossed. "The only thing I'm interested in is the Redeemers. I'm going to find out why they want me dead."

"But you know why," Jack said.

Annie stamped her foot. "No, I don't. And don't give me more of that Reader garbage. This is a plain old logical problem. Governing and teaching are trades like everything else, right? I'll learn where the Redeemers train their apprentices and sneak in there to look at their history and rules. No one knows anything about the Redeemers, really. When I know how they think I can figure out how to stay out of their hands."

"I know where." Siobhan flared tomato-red.

"You do?" Jack said. "Where?"

Annie took a step away from Siobhan. "If you told me the sky overhead is blue, I'd look for myself to make sure."

"Annie?" Jack's head swiveled from her to Siobhan and back. "I don't know what's wrong between you two, but Siobhan told the truth. About Readers and Pages and everything."

Annie ignored him and said to Siobhan, "If you're so on my side, why didn't you tell me this before?"

Siobhan pinched her lips between her teeth. The silence lengthened. She twisted her hands in her lap, looked up, and looked down again. "I'm afraid."

"Of me?"

"No."

"Of what, then?"

Something about the tension in Siobhan's hands made Annie crouch in front of her and tilt her head to see Siobhan's face. "Tell me. If you're not scared of me, then what?"

Siobhan unlocked her hands and took hold of Annie's damaged left one. She pushed up the sleeve just enough to reveal the scar.

"Of this."

# CHAPTER TWENTY-THREE

Annie freed herself and shook down her sleeve. With her scar revealed, she felt more naked than if all her clothes had vanished off her body. "Don't touch me again."

Jack's face became all eyes and open mouth.

"I saw them when you hit your head on the floor," Siobhan said.

Annie got an image of herself in Siobhan's kitchen, Eamon and Nora peeling off her clothes. Like the Redeemers did in that dark, echoing room. She heard the leader's voice talk about stripping clothes...

She shook herself like a wet dog. *Have some guts. Don't let it suck you in again.*

"What did your family do to me, Siobhan?"

Siobhan bit her lips. "Mom said we had to make sure. We took off your boots and socks and unbuttoned your sleeves."

"Who?" Anger heated Annie's face. "Who took my clothes off?"

"Mom and me."

Annie clutched her wrists tighter, ghosts of the old agony making them throb. Fury tied her tongue. There weren't enough words to say what she thought about Siobhan and her family. Or there were too many, and she couldn't say them all at once.

"Annie?" Jack said. "What's wrong with your arms?"

Annie heard the sound of his voice, but not the words. She stared past both of them at the river, willing the sounds of hammers and nails and splashing blood out of her head.

"Siobhan? Annie?" Jack touched Annie's shoulder and she jerked away. "One of you talk to me, please?"

Annie's fingernails were trying to poke through her shirt. She supposed she ought to let go. Her scars weren't going anywhere. They didn't need protecting.

*No, but I could use some protection. Grow prickers all over my skin like a raspberry bush, maybe. So people would keep off.*

"Matthew's balls." Jack pried at Annie's fingers. "Annie Cook, what's going on?"

Annie swatted at him, but he jumped away. At that moment she knew how to get rid of him. How to crush the hero-adoration out of his face. *Strip myself. It doesn't matter. I have nothing left to be shy about. I'm dead.*

"You think I'm something special? I'm damaged goods, nothing more. Look."

Annie unbuttoned her sleeves and yanked them up to her elbows, then unlaced her boots and pulled off her socks. The scars glared red and angry in the morning light. The ones on her feet ached in the cold air. Her mouth twisted when she heard Siobhan's stifled gasp.

"What's your problem? You've seen them before. Did your family enjoy the sight? Was it better than a Halloween play?"

"No. We didn't do it to... I mean, we weren't trying..."

"To inspect me like the sheep you pick out for New Year's supper? You didn't get the chance to nail me to your barn wall but you sure knew how to save your own skin in Walt's cellar."

"Stop rubbing my face in it." Siobhan slammed both hands on the ground, sending her fork and knife flying into the cattails.

"Both of you shut up." Jack's bass voice cut through theirs like scissors through hot glass.

Annie ground her teeth together a moment before Siobhan's mouth clacked shut.

"Thank you. Siobhan, is Annie saying that you didn't tell her you were a Reader too?"

"That, and other stuff."

"All right. Annie, you should know that Readers are a skittish bunch. Did your husband tell you about Readers before you found his Page?"

"No, and he—"

"Wait. But he told you afterwards, right? My dad said that he and mom had the biggest fight about that. Turned out both were Readers and didn't know it 'til they'd been married a whole year."

Annie deflated. "No, he didn't tell me afterwards because he was dead."

Jack's mouth fell open again. "Oh, wow, Annie, I'm sorry."

Annie covered her foot scars with her hands. "He hid it so well I would never have found it if I hadn't been cleaning the shop top to bottom. I wonder what else he kept secret from me. If that story the tanner told me about Hank getting drunk and robbed and killed was another Reader lie, maybe the Redeemers got him, too." She glared at Jack. "Readers are good at lying."

"Wait, wait, wait," Jack said. "You're really not a Reader?"

"For the hundredth, time, no, I'm not a Reader. My mother raised me not stab people in the back."

Jack flinched. "We're decent people, most of us. Right, Siobhan?"

"I've been trying to tell her that for days," Siobhan said.

Annie's laugh had a sad sound. "Siobhan, Matthew himself would have to appear in the sky above us before I would trust you."

"Secrecy is a habit, Annie. Readers have been keeping themselves secret since Matthew saved the world." Siobhan retrieved her knife and fork. "It's the second thing we all learn."

Annie pulled her stiff hands away from her feet. "What's the first thing?"

"Annie?" Jack's voice was only an echo of itself. "What did the Redeemers do to you?"

*Pigs on stage. Except I'm the pig and these woods are the stage.* "You don't know?"

Jack turned to Siobhan. "Do you? Dad was kind of a solitary Reader most of his life. I've been staying that way, too, especially around Walt."

Siobhan kept her eyes away from Annie's feet. "We guessed, but no Reader I ever met knows for sure. No one's ever come back."

Annie said, "You must have a Page about it."

Jack looked at her like she was a backward student. "Pages aren't about the Redeemers."

Annie returned the look. "There's obviously a connection between you. Why not Pages?"

Siobhan's hands came up in a "stop" gesture. "Pages are what the Readers are all about. They're ours, kept hidden from the Redeemers. They're our connection to the Readers who lived before the Last War."

"Dad and I used to try to figure out what his Pages meant those nights we camped in the biggest old cities. We never could, though. Dad's Pages are really small ones, sometimes just a sentence. They don't have enough information."

"Speaking of Pages," Siobhan said, "do you have your husband's Page?"

Annie shook her head. "My friend the lying, gutless Reader borrowed it the night the Redeemers took me." She kept her eyes on the river sparkling in the sun, so unlike that foggy May night.

"You let someone borrow your Page?"

"Spare me the attitude, Siobhan. It was just a piece of paper."

"Are you crazy? It's more than—"

"Stop it," Jack said. "Forget the Pages for a minute. Annie, what made those scars on your feet?"

Annie moved to cover them again, then stopped herself. *I'm going to use them to scare Jack away? Frighten him and Siobhan back to Abilene. They won't be as frightened as me, but then again, I'm dead. Never forget that. The rules are a different for dead people.*

"Ever hear the word crucify?" Annie said.

"No," Jack said.

"Yes," Siobhan said, "but no one knows what it means."

"It means me."

Puzzled stares.

*Do it.* "They talked a lot in some language I didn't understand, but they said that word, crucify, in English. Then they held me down on two crossed boards and hammered nails through my hands and feet into, into the boards." The remembered sounds overpowered the river flowing, the birds singing, her own breathing. "They picked me up—me and the wood—and hung me on the wall like a picture. They recited something else when I stopped screaming. I don't remember what. They took the torches and started to sing something in that other language. Then they left. They left me alone in the dark to die."

Fear burned into her throat. She heard the hammer strike. Heard her voice screaming as the torture sent agony blazing through her arms and legs. Tasted her own bloody vomit. She put her head on her knees and breathed deep and slow to stop from puking fish and apples and coffee onto the grass.

When breakfast retreated into her stomach again, she raised her head. Jack's hand was an inch away from her exposed wrist. He flinched when she met his eyes.

*Do it.* "Need to touch it to believe me?" She took his hand and pushed his finger and thumb on her left wrist's entry and exit scars. "They used me like a piece of wood they needed to prop up their wall. See these fingers?" She flopped them. "Another gift from the Redeemers."

Jack swallowed, but didn't say anything.

*He's not scared enough.* "Don't miss these." She took his hand off her wrist and planted her right foot into it. "They used longer nails on my feet, I think. I couldn't see them too well then, because my arms were pinned to the wood and my eyes got blood splashed all over them and I was puking on myself."

"Annie, I... we..."

She yanked away her foot. "Listen, Reader. You think it's some kind of adventure, following me? You think you'll meet new Readers and see some more of your precious Pages? Pig shit. The Redeemers want me dead. And I'd bet a year's salary there's only one way they kill people."

"Annie," Siobhan said.

"Do you want to risk dying like this?" She pushed her hands in Siobhan's face. "You were so eager to see these when I lay helpless on your kitchen floor. Think about it, Reader. My blood hit the Redeemers in their faces. It splashed all over their robes. I don't remember it all, Redeemers be thanked." She laughed at that. "I fit in so well, don't I?" She heard a wrong note in her laughter, and squelched it. "I'm dead. It's supposed to be easier now."

"What?" Jack said.

"Dead. Get it? If the Kansas City Readers hadn't taken pliers to the nails—at least I assume they used pliers—I'd be rotting on a wall with the rest of the Redeemer's victims. Dead. No one to fear. No more running away in the night."

"The rest?" Siobhan said, holding Annie's hand like a dandelion at peak flyaway stage.

"I had company on the wall. A skeleton, just like the drawings we learned from in school. And someone who'd died not quite as long ago, because his or her skin was rotting. The maggots dripping from the open mouth were a nice touch." *How am I remembering this all of a sudden? I don't want to remember it. Go away, memories. I have a beautiful cell in my head waiting for you.*

"Stop it. Just stop it." Siobhan dropped Annie's hand. "You're just trying to scare us. Stop making up Halloween stories."

Annie really laughed this time. "Sure, Reader. That's exactly what I'm doing. Plug your ears and pretend you can't hear me."

Jack said, "I'm strong, you know? When I chased after you, I said it'd be to protect you." He spread out his hands. "I'm an idiot."

"She doesn't need protecting." Siobhan stuffed her plate and utensils into her knapsack with enough force to rip the material. "When I chased her, I wanted to protect Readers. I thought—my whole family thought—that the letter was exaggerated. There was no way Redeemers would do something that left those kinds of scars." She dragged her eyes up to meet Annie's. "It was Walt in the cellar who did it. He terrified me. When you brushed him off like a mosquito I knew I didn't understand anything."

Annie thought she sounded miserable the night before. "Poor Siobhan. All your illusions shattered. Welcome to every day of my life."

"Jack, would Walt really have used his knife on Annie?"

"Probably. If Gail and her husband didn't stop him."

Siobhan's fingers knotted around themselves again. "I've sold apples and wool along the river and up north for years. I thought I'd seen every kind of good and bad in people. But seeing a Reader get that crazy woke me up. If Readers can want to kill each other like something out of a Last War horror story, then I can't doubt what the Redeemers could be capable of."

Annie rubbed her hands over her face. "What did you think could make these scars?"

"I was sure whatever happened to you, it couldn't really have been that bad."

"Not really that bad?" To Annie's own surprise, she began to laugh. "Even—what—but—" She laughed harder. Her stomach began to ache and tears ran down her cheeks.

"Annie, stop, please." Jack said.

Annie caught her breath for a second, but laughter overpowered what she wanted to say. Finally, when her lungs felt empty enough to be inside out, she fell onto her back and stared up at the blue sky.

"Go home, Readers," she said between gasps. "You don't know what you're getting into. Go home and lie to yourselves and play with your little pieces of paper."

Jack hauled her to her feet and planted her in front of him. "Listen to me, Missus. This isn't just about you. We're going to find the Redeemers' hideaway together. You have reasons? So do I. My best friend disappeared in Colorado Springs last year. If you're right, and the Redeemers kill everyone they take like they tried to kill you, then I'm going to kidnap a Redeemer and you're going to show me how they do it. You want revenge? I'll help you get it."

Annie stared at this new side to sweet, eager Jack. A moment later it was gone, and he picked up her hand. His long fingers touched the scars and his mouth quivered.

"I'll protect you whether you think you need it or not, Annie. If they find you, I'll fight them off. I look skinny but I play football and I chop wood for the blacksmith for extra money. See?" He pointed to his arm.

She rebuttoned her sleeves when he released her. She couldn't desert him. Where would he go—back to Walt? No. And Better to travel with Siobhan than waste time and energy trying to outrun her. Keep your enemy at your side.

"Where are we headed, Siobhan?"

"Colorado Springs." Obvious relief filled her voice.

Annie put her socks and boots back on. "Isn't it miles and miles from here?"

"Less than a hundred. The only towns in between are Plainville, a little place called Smoky Hill, and Cheyenne Wells."

"How do you know it's where the Redeemers go to ground?" Jack said.

"I met with some Readers in Cheyenne Wells once. They had an old letter from someone who had poked around the abbey. It has four floors. The third and fourth floors were all bedrooms. The second floor had more bedrooms, a kitchen, and dining rooms. The entire first floor and one end of the second had some kind of open space with only one door on the second floor and one on the first. The clincher was the cellar. It had rooms full of books and desks, just like a school."

Annie ticked the points with her. "You momorized the letter?"

"My friend wrote it out for me. It's in our cellar back home. We never show it to anyone."

"Of course you don't." Annie packed her dish and utensils. "Do either of you know how far it is to Plainville from here?"

"Thirty miles, maybe," Jack said.

"That's at least two days of nothing but fish to eat, unless you packed something else?"

Siobhan shook her head. "We already ate everything I grabbed. I left in a hurry too."

"I have the jerky and some dried fruit," Jack said. "But I always bring my bow."

"Excellent." Annie hefted her knapsack. "I'll look for basil and wild onions. I make a mean stuffed rabbit."

# CHAPTER TWENTY-FOUR

"Here are the books I found." Annie set them on the grass at noon while Jack turned a stuffed rabbit on a spit over their fire.

Siobhan scooted backwards. "Are you sure they're safe?"

Annie rolled her eyes. "As sure as anyone can be. This is only a cookbook, but it has ingredients I never heard of. Look at this." She turned the browned pages of the dessert book. "See this white ball on the piece of apple pie? It's called ice cream."

Jack tested the rabbit. "I saw ice once when it snowed overnight. It's hard, like a rock, but cold."

"But how would you combine it with cream?" Siobhan said. "The ice would make the warm cream separate."

"Here's another one. Lemon Coolers."

"Lemon?" Siobhan said.

All these unknown ingredients drove Annie the cook crazy. "It's a kind of cookie. I don't know why they're cool, either. But the instructions say to roll them in powdered sugar. Most of the recipes call for sugar. I think they used it like honey back then."

"How did they make it? Maybe bees changed after the Last War." Jack turned the rabbit as the fire flared in a gust of wind.

"It'd have to be dry to grind it to a powder," Siobhan said. "So it must've been a spice or herb."

Annie closed the book with care. "I have a cook's treasure, and I can't make half of these recipes. I don't even know where to begin to find substitutes for some of these things."

"What's that on the other cover?" Jack said.

"Look at this painting." She motioned them in.

"I've never seen a painting that good," Siobhan said. "I can count the stitches in the shirt."

"Rabbit'll be ready in a minute," Jack said. "Anyone know what cinematic means?"

"Something to do with theater. The book talks about the word like it means some kind of plays. It calls them 'movies' but doesn't explain what either word means."

"Done." Jack slid the brown, fragrant rabbit from the spit onto his plate and cut it into several pieces. "Let's eat something normal."

Siobhan took a leg. "What I really want is a regular old baked potato."

Annie cut through the ribs. "They don't grow wild. You'll have to wait until we get to Plainville."

"That's another whole day."

"No one said life on the road would be easy."

Siobhan threw a dead leaf at her.

* * *

"Happy Halloween!" the Plainville innkeeper raised his wineglass.

"Happy Halloween!" the guests and musicians answered, and everyone drank.

Decorations covered all the downstairs rooms in the inn. Everyone wore costumes—even the band. Sheaves of dried cornstalks sat in doorways and corners. Carved pumpkins glowered or smirked on tables inside and out, the candles in them guttering as dancers whirled past. Piles of sandwiches, cakes, and cookies crowded the jack-o-lanterns; beer barrels and casks of wine sat beneath the tables. Lanterns hung on poles in the garden and from the walls outside. Rag dolls, ghosts, animals, and some unidentifiable creatures crowded the dining and living rooms and spilled onto the patio.

"Here's to gainful employment." Annie raised her wineglass. Jack and Siobhan clinked theirs with hers and they all drank.

Annie licked her lips. "I want the spice recipe for this wine."

"Good luck," a wheezing ghost said at her elbow. "Lou's family only passes on their secrets to the next heir when the oldest winemaker is on his deathbed."

"Who was that?" Siobhan whispered.

"Glen, my new boss. He should've picked a different costume. He's too fat to breathe in that sheet. He must be sweating like a pig."

"And you get to wash it tomorrow," Jack said.

Annie stuck out her tongue at him.

"And Jack's, too," Siobhan said. "Where did you get the black shirt and trousers, Jack? And what did you use to draw on the bones?"

"They're some of the doctor's herb-grinding clothes. Her husband thought of the skeleton idea because I'm so skinny. I used a piece of chalk her son borrowed from the weaver."

"At least my ghost costume is easier to move in than Glen's." Annie flipped the twisted sheet-end around her arm.

Jack ducked. "You'll smear me."

"I keep losing straw," Siobhan said. "Some scarecrow. I'll be picking bits out of my hair for a week."

Annie tucked in the loose end. "At least I don't have to sweep or do the dishes. Costume washing on top of regular inn laundry is bad enough."

The fiddler, flute player, and drummer began a new song.

"A reel at last," Siobhan said. "Come on, Jack." She handed Annie their glasses and dragged him into the center of the room.

A chubby stranger with pointed ears tied to his head tapped Annie on the shoulder. "Want to dance?" He wiggled the whiskers attached to his nose.

"Sure." She smiled at him. He flipped his long, stuffed rat tail over his arm and they joined in.

A square dance followed. Most of Siobhan's straw littered the floor afterwards and Annie pulled her outside to fix her up.

"What this needs is a needle and thread." Annie removed a safety pin from her own sleeve and pinned Siobhan's sleeve tighter around the straw.

"Here; I have an extra pin in my pocket."

Annie slapped her hand away. "I just fixed that sleeve. Let me." She pinched Siobhan's other cuff and worked straw onto the pin.

A hooded figure stepped into the lantern light at the corner of the building.

Annie backpedaled into the wall. Siobhan turned, then stepped in front of her like a shield.

The figure walked closer. Annie edged toward the street. *About fifty feet. Can I run fast enough in my costume?*

The figure raised its hands and removed the hood. The light revealed a smiling, wrinkled face covered with paintings of constellations.

"Didn't mean to scare you ladies," the old man said. "Some spooky costumes in there, eh? Give you the willies?"

He walked inside and several voices hailed him. "Lou!" "Wouldn't be a party without the best winemaker in Plainville!" "About time you showed up, Lou!"

Annie slid down the wall and covered her face. *I got distracted and forgot. Never forget. They're always after me.*

Siobhan sat next to her. "We need to relax."

"No. If I relax they'll catch me."

"Annie."

"No." She clenched her right fist and as much of the left as she could. "Do you see that?" She shook the loose fingers. "Do you remember this?" She pulled the ghost wrappings back enough to show the scar.

Siobhan reached out and covered it again. "Stop it."

"No. It's who I am. The old Annie didn't need to think too far ahead; didn't keep a constant lookout for them; didn't wake up screaming every night." *Slower. Quieter.* "You know what's different about me now? Besides the white hair that showed up afterwards, that is. I used to be happy." She laughed, but there was no humor in it. "You probably wouldn't have recognized the old me."

Siobhan poked more straw into place. "You carved me for supper pretty well."

Annie propped the back of her head against the brick wall. "Readers and truth don't get along. I trust no one."

"Talking us out of Abilene wasn't enough?'

"Not when you remember to tell me later how you threw me to Walt like a bone.'"

"Matthew's balls, Annie, I already explained that." Siobhan stood and walked halfway down the garden fence.

When Siobhan stopped walking away, Annie said, "You all claim to be one thing and act like something else."

"And?" Siobhan turned to face her.

Annie stood. "And there's your family. You."

"And?"

"What they do and say isn't your fault. But what you say is."

"What did I say? When?"

"You called yourself my babysitter. But when that woman in the cellar asked you what you'd do if the Redeemers came for me again—" Siobhan made an exasperated noise— "you said you'd let them have me so you could save yourself."

"What did you expect me to say?" Siobhan walked back to Annie. "I would've burst into song and dance to get away from Walt. Join the real world, Annie. Stop going on and on about what a victim you are."

"Eat sheep shit, Reader."

Siobhan put a finger to her lips. "Too loud. Never say that word where people can hear."

"You grow up knowing all this secrecy stuff, didn't you? How nice for you. No one put masks over their heads to teach you how the world works. Well, I didn't. I thought the," she whispered the word, "Redeemers were everything good and right and wonderful until they did things to me no Halloween play writer ever imagined." Annie took two steps and stood nose-to-collarbone with Siobhan. "When I get used to living upside down and breathing without puking up blood, I'll let you know. Until then, either come with me or go home, because I'm not waiting to see which Siobhan you turn out to be."

They faced each other in silence for a minute. The band inside started a polka.

Jack came to the door with a plateful of pumpkin-shaped cookies and three full wineglasses. "Here. Gotta eat something to soak up all this wine. Did you see the winemaker's costume? His cloak is covered with star patterns. It's the best one here."

They stiffened. "Yeah."

Jack squinted at them. "Something wrong?"

"Nothing."

# CHAPTER TWENTY-FIVE

The band went home around two a.m. Glen found Annie telling ghost stories in a corner with Jack, Siobhan, and the cook.

"Dom, breakfast at nine and remember to make extra coffee. Annie, don't collect laundry 'til ten. They'll all sleep late." He struggled out of the sheet. His bald head dripped sweat. "I need a new costume next year." He turned away from them. "Louise?"

A tall rag doll waved from the wine table. "I know. Clean up tomorrow morning and leave the wine out 'til three."

Dom leaned over to Annie. "His annual fit of generosity."

\* \* \*

*Tick. Tick. Tick.*

*Footsteps? She's not alone?*

*She peers into the gloom. No one.*

*Tick. Tick. Tick.*

*She looks down. A dozen plump rats lap at a dark puddle spreading out from the wall. Liquid drops into the puddle at a steady rate. She raises her head.*

*No holes in the ceiling. She doesn't hear rain on the roof.*

*She looks sideways. Blood drips from her hand. She looks down. A drop of blood plunks in front of one furry head.*

Come and get it!

*She giggles. Her lungs won't pull in enough air. She pushes against the wood. Pain flames through her legs. Blood drips faster from her insteps.*

*A squeak. She looks down. A bold rat puts its forefeet on the plank and bares its teeth.*

\* \* \*

"Wake up."

Annie opened her eyes and Siobhan stopped shaking her.

"You were screaming."

"Sorry." Annie gulped. "Sorry."

"What were you dreaming?"

"Rats." She shuddered.

"What's so bad about rats? They're just gross."

"They were drinking...there was one big one..." Annie rubbed her face with her hands. "I'd forgotten this. My blood made a puddle on the floor. These rats were lapping it up. One of them got on his hind legs to reach my feet. I thought he was going to bite me and I screamed and scared him away."

"Disgusting."

She found a small smile. "I don't know why I'm starting to remember more. Sorry I woke you up."

"No problem." Siobhan yawned and went back to her own bed.

At breakfast Siobhan said in the middle of a bite of toast, "Annie, did you mean there was a puddle of your own blood on the floor big enough to feed a pack of rats?"

Jack's coffee went down the wrong pipe. "What?" He grabbed his napkin and coughed into it.

Annie looked around. The only other early risers were three old ladies at the opposite end of the dining room. "This is not breakfast conversation."

"But what—" Jack said.

Annie held up her fork. "I'm eating."

"I know, but..." Siobhan said.

"Can we please discuss this later?"

Jack leaned over to see the clock in the lobby. "It's eight-fifteen. I have to be at work at nine."

"Me, too," Siobhan said.

*Whatever it takes to shut her up.* "Fine. Our room right after breakfast."

"I'd forgotten about the rats," Annie said from the corner of her bed. "I wonder what made me remember?"

"I bet it was the waiter's costume," Siobhan said from her own bed.

"Ah. Could be."

"What did I miss?" Jack said.

"Annie had a nightmare last night."

"About rats? You mean there were rats where they tried to kill you?"

"The wall of the big room where I was had other bodies and skeletons hanging on it too. The whole place reeked. Like a carnival for rats, you know? When enough of my blood got onto the floor, they came out to drink it."

"Did one really try to bite your foot?" Siobhan said.

Annie nodded. At least this time the story wasn't rattling everything in her head's locked room. "The Readers must've come to rescue me right after that."

Jack leaned forward. "Did they slip in the blood? How did they get the nails out? How did they get you out?"

*Shut up, Jack.* "I don't know. To all three."

"But you have to remember something. What did they look like? Did they talk?"

"Jack." Annie kept her voice steady. "I was…it was…" She took a breath. "I wasn't thinking straight."

She had to end this before the cell changed its mind and nails and blood and—*Stop.* Before it all tried to escape. She slid off the bed. "I have to get to work."

Annie stopped at the cellar door. All those costumes to wash. And Siobhan got to sit in a comfortable chair, embroidering flowers on rich women's dresses. At least there would be no one down here to grope her. And no Redeemers would be lurking in the sinks, spying on her.

She peeked into the rooms along the short cellar hallway. Preserves and pickles behind that one, tools and broken furniture across the hall, spare dishes next to that, the stone-lined meat and butter storage room. Laundry room at the end.

Clotheslines covered the entire back half of a room half as large as the entire first floor. Washtubs crowded next to two sinks with pumps, and tables for sorting and folding filled the rest. Two laundry chutes emptied onto the tables, a heap of tablecloths and napkins piled under each of them.

Annie climbed to the second and third floors and emptied the hampers at the ends of the hall. Sheets, underwear, and Halloween costumes all down the chute, oh joy. Two full days' work.

By suppertime she wanted to sleep right there on her napkin.

Siobhan clanked her spoon on her empty pudding dish and Annie jerked upright.

"Go to bed. Unless you want to go to the theater with Jack and me."

"I only want a pillow under me and a blanket over me."

They all stood and headed for the main stairs. Jack and Siobhan went out the door as a woman wearing a fur-lined cloak entered. Annie trudged up to her room, wondering what plot Siobhan and Jack would hatch during intermission. If they even went to the theater. More likely Siobhan went out to pass the "Stop Annie by any means necessary" letter to Plainville's cache of cowards and bullies. Also known as Readers.

At first Annie dumped her clothes on the floor, but remembered Abilene and packed her knapsack for a quick escape. Fatigue triumphed over her jangling nerves and she fell asleep almost at once.

A slight pain woke her. Her arm had worked out of the covers and hit the wall. She looked upside down at the door. A tall shadow stood in the doorway.

# Chapter Twenty-six

Annie shrank against the wall. *The image. They'll make me—*

"Annie." The tall shape knelt on the bed. "You're having a nightmare."

*The image. Get away—*

The shape patted her shoulder. "Wake up."

Annie shoved the shape off the bed and scuttled to the far end.

"Ow! Annie, wake up." The shape got to her feet, rubbing her tailbone. "It's me."

The chanting in Annie's head faded and the tall shape in front of her changed into Siobhan.

"Why do I keep hearing 'the image' in my nightmares?"

"I don't know. Are you awake now?" Siobhan lit the lamp on the dresser.

"The door was locked but they still came in. There were two of them. The hoods hid their faces... It was that woman in the hooded cloak. She reminded me."

The nightshirt exposed her wrists. Her feet. The light emphasized the way the holes—scars—had kept the shape of the nails. The cell in her head rattled and groaned. Blood seeped under the door. A table floated out and mushroomed to life size. *T*-shaped boards appeared on it. Five hooded and cloaked killers waded through the blood, singing, and hurled her on the cross.

"I tried to escape. I hit one, I think, but I couldn't fight all five of them." She didn't want to remember this, but the words spewed from her like vomit. She put her hands over her ears. "They picked me up and carried me like, I don't know, like a trophy. They sang while they carried me. No, not really sang, more like reciting poetry, the way first-graders recite the alphabet. I couldn't understand a word of it. But when they dumped me on to the wood, the leader said something odd in regular English."

"Odd how?" Jack's voice.

Annie looked up. *When did he come in?* "Like a Page. I didn't know that back then."

"Wait a minute." Jack ran across the hall to his room and returned with his knapsack. "I keep them in a pouch on the bottom." He upended it over the bed, stuck his arm inside, and came out with a flat wooden box about the size of his palm.

Siobhan gaped. "This is your collection."

"Annie, do you remember what they said?" He popped a hidden catch to reveal a stack of thin papers of different sizes.

"No. Only that it was something about an image."

Jack lifted up the papers one by one. "Here it is. Listen: 'We shall also bear the image of the man of heaven.'" He looked up. "Was that it?"

"No. Yours is missing some words." She rocked on the bed, punching her forehead with the heel of her hand. "Get out of my head. I don't want to remember. Get out. Leave."

Their hands were cold and dry and strong. Like they lifted heavy weights all the time. Well, of course they did. They lifted her and her friends up to hang on the wall.

*Stop it. They're staring at me. They'll think I'm crazy.*

Annie looked over at Jack. "They said something else. Maybe it's in your collection."

"What was it?"

"Something about cutting up clothes."

He didn't glance down. "No. I don't have anything like that."

She shrugged. "Maybe it's their own bizarre little ritual."

"What ritual?" Siobhan asked.

"The Redeemer who wasn't holding me cut off my trousers and shirt and split them into four pieces."

"You were naked?" Siobhan plucked at her own shirt hem.

Jack reached across to Annie, but pulled back his hand.

Annie nodded. "Then the same one pulled out a hammer—no, a mallet—and nails. I yelled at them. I asked the woman—"

"One of them was a woman?" Siobhan said.

"She ignored me. She held my hand so he could place the nail where it belonged." *Keep going. Get through it.* Not much more. Already the hammers pounded the cell door. The deadbolts squealed, but they held.

"When they finished, they picked me up again—me and the wood—and carried me to the wall behind them."

"You could see where you were?" Jack said.

"There were some lamps. But it was a big, dark place. The light only reached a few feet. They hoisted me against the wall and let go. There must have been hooks or something on it, because the wood only fell a little ways."

"But you were—hanging—" Siobhan said.

"I, um, dropped down but the nails held me there."

Blood running down her arms, over her ribs, between her toes. Dripping. Dripping. Counting time like a clock. *The baby dying. Ripped out of my womb like knives shredding my stomach.*

Jack's voice. "What happened next?"

She jerked in a breath. "Sorry. I heard them walk away and I opened my eyes. I remember that, so I must've shut them. They were standing in front of me again. I could've seen their faces if their hoods were off. Their heads were only a few inches below mine. They recited that image phrase."

"Want to look at my Pages?"

"No. I wish I could remember every word, because then I could search for it. They used big words. More words I hadn't heard before."

"When I woke you up just now, you were saying the image word," Siobhan said.

Annie stared at a corner of the ceiling. *What was it?* "The image of..." Her head drooped. "It's still gone."

"Did you talk to them?" Jack said.

"What would I have said?"

"Ask them why? They might've told you if they thought you were going to die."

Siobhan elbowed him. "Jack."

Annie gave him a crooked smile. "I didn't think of it that way."

"We know they're crazy. Sometimes weirdos in scary books like to explain why they're killing their victims just before—"

Siobhan clamped a hand over his mouth. "Ignore him. What did they do after they recited that bit about the image?"

"I must have closed my eyes again, because when I opened them there was a ray of sunlight. I think from a hole in the roof, but I couldn't see that high."

Siobhan said, "You were in the Abbey, you know."

Annie stopped breathing. "Of course. Where else would the Redeemers have taken me? Of course."

Jack pushed Siobhan away. "I gotta ask. How did the Readers rescue you?"

"No one ever told me."

"Did they talk when they did it?"

"I don't think so. I didn't hear them walking, either."

"Annie, there was no one else there but you and them. How could you not hear anything?"

"I was screaming." She lowered her gaze to the piece of blanket in front of her feet. "I screamed until my voice gave out. It hurt." She nearly laughed. "That's so inadequate. It was hard to breathe. I had to keep pushing myself up against the wood with my feet. Later on, the doctor had to take dozens of splinters out of my shoulders and my butt. Anyway. They must've had pliers, because all I remember is a hard pull on my wrist and the cold nail sliding through the hole."

Siobhan inhaled sharply.

*It's over. I'm dead. Telling the story can't hurt me.* "The next thing I remember is waking up in the hidden room."

The downstairs clock bonged midnight.

Jack said into the silence that followed, "When they took my best friend last year. I looked everywhere. I went to Plainville and Topeka and Great Bend. Nothing. When I came back, Walt took me into his office, threw me into a chair, and told me never to talk about Van again. I asked him why. You saw how he hates it when people stand up to him. He tried to slap me around. I kicked his knees out from under him, pinned him to the floor, and demanded a reason." He gave a short laugh. "He called me some names I'd never heard before, but in between them he said that when a Reader disappears, we always give out that they've moved away. Their Page goes to someone in their family."

"What if they're the only Reader in the family?" Siobhan said.

"Then the group gets it. Efficient, huh? He told me to quit looking and follow the rules."

"Did you?" Annie said.

"He thought I did. Ten months later, you came to town." He

rearranged himself on the bed. "So I followed you. You were the only one besides me and Van who'd ever stood up to Walt. And I thought you'd be able to tell me about Readers in other towns so I could find a better group."

"But?"

"You said that Redeemers only kill people one way. Are you sure?"

"No, I'm only guessing. But if I try to look at it objectively—" *Like that will ever happen*— "it almost reminded me of a play. Memorized, rehearsed. They were too good at it."

Jack folded in half and covered his head with his arms.

"We need to stop it," Annie said.

"How?" His voice was muffled.

"Colorado Springs, like you said, Siobhan." She climbed over to Jack and put her arms around him. The memories backed off. "Jack, we both want revenge. You for your friend. Me for the baby and maybe Hank. Come with me to Colorado Springs now, no extra stops along the way. We'll make revenge happen."

"It's a week, easy, from here to there," Siobhan said. "We'll need supplies."

"I'm getting eight-fifty a week," Annie said.

"Nine," Siobhan said.

"Eight." Jack sat up. "Sorry I kind of lost my balance there. I'll work on travel plans tomorrow."

"Today, now," Annie said. "It's my day off. I'll get prices for jerky and dried fruit. And I'll mend all our socks." *Siobhan and Jack and Annie. Three friends traveling together, exploring all the towns along the Smoky River. All the towns in the world, that is. It's the perfect cover for my revenge journey.*

"The weaver has a big stock of ready-made clothes," Siobhan said. "I'll see about coats and hats. Colorado Springs is in the mountains."

One chime.

Annie stood. "Jack, it's twelve-fifteen. What are you doing in a lady's room at this hour?" She waited a beat and winked at him.

"I—I—" He saw her face and smiled. "I'm out of here. Good night."

# CHAPTER TWENTY-SEVEN

"Jack, what happened to you?" Annie's cider glass hit the lunch table.

Jack fumbled for his chair and plopped into it. His eyes were swollen to slits and pink hives covered his arms.

"It was something with blue flowers and long, serrated leaves. I had it ground to a powder and took a pinch between my finger and thumb to test the fineness. Suddenly I started to sneeze and couldn't stop. The next thing I knew my eyes were swelling up and my neck and arms itched like crazy." He scratched his neck. "My boss came in and dragged me to the sink. She doused me with cold water and rubbed cream all over me. She said to go home and not come back until tomorrow." He sneezed twice into his napkin.

Eva, the waitress, came over with three bowls balanced on one arm. "You look terrible Here. Chicken soup today. It'll make you feel better."

Siobhan followed her in. "Jack! What happened?"

"Allergy." He sneezed again. "She said it'll clear up by tomorrow. I'll finish our travel plans this afternoon instead."

The family at the next table moved their chairs away from Jack as though he'd infect them.

Annie's own arms itched in sympathy. "You will not. Take a nap after lunch. You look like you need it."

"Did she give you cream to rub on the hives?" Siobhan said.

He nodded.

"Then go take care of yourself. We're not in that big a hurry."

"Okay." He found his spoon and started on the soup.

"Did you tell the weaver we're leaving?" Annie asked Siobhan.

"Had to. She saw me looking over the coats and hats and asked what I wanted. She wasn't happy."

"Is she short-handed?"

"No, but I have this cattail design I sketched on a dress pattern and she sold it this morning to one of the rich women on the north side of town. Now I'll have to teach it to the other girls or she'll lose the sale."

Jack scratched his neck.

"Jack, stop," they said together. He jerked his hand away.

"Why's it so important to have your design?" Annie asked. "Can't she pick another one?"

"She's kind of wide and says the cattails flatter her figure. The weaver doesn't want to lose her business to the shop on the west side." Siobhan sighed and finished her soup. "I'll have to work late."

Eva came back with pot pies and tea. "You want wine instead?" she said to Jack. "Might make you feel better."

He shook his head and pointed to the teapot. "Peppermint?"

"Yeah. I figured you'd need help clearing your head."

"Thanks."

"You call me if you need anything. I'll be in the kitchen." She patted Jack's hand and left with a flip of her short black hair, carrying the soup bowls.

Annie smiled. "I think Jack's made a conquest."

"I agree," Siobhan said.

"Huh?" His watery eyes peered at them.

Siobhan and Annie became very interested in their pies.

After lunch, Annie knocked on the innkeeper's office doorframe. "Glen, do you have a minute?"

He looked up from a desk covered with papers, pens, and empty plates still holding breadcrumbs and pie crust edges. "You're quitting."

"Yes, I'm afraid so. How did you know?" She closed the door.

"You're the third one this year. What is it this time? Too much to do? Not enough money?"

"Things haven't worked out for the three of us, so we're moving on."

"What are you, joined at the hip? Let your friends move on and you stay here. I like your work. You want a raise? I'll see what I can do."

"It's not the money. We prefer to travel together. I'll be here to collect and wash through Wednesday morning."

He grabbed the few hairs left on his head and made a noise that sounded like "urrggh." "Fine. Fine. I'll pay you Tuesday for the work you'll do Wednesday."

When Annie and Siobhan sat down to a late supper, Eva came over with two glasses of wine.

"I checked on Jack a couple hours ago," she said. "The hives were still bad, so I helped him rub in the ointment and tucked him up. I'll bring him a tray later."

"Thanks," Siobhan said. She waited until the kitchen door had closed before saying, "Well."

Annie grinned. "We're going to break up a budding romance."

"Nah. It's a week to Colorado Springs, maybe another week to get what we need to know, then a week back. Winter's coming, so there'll be fewer travelers. No competition." She wagged her eyebrows.

"We'll get enough supplies there so we won't have to stop at the towns in between on our way back. I'm glad Eva likes him. Have you seen the way he looks at me?"

Siobhan nodded. "Starry-eyed. You're his hero."

"He's sweet, but, he's not Hank. Eva will be good for him."

"Should we tell him the plan?" Siobhan said.

"Let's tell Eva."

"I agree."

Jack looked almost normal the next morning at breakfast. Eva brought four fried-egg sandwiches and set two in front of him. The white lace at the low neckline of her bright green dress hovered in front of Jack for an extra moment.

"You didn't eat anything last night. How are you going to work on an empty stomach?"

He smiled at her. "Thanks, Eva."

Annie and Siobhan batted their eyes at him after she left.

"What?" he said with a scowl.

"Nothing," Annie said.

"Nothing," Siobhan said.

After supper, they gathered around a table in the living room. Jack unrolled a long sheet of paper and set cups on the ends to hold it open.

"Eva and I are going to the theater when she's done with the dishes, so I'll be quick. The doctor's youngest is into maps, so he did this for me. Here's Plainville, and here's Colorado Springs. The scale is about twenty miles to the inch."

"That makes it..." Annie measured with her thumb, "one hundred forty miles."

"Seven days, twenty miles a day," Siobhan said. "We can do that."

"The weather shouldn't turn to rain until the end of the month, if the patterns for the last few years hold true," Jack said.

They looked at him.

"It's a hobby. It snowed once when I was a little kid. Ever since then I've kept track of winter weather cycles."

"Brrr. Snow," Siobhan said. "I hate the cold,"

Jack pointed with his index fingers to two spots on the map. "Here's Smoky Hill and here's Cheyenne Wells. They're pretty evenly spaced between here and Colorado Springs. We might want a night at an inn on the way."

"We have three dollars left after paying for our rooms this week," Siobhan said. "We'll have another twenty-five between the three of us on Sunday."

"I brought four," Jack said.

Annie frowned. "I didn't bring anything."

"Didn't you have a job in Topeka?" Jack said.

"Sure, but I got ambushed one night and had to leave everything behind. And you know what happened in Abilene."

"Then don't be silly," Siobhan said.

Eva appeared in the doorway, a red hat on her black hair and wearing a short red dress to match.

Annie nudged Jack. "See you later."

He looked up. "Hey, Eva." He ran his fingers through his thick, twisted hair and straightened his shirt.

"You look fine," Siobhan said.

"Have fun."

He frowned at them. "What's with you two?"

"Nothing."

"Nothing."

That night, Siobhan stood at the dresser and tallied their funds.

"Twenty, twenty-two, twenty-five and fifty cents. Plus my three and Jack's four, thirty-two fifty. Okay. Coats are three dollars. Hats and gloves are fifty cents each."

Annie tapped a pen on her list of supplies. "I need opinions. Do I get food for the whole week or hope Smoky Hill is big enough to have a grocer's?"

"What's the price difference?"

"Crackers, cheese, fruit, and vegetables for the three of us for a week: Three. If we want wine, add two and a quarter."

"I'd really like to add the wine," Jack said.

"Me, too," Siobhan said.

"Okay, then, four-fifty." She rubbed the tip of her nose. "I know we're pooling our money, but I'd really like to replace the salve I lost in Topeka."

"Salve for what?" Jack said.

"The scars ache by the end of the day. I rub it into them."

Jack's eyes went to Annie's wrists, then shied away. "What's in it?"

"Peppermint, black cohosh, slippery elm, white willow."

"That sounds familiar. Lanolin base, right? I'll check at work. I think she has some on her shelves."

"We're forgetting Colorado Springs," Siobhan said. "How long are we going to be there?"

Annie looked at Jack, who looked at Siobhan.

"A week?" Annie said.

"Sounds good," Jack said. "Seven for that?"

Siobhan frowned. "Can't be."

"I paid seven in Topeka for a week with meals for just me," Annie said.

"Ouch," Siobhan said. "Maybe we won't stay a week."

"We could try to get jobs."

"For a week?" Jack said.

"It'd be the perfect disguise," Annie said. "We can go into as many shops as we want, talk to shopkeepers and apprentices." She paced between the table and the fireplace, talking faster. "Siobhan, you could try the weavers and maybe the farmers. Jack, the doctor and the chandler. I can go to the bookseller and the leatherworker. Maybe the innkeeper, too. Even if we end up only staying two or three days, between the three of us we're sure to find some clues."

"All right." Siobhan started a new column of figures. "Twelve for the clothes, four-fifty for traveling food, three for a bed and meals in Smoky Hill."

"Another three for a night at Cheyenne Wells?" Annie grimaced. "Maybe we should sleep in the woods and save the money for Colorado Springs."

"If the weather gets too cold in the mountains, I am not going to be a pleasant traveling companion," Siobhan said. "Consider yourselves warned."

"It's early November, Siobhan," Annie said. "How cold can it get?"

"I can look for deer spoor," Jack said. "Packing the meat will be messy, but one good deer will feed us for a week."

"Jack, you're my hero." Siobhan separated the coins into three piles. "I'll get the coats after breakfast tomorrow."

"I'll take care of the food after I sort and soak the laundry."

"I told the physician I'd do one more day of grinding," Jack said.

"Then we'll leave after supper tomorrow?" Siobhan said.

Annie folded the list and put it in her pocket. "With after-supper coffee in us, we can get in five or ten miles before camping for the night. Sounds good to me."

Wednesday at lunch, Jack pulled out his chair but stopped mid-sit to stare at Annie.

She paused with her mug of beer at her lips. "Has my hair turned blue?" She drank and set it down.

"No. I was supposed to remember something." He sat and his trousers went *klunk*. "That's it." He pulled a small glass jar from his pocket and handed it to her. "There were lots on the shelves. She says everyone uses it. There's aloe in her version."

Annie unscrewed the lid and sniffed. "Phew. That's the smell. How much was it?"

"She gave it to me."

"Great. Thank her for me."

Siobhan came in just then, lugging three coats: plum, deep blue, and grass green. "Gloves are in the pockets, hats in the sleeves."

"What gorgeous colors." Annie pulled out a hat. "And the hat matches perfectly. Do they have special formulas for dyeing?"

"I think so. No one goes into the dyeing room except the weaver and one apprentice." She put her hand on the middle coat. "I love this green."

"I like the plum," Annie said, "but if Jack wants it, I'll take blue."

"I don't care," Jack said. "My mother was interested in things matching like that, too. It must be a girl thing."

Siobhan laughed. "It must be."

\* \* \*

Jack met them at the back door that night as the moon started to rise.

"Sorry. I was saying goodbye to Eva."

"You told her we're coming back, right?" Annie pulled her knapsack strings tighter.

"Yeah. She asked how long and I said about three weeks. She said Glen will probably beg you to do the laundry again."

He bent down to adjust his boots and Siobhan winked at Annie.

They turned right at the end of the gardens and aimed for the river.

"Wait a minute," Annie said. "I think I remember a shortcut behind the grocer's. Just a second." She detoured left and jogged two blocks. *I have to stop being jealous of Jack and Eva. Admit that I'm attracted to Jack and squash it. I have work to do. Besides, Hank hasn't been dead six months yet. What am I thinking?* The moon went behind a cloud. When it reappeared, she faced a row of trash cans against a stone wall.

"Idiot." She turned around. "Never mind! I'm coming back!"

Two hooded figures blocked the end of the alleyway.

"You will come with us, heretic."

Without hesitation she ran at them and battered her shoulder into the one on her left. The one on her right grabbed her by the waist and pinned her arms to her sides.

"Help!" She kicked and squirmed.

*He bit my neck. No—that was a needle. Gotta... get...*

# CHAPTER TWENTY-EIGHT

*The Redeemers appear before her, singing in that unknown language. The hems of their robes soak up her puddled blood.*

*Inside her womb, the baby whispers, 'Mama?' and a Redeemer holds up the knife.*

*She tries to back away, merely pushing her shoulders harder against the wood, and the nails drive themselves deeper.*

*The Redeemer slices open her stomach. She shrieks. Another Redeemer pushes his hands through the smooth gap and pulls out the baby.*

*The baby whispers, "Mama, help." and the circle of Redeemers lower their hoods to it. The noise of their feast reaches through her blinding pain. The baby's voice wails with her, once, and then she hears only her own endless screams.*

*The Redeemers drop the gnawed skeleton at her feet. Her blood covers it. The tiny mouth still cries, "Mama."*

Annie rolled off something and onto a floor, screaming. Her hands clutched at her trousers, pushing and pushing together her ripped stomach. She knew it was ripped—what was covering the gash? The baby's whispery voice wriggled into her head. *Have to save the baby. Have to put little Hank back. Have to—*

Hands steadied her from behind.

*They can't take the baby—* "Let go!" She flailed at the hands.

"Annie, it's us."

Annie's muscles locked. *That's not a Redeemer's voice. I'm not hanging on the wall. I'm not? Where's little Hank? He's gone. He's dead. The Redeemers killed him. Why aren't I dead? I am dead. I remember. Wait. That was Jack's voice.*

She opened her eyes. "Jack?" She must be crying; the room was all wavery.

Jack squatted in front of her. Moonlight shone through a window behind him. She lifted one hand and touched his hair. She wasn't hallucinating. This was Jack's head. "What happened?"

"We were heading for the river," Jack said. "You said you knew a shortcut and took off. A minute later we heard you call for help and we ran. Two Redeemers were carrying you out of an alley."

*I'm empty. There's just a hole where little Hank should be. I'm so tired of listening to the empty me.*

Jack took her hands and pulled her to a sitting position. Other hands supported her from behind. Annie looked over her shoulder. "Siobhan?"

Siobhan gave her a bright smile. "About time. This place reeks of cow."

Annie moved her gaze past Siobhan and saw wood ceiling beams meeting at an angle above their heads. Loose hay filled three-quarters of the loft. Somewhere below a goat bleated and a cow mooed back.

"Are you dizzy?" Siobhan asked. "Do you have a headache? You've got a nasty red bump on your neck."

Annie slumped onto the floor again. "They poked me with something. Like they did before." *They almost got me. Redeemers help me. They were this close.* "How did I—we—get away?"

"Jack has some impressive muscles." Siobhan scooted around to face her. "He socked the one carrying you right in the stomach."

"And Siobhan kicked the other one in the groin, and when he bent over she probably broke his nose."

"I was only imitating you." She grinned. "It's lucky Annie didn't have far to fall."

"Yeah, sorry about that, Annie. I was so into making sure they wouldn't follow us, I forgot you'd fall when they let you go."

"Did they follow us?" Her voice shook. *Weakling. Show some guts.*

"Absolutely not. When they were both down and moaning, Jack chopped the backs of their heads with one hand and they went out like a snuffed lamp." She picked up his hand and felt the edge. "You have to teach me how to do that."

"We carried you out of town and found this barn," Jack said. "We're in the hayloft. Siobhan says no one will be out here until sunup."

"How long was I out?"

"A few hours."

Annie shuddered. "They were going to—"

"Yes, well, they aren't now, so don't worry about it," Siobhan said.

Annie couldn't think straight. "I have the worst headache." She rubbed her wrists, one after the other, over and over.

*Wait. They came for me. Siobhan's still here. She didn't throw me to the Redeemers and run away.* She met Siobhan's eyes. "You didn't leave."

"What?" Jack said.

"I told you I wouldn't." Siobhan said.

"I'm sorry."

Siobhan grinned. "Almost worth it to hear you say that."

Annie chuckled, then stopped. "Ow. Bad for the head." *Bad for everything. Is it scary that I can laugh without meaning it? What did they drug me with? It must be the same mixture. I don't remember wanting to laugh the first time. But I was alone then. So tired of being alone.*

Siobhan and Jack were staring at her, worry wrinkling their foreheads.

She put on a strong face for them. "Sorry. Still a little woozy. Should we get out of here?"

"Are you up to it yet?" Siobhan said.

"Yeah." Annie got to her feet but swayed like a wind-blown sapling . "What I meant was I'll be up to it in a few minutes."

Jack held her while she regained her balance. Then without warning, he kissed her.

*Whoa—what—* she pulled her head away, but he didn't release her.

"Thank the Redeemers you're all right." His deep voice grew husky. "You looked so pale and limp. I thought you—" He kissed her again.

Hank kissed her before leaving for Liberty, so long ago. Jack's lips were bigger than Hank's, and softer. *He almost makes the emptiness fade.*

She held him, returning the kiss for just a moment. Then she heard the drug-nightmare voice of little Hank and she pulled away. *What am I doing?* "Jack."

He closed the gap and hid his face in her hair. "I love you, Annie. I've loved you since the night in Walt's cellar. I don't know what I'd do if I lost you."

She slid down, out of his embrace. "Jack, I didn't mean, that is, I never..."

He stared at her for a long moment before he hit himself in the forehead. "Why don't I keep my big mouth shut?"

She touched his arm and he looked down at her. Her throat closed at the hurt and humiliation in his face. "Jack."

"Forget it. Forget I said anything. It was stupid. I'm a jerk." He pulled away.

"You are not." She gripped his wrist. "You're sweet and incredibly brave and I'd have been dead in a few hours without you. But the baby."

He gulped. "Are you pregnant?"

She shook her head. "Not anymore. Little Hank," she drew in a deep breath, "little Hank died inside me while I was nailed to the abbey wall."

Behind her, Siobhan said, "Oh, no," in a small voice.

*I sound like a bad dramatic play. No one wants to hear that. I'm tough. I can handle this.* "It's taking me a little longer to get used to things than I figured. So, I don't think I could, I mean, it's not you, it's the baby." She rubbed the back of her neck. "That came out all wrong."

Jack held her like she was as fragile as a Page. "You're tough, Annie, but you need me—us. We'll get you into the Colorado Springs abbey. Trust me." He kissed the top of her head.

With that kiss, just for a moment, Annie didn't feel decades older than Jack. Little Hank's voice faded from her ears and her perpetual hate receded.

*I have to keep my guard up. I have to remember that I'm dead. But... I don't want to be dead.*

Siobhan cleared her throat. "We have an hour or so 'til dawn. Here." She uncorked her wineskin and handed it to Annie. "You need this."

Annie needed more than wine, but at least a few swallows took away the lingering chill from the Redeemers' drug. "You're right. I did need that. I'm hungry too. Anyone want cheese and apples?"

They picnicked on her bed of hay.

Annie stopped in the middle of another swallow of wine. "That word."

"What word?" Siobhan said.

"Heretic. They called me that when they blocked off the alley, and the ones in Topeka called me that when they tried to grab me. Do you know what it means?"

"Uhn-uhn," she said through a mouthful.

"Is it in one of your Pages, Jack?"

"I don't think so. Let me look." He wiped his hands on his trousers and reached into the bottom of his knapsack.

Siobhan shoved her wineskin into the hay and hovered over his shoulder. "Don't make me drool. Please, please, may I have a look?"

He took out half the sheets and handed the box to her. "Dad told me not to let them out of my hands, but you two are different."

"Ohh..." Siobhan held the fragile piece of paper up to the moonlight shining through the window.

"Annie?" Jack offered her the top four scraps of different-textured paper.

She cleaned her hands and took the sheets gingerly, squinting at the small, re-inked print on the first one. "That except your righteousness shall exceed the righteousness of the scribes and Pharisees, ye shall in no case enter into the kingdom of heaven." She handed it back. "More words I've never heard. Let me see another one."

A few minutes later, Jack packed all the papers away.

"All right, your papers don't have the word." She looked out the window. "Moon's setting."

Siobhan gathered the apple cores. "I'll toss these into the pig trough on the way."

Jack pitchforked the hay back into the corner pile while Siobhan tied her own pack. "Annie, how's your head?"

"Better. The food helped." She looked down into the barn. "Will we wake up the cows?"

"Nah. It takes a lot to rile a cow. They won't even moo unless we make too much noise."

They climbed down and scuffed out their footprints in the dirt floor. The cows didn't budge. Siobhan cracked the barn door.

"No one stirring. Let's get out in case someone in the house is an extra-early riser."

They slipped through the barn door and away from the house.

The sky was just beginning to lighten toward the east as they weaved through rows of vines covered in heavy clusters of purple grapes. Soon after sunrise these gave way to pine trees and willows. They covered more miles by noon than Annie had expected.

"My stomach is talking to my spine," Jack said when a gap in the reeds showed several feet of river. "And it's saying Trout."

Annie dropped her pack and fell backward onto the grass. Siobhan followed.

"Someone call the waitress to bring lunch," Siobhan said.

Annie raised her hand. "Find me something to use for a fishing pole, since you two couldn't manage to carry me and our old ones."

Jack stuck out his tongue at her. He took out his pocketknife and returned in a few minutes with three long ash branches. She tied string around their bases and wrapped it in spirals all the way to the tips before baiting them.

"I'll see if the trout are in the mood for cheese. I owe you one."

"Don't be silly," Siobhan said. "Give me a pole."

The fish refused to cooperate, so Jack went foraging and returned with his shirt full of tiny pears. She built a fire and they roasted the fruit on more ash sticks.

At dusk they stopped for the night and caught five trout. Annie skewered three for roasting and Jack built a small tripod to smoke the others. Siobhan wove some thin willow branches into a grid. When the moon rose, they banked the fire. Annie filleted and salted the remaining fish and set the grid and tripod over the embers.

"Hat and gloves for me tonight." Siobhan pulled out her blanket.

\* \* \*

"Annie. Annie."

A hand shook her shoulder. She opened her eyes. Siobhan crouched above her, half her face white in the moonlight, the other half orange from the glowing embers.

"You were having a nightmare."

"I'm sick of this." Annie pulled out her handkerchief and dragged it across her wet cheeks.

Siobhan yawned in her face. "Sorry. Tired."

"Go back to sleep. Thanks for waking me up."

When Siobhan was wrapped up and snoring, Annie checked the embers and turned over the fish. Wide awake now, she felt in her bag and brought out the salve jar. She slipped off her socks and rubbed it into the four scars. At last she cocooned into her blanket and stared at the moon for a long time.

\* \* \*

"Good fish," Siobhan said, licking her fingers.

"Hey!" Annie pulled the grid out from under her hands. "Catch some fresh. This is for walking."

"If you can take my jerky, Annie, I can fit both fish into my pack," Jack said.

Whippoorwills and chickadees filled the woods. Red-winged blackbirds swooped along the riverbanks and between the willows. Annie paid attention to them and locked up her nightmare. Siobhan found wild carrots at lunch and Jack brought down two squirrels. Late in the afternoon, he shot a fat rabbit and they used the smoking grid for the leftovers.

\* \* \*

"Annie. Annie."

"What?"

"Nightmare." Jack's voice.

"Sorry." She inhaled a noseful of snot and coughed.

"Want my handkerchief?"

She shook her head and found her own wadded up in her pocket. She honked into it.

"What was it this time?" Jack said.

*Don't tell him. It'll go away faster if I don't repeat it. It wasn't that bad. It wasn't—* "They stretched me out on the wood and picked up the hammer and nails. The nails stretched like taffy. They looked a foot long. They held me down and I screamed at them to stop. They raised the hammer and pounded the nail into me. My blood sprayed out and they kept hammering and hammering—"

Jack put his fingers on her lips and she stopped. He brushed tears from her cheeks with his thumbs and put his arms around her.

*Don't give in. I'm stronger than this. Stop blubbering. Get out of his arms. I am not his true love.*

"I'm sorry." She backed out, drying her face on her coat sleeves.

"That's okay. Think you can you get back to sleep now?"

"Sure. Thanks for waking me up."

"No problem."

\* \* \*

"Look at me," Siobhan said to Annie at lunch.

"What?"

"You have circles the size of dinner plates under your eyes."

"So?"

"There's more white hair, too."

"Thanks."

"You're still having nightmares, aren't you?"

"So?"

"So wake one of us up. We'll sit up with you 'til you can shake 'em off."

"Why should you lose sleep too? I squashed this before. I can do it again." She stood and went to the river to wash her plate.

Later that afternoon, a gaudy figure popped out of the tall cattails near the river.

"My river!" it shouted in an old man's voice. "This is my river. If you want to walk here you have to pay the toll."

He wore several different shirts and trousers, one on top of the other. A straw hat held down long brownish-gray hair, its wide, multicolored band falling over his eyes.

"Why is it your river?" Jack said.

"My family owns it. Just like in the towns. Butcher. Chandler. Weaver. Ever since my great-great-great grandfather came here. You three have to pay the toll."

"What is the toll?" Siobhan said.

"A lock of hair from each of you. Haven't you heard of locks on the waterways? It's a fine tradition. Must keep the uniform ready for inspection." He doffed his hat and tumbled it down one arm like a showman.

Jack cleared his throat. "It's colorful."

"I have every kind here: gray, blonde, white, red, black, and every shade of brown." An ancient pair of scissors appeared in his hand. He held them out to Jack. "Young sir?"

"Not worth a confrontation," Jack whispered. Siobhan nodded. Annie shook her head.

"What?" Siobhan said in her ear.

"I don't trust strangers."

"He looks harmless enough."

"No one's harmless."

Siobhan rolled her eyes.

Jack took off his hat and snipped one of his twists of hair.

The old man grinned. "Excellent; excellent." He held it up to the sunlight. "Thick and sturdy. This will last several winters."

Jack passed the scissors to Annie and she snipped a long curl. Siobhan cut several strands of her straight, dark hair and handed them and the scissors to the river warden.

"Thank you kindly, travelers. You are free to continue along my river. A good journey to you." He disappeared into the abundant cattails.

They walked in silence for a long time before Jack felt his missing hair. "That was nuts."

Further on, Annie said, "Someday my grandchildren will ask, 'Grandma, what was the weirdest thing that ever happened to you?' I'll be able to say, 'Kids, I once met a crazy old man by the river who said that I couldn't walk there until I gave him a lock of my hair as a toll.' Then they'll pat my wrinkled knees and whisper to each other that grandma's mind is going fast."

*Grandchildren. I have to marry again and have my own children first. Not easy for a dead woman to accomplish.*

# CHAPTER TWENTY-NINE

"Like this?" Annie nocked an arrow onto Jack's bow.

Sparrows and chickadees called from the surrounding pine trees. They'd reached the Smoky Hill Inn the day after paying their river toll. The aroma of roasting pig from the kitchen came and went with the breeze.

"No; turn sideways to the target," Jack said. "Now pull harder. You want your hand to touch your shoulder."

"My shoulder?" The arrow twanged, flew a wobbly arc, bounced off the pine needles on the ground, and fell over.

"Ouch," Siobhan said.

"An entire family of squirrels is behind that tree, laughing," Annie said. "I just know it."

"Try again," Jack said.

"My fingertips are throbbing." She clenched her teeth. This time she pulled the arrow within six inches of her shoulder before she released it. Its flight was truer, but the shot had no power behind it and the arrow clunked off a tree trunk into the grass.

"That was better."

She looked up at Jack. "You're humoring me. Here. Take your bow. I quit for the day. This is harder than trimming shoe leather with a dull knife.

"Isn't it time for supper anyway?" Jack said. "We can't hear the bell out here."

"I'm for heading back," Annie said. "Let the squirrels amuse themselves for awhile."

They skirted trees back to the path and walked to the inn's vegetable gardens, now plowed over for the winter. The waiter rang the bell as soon as Jack opened the door.

"The play starts in an hour if you want to go," the waiter said to them after supper. "They're doing *Snowbound.* It's a musical comedy. The lead is that blonde just walking out the door."

They looked. Jack whistled.

The waiter smiled. "Everyone has that reaction. Leave soon if you want to get good seats."

"Can we afford it?" Jack asked Siobhan.

Siobhan wrinkled her forehead and muttered numbers. "Shoot us a deer so we don't have to buy jerky and we can squeak through."

"It's a deal," Jack said. "I'm tired of fish, anyway."

\* \* \*

"It wasn't *Double Trouble,* but it was fun." Annie raised her voice above the cold wind as they ran back to the inn afterwards.

"You've seen that?" Jack said.

"In Abilene. Our last night there."

"Oh. Yeah. Uh, did I ever apologize to you for that? Walt and the flour sacks and everything?"

"It wasn't your fault. Don't worry about it."

Siobhan reached the front door first and they crowded in behind her.

"Heat." Siobhan made straight for the fireplace in the living room. Mulled wine and spiced cider simmered on the hob. She poured wine for the three of them and they commandeered the opposite corner of the hearth while the rest of the theatergoers got drinks.

"The male lead was very easy on the eyes." Siobhan said.

"So was the blonde." Jack said.

Annie sighed. "Poor Eva. Forgotten so soon."

"I haven't forgotten her." Jack's eyes grew big and sincere. "We have a date for when we all get back to Plainville."

"Good. Eva's sweet and a lot of fun."

"But, Annie, Eva's a nice girl to hang around with and all that, but..." He reached for her hand. "It's you who...I mean..."

"Jack," Annie said, her voice firm.

Siobhan held out her hands for their cups. "I'll get refills."

Annie inspected her cuff buttons for loose threads and Jack

picked at the edge of the hearthstones until Siobhan returned.

"We can still afford breakfast here tomorrow, right?" Annie asked her.

"Yeah. I subtracted that when I was figuring if we could pay for theater tickets."

"Great," Jack said. "I'll get up before dawn and scout the woods. It'll be easier to skin and chop up a deer here in the kitchen. They have better knives."

* * *

The next morning, Annie and Siobhan were halfway through bowls of oatmeal by the time Jack came to their table. He bowed to the floor, flipping his hair over his head and spraying them with water.

"Don't water down our coffee," they said.

"What's a little water when there's a pile of neat packets of meat from a ninety-pound deer being kept cool for us in the cellar? Sorry I'm late. Cleaning and skinning is messy. I had to take a bath."

They applauded and he bowed again before sitting down and slurping hot coffee.

"I saw deer spoor when we got near here yesterday, so I climbed a huge oak after the moon set and waited. He came past me after sunup. I got him right behind the shoulder and it went straight through to the heart. He didn't even run a hundred feet." He poured honey over his oatmeal and swallowed a massive spoonful. "This is exactly what I need to warm me up. The hostler saw me dragging him back and gave me a hand. The inn's keeping the skin and a third of the meat."

Annie calculated the weight of her knapsack. "We each have to carry twenty pounds of meat?"

Jack shook his head and gulped more oatmeal. "No, ninety pounds was the weight with bones and skin and antlers. We'll end up with about twelve to fifteen pounds each. We'll hardly notice the weight."

"Does anyone mind if I work on that jigsaw puzzle in the living room before we leave?" Siobhan said, adding honey to her coffee.

"Is this an obsession we should worry about?" Annie said.

Siobhan screened her face from the other guests with her napkin and thumbed her nose at Annie. Jack coughed on a mouthful of oatmeal.

The cook sold Annie spices, an old frying pan, and a spatula while Siobhan and Jack attacked the puzzle. She perched on the windowsill afterward to watch them.

"Ten pieces...seven...two..." Siobhan snatched the last piece from Jack's hand and snapped it into place. "I win."

Annie looked at Jack and bit back laughter.

Siobhan's face turned the deep red of a ripe tomato. "It's my secret addiction. I have a stack of them at home."

"Hey, whatever makes you happy." Annie jumped to the floor. "I packed us both up. Can we go now?"

* * *

Annie wiggled her fishing pole in the river at lunch and stared at the moving water. She was getting too comfortable with Jack and Siobhan. She was starting to trust them.

*Siobhan didn't tuck her tail between her legs and run when the Redeemers showed up in that dead end alley because Jack was there too. It wasn't a change of heart. It was the need to keep Jack believing her protestations of how she's on my side.*

A fish broke the surface. Annie did her best to make the bait as attractive as a fat dragonfly.

*Jack is either a bigger puzzle than Siobhan or the best actor on the Smoky River. As a problem to be solved, he doesn't matter either. I will not trust him. I will not trust Siobhan. I will remind myself every morning and every—*

"Whoa! Caught a big one." She wrestled with the line and yanked an eighteen-inch catfish onto the grass.

"Delicious," Siobhan said. "Wish we had a frying pan."

"We do." Annie pulled it out of her knapsack. "You may applaud now."

"Dare I hope for butter?"

"Is lard acceptable? I have pepper and thyme, too."

Siobhan bowed to Annie. "From now on, I'm always traveling with a cook."

"I've got one too." Jack pulled a smaller catfish out of the water. "Annie's will feed all of us. We can smoke this one."

"I'll build the fire if you'll gut, Annie," Siobhan said.

"Anything to get out of gutting?"

"You know it."

"Wait a minute," Jack said. He picked up a rock from the river's edge and smashed both fishes' heads.

Annie flinched. "What was that for?"

"These guys are tough. I hooked one last year and when I

went to skin it, it tried to bite me. I don't take chances with catfish anymore."

Annie slit and disemboweled both fish, seasoned and filleted both and gave the bigger one to Siobhan to fry.

*What a happy little group we make.*

# CHAPTER THIRTY

Annie stopped by a chestnut tree and puffed. "Have we been walking uphill all day, or is it me?"

"It's not you," Siobhan said. "My ankles feel it, too."

"The willows are gone," Jack said. "And the air is, I don't know, crisper."

"Could just be winter coming," Siobhan said.

Annie touched the ground with her palms and her back cracked. "I wouldn't mind soaking my feet in the river. Anyone else feel like quitting for the day?"

They walked through barberries and yews to look down a three-foot-high bank at a narrower, faster Smoky River.

"I think we need to cut the fishing lines longer," Annie said.

Siobhan made puppy-dog eyes at her. "If you clean the rabbit I caught, I'll cook."

"Is this supposed to be a deal?" Annie shrugged. "I don't mind."

Siobhan speared alternating pieces of rabbit, onion, and deer on three sticks for supper. Afterward, Annie sat cross-legged near the fire and stretched.

"Siobhan, that was a good bargain. I enjoy being served for a change." She counted the bumps in the front pocket of her knapsack. "I'm still carrying a dozen apples. Want dessert while there's still enough light to see?"

"I always want dessert," Jack said. "I'll wash."

"How? The river is too far down."

"For cute little girls like you and Siobhan, maybe. I'm a man."

They both clawed at him and he slid down the riverbank, laughing.

The apples finished shortly after he returned. "I suppose you deserve this," Annie said, handing him one. "You'll notice that a short stick cooked your apple just fine."

"I didn't say everything short was useless." The apple skin popped. He blew once, bit into it, and with a yell flung himself down the bank again and plunged his face into the shallows.

After the splash Annie heard a full minute of coughing. She and Siobhan laughed so hard they dropped their own apples. Siobhan leaned over the edge and handed them to Jack. "If you're done scorching your tongue, can you rinse these, too?"

Jack had just squeezed his drenched hair over the fire when Annie pointed ahead of them. "Quiet."

A metallic ringing and clattering came nearer, like cowbells swinging against an anvil.

Annie leapt to her feet. *Don't wait for them to surround the fire. Go.*

Siobhan put a hand on her arm. "Relax. They don't announce themselves like someone dropping pots on the kitchen floor."

The noise increased. "Greetings, fellow travelers," a voice said from the woods.

A lumpy, puffing shape came into the firelight. He wore a rabbit-fur hat and a dark coat with a small cast-iron pot and three-legged stand strapped to his back.

"May a cold and weary tinker share your fire on this November night?"

Annie remembered to breathe. Siobhan and Jack would probably protect their prize against any poacher. Letting the tinker stay wasn't much of a risk. "Of course." She pried her fingernails out of her palms and sat.

Jack sat next to her and whispered, "We got your back."

The tinker held out his hands to the fire. "Ahh." He beamed a smile made crooked by an old scar on his bottom lip. "Allow me to introduce myself. I am Nick, mender of pots and merchant of spices. Please call me Nick. Everyone does. I had thought to reach Fountain today, but the weather has not been kind to my tired feet."

"Please sit down," Annie said. *And turn off the patter. It won't make me trust you.*

Jack and Siobhan eased away from her into positions that flanked the stranger.

"Thank you kindly." Nick wriggled the stand and cauldron off his shoulders.

"Would you like an apple?" Annie held out her cooled one.

"I am much obliged." He took a bite.

She skewered another and started roasting it. He seemed harmless. She caught Siobhan's eye and cocked her head in an unspoken question. Siobhan gave her the tiniest of shrugs.

"It gets harder to earn my living as the weather turns," Nick said. "Pots need mending sun or storm, but once Halloween passes, my feet stay cold until May."

"I remember you," Jack said. "You used to repair my dad's mixing pots. He made dyes. Big guy, bald, all his jokes started with 'three guys walk into a winery.'"

"And you used to travel with him? Yes, yes of course! John and little Jack. You're no longer working together?"

"He died last year."

"Please accept my sympathy. Are you carrying on his business?"

"No. I'm traveling with my friends here."

"And where would you be headed at this time of year, if I may inquire?" Nick said, already halfway through his apple.

Annie stopped turning hers. *Why did he want to know?*

"Colorado Springs," Jack said.

"Ah. I've just come from a six-week sojourn north of there," Nick said. "I mended more pots than I could count. The labor was well worth it. I earned enough to see me through most of the winter. I shall spend the next month in Fountain. Perhaps longer, if the rains turn to sleet as they did last year." He bit into the last of the apple. "Have you even been there? Lovely little town with the most charming doctor. The blacksmith creates delightful iron flowers. Everyone decorates their garden fences with them." He slurped juice from his fingers. "But don't you know that the Redeemers began arriving on the first? Colorado Springs has already pulled into its shell."

"The Redeemers arrive?" Siobhan said.

"Indeed. Have you never been to Colorado Springs?"

"Not since I was six or seven," Jack said.

"I see. Every year in early November as many Redeemers as possible, it seems, come home to Colorado Springs. The abbey where they are born, or trained, or possibly both, is there. The November gathering has always looked to me like a family reunion. That is, if one may regard the Redeemers as a family."

"What do they do?" Jack said.

"That, little Jack, is quite possibly the world's most unanswerable question." He grinned at him. "I have been to Colorado Springs many times in the last twenty-odd years, and the pattern is always the same. Their, let us say, reunion is a two-week event. It takes a week for all of them to arrive. In my younger days I once counted as many as one hundred and thirty."

Annie's stick started to tremble, so she planted it. "More than a hundred?"

"Indeed. You would not think it, the way they are seen only in twos or threes everywhere else. But I assure you it is true. They go directly to the abbey and are not seen again until the end of the second week. Then they leave in the same manner."

"What does everyone in Colorado Springs do?" Siobhan said.

"Scurry into their homes like rabbits when a fox appears." He laughed. "But I must not criticize the good people of Colorado Springs too harshly. What would any of us do when confronted with awe-inspiring figures by the dozen? I doubt we should repeatedly bow as actors do after a performance, but neither does it seem right to pass them in the street as though they were the same as the rest of us."

Annie blew on her new apple. *Let's see how he reacts to the superficial part of our plan.* "We're looking for work there. Should we give it up until after the Redeemers leave?"

He nibbled the last morsels of his. "I should say it all depends on the kind of work."

"The weaver," Siobhan said.

"The doctor," Jack said.

"Laundry or waitressing at the inn," Annie said.

"Dear lady, the inn will be so empty they shall be hard put to use their store of milk before it goes sour. I believe the only guests still there are a few elderly residents who have no family left." He tossed the apple core into the fire. "The weaver might be possible. I have repaired pots for the brother and sister who run the shops at the north and south ends of town, and they are always busy. The doctors, now. There are two, on the east and west sides. I did not encounter the winsome lady on the west side this season. The older man on the east side was training his grandchildren to make tinctures this summer, and he had two dozen small cauldrons and pots for me to repair."

Siobhan looked at the crowded trees. "If we get really desperate, we could sleep in the woods until the town opens up."

"I know. Bad timing." Annie finally took a bite.

"Kind hosts, do not despair. I know of travelers who have requested a room at the inn during the Redeemers' arrival week and paid barely half the usual price for it. If you possess a few dollars among you, the loquacious Margaret will not turn you away."

"It'll be one more day before we reach Colorado Springs," Jack said. "What'll be the date then?"

"The eleventh," Annie said through a mouthful.

"A mere two days after that the town will return to normal," Nick said. "Without doubt you and Margaret will reach a mutually beneficial agreement. She is unhappy when her inn does not echo with the sounds of satisfied guests."

*Enough conversation with the unknown traveler who just happened to be walking in the woods in the exact same spot as us.* "All right, then." Annie collected the rest of the apple cores and skewers, and set them and the newspaper meat-wrappers on the fire. "We'll be heading on to Colorado Springs in the morning, Nick."

"And I shall continue to Fountain. Your fire and companionship are most appreciated this night. Traveling alone is a tedious business."

He removed his top coat, folded it for a pillow, and donned a rabbit-fur scarf and mittens. The identical coat underneath it bulged and puckered from dozens of odd-shaped lumps on the inside.

Jack banked the fire and Annie settled between him and Siobhan.

*Keep an eye open. Jack's snoring should be enough to keep you awake. Just in case.*

# CHAPTER THIRTY-ONE

Annie stared at the stars, trying to figure out what woke her. "In my thoughts, in my words..." Nick's voice, distant in sleep. She wasn't the only one who had nightmares.

"My brothers and sisters..."

She turned her head his way. He had rolled away from the fire and grass surrounded his head.

"Conformed to the image..."

She scrambled on hands and knees to his side and shook him.

He sat up, wild-eyed. His coat fell in a heap around him. "What? What is it?"

"You were talking in your sleep."

His gaze took in her, the fire, and the curled-up humps of Siobhan and Jack. "I apologize for waking you. I must have been quite loud."

The fire crackled behind Annie, giving the illusion of comfort and safety. After a moment, he said in a casual voice, "What did I say?"

She kept her gaze on him. "Something about brothers and sisters. Do you have a big family somewhere?"

"A very long time ago, my dear. I am older than I look."

*Here goes.* "Then you said something odd: 'conformed to the image.'"

He refolded his coat pillow. "Indeed. That means nothing to me.

Who knows what our brains conjure when we're asleep?" He pulled his sleeping coat up around him and stared straight at her.

She met him squarely but she blinked first. "I've had odd dreams myself once or twice."

"Good night to you, then." He lay down and closed his eyes.

She returned the few steps to her knapsack and stirred the embers of the fire. *I'm not the tough broad I think I am.*

The renewed fire threw light onto Nick's face and he turned his back to it.

*Memorize the lesson, dead woman. Trust no one. No one at all ever again.*

She tugged her hat down over her ears and wrapped herself in her blanket. This time she faced the fire and Nick the tinker beyond it.

\* \* \*

Annie was up before everyone else. An easy accomplishment since she didn't sleep after Nick's nightmare. The fire perked up after she fed it several twigs. She dumped last night's coffee grounds beneath a wild raspberry bush, rinsed and refilled the pot in the river, and started a fresh pot. Then she strung and baited a branch and sat on the riverbank waiting for sunrise.

*He's leaving this morning. He doesn't know my name. He didn't recognize me. I'm safe.*

A fish tugged at her line. She landed a perch and re-baited the string.

*Maybe one day I'll actually believe I'm safe. Right. And I'm not dead, either.*

Siobhan appeared next to her. "The coffee was boiling, so I moved it."

"Sorry. I forgot about it."

"You forgot coffee? Someone tell the newspaper." She sat down and ran her fingers through the tangles in her hair. "I have to remember to braid this mop before I sleep. What's on your mind that could be more important than coffee?"

"Later." She flicked her eyes toward Nick. He sat up and yawned.

"Got it. I'll get another pole."

Soon they had four perch sizzling in the pan. Nick seasoned them from rows of bags sewn inside his coat.

"This is good." Jack took another bite. "What's the green spice?"

"Marjoram. It's not as versatile as basil, but its difference makes it popular," Nick said. "During that particularly long winter a few years back, the inns were desperate for something else to put into the stews. Enter my humble self with marjoram and oregano. They funded my new cauldron."

Annie cleaned the dishes afterward and Siobhan doused the fire. Nick strapped on his cauldron and stood.

"Would you like some deer meat?" Jack asked him.

"I would be delighted." He removed three spice bags from an inner pocket and slid two damp packages in their place. "Please accept this in return." He held out one of the bags.

Jack opened it and sniffed gently. "Allspice?"

"Indeed. Have you ever tried it on roasted apples?"

"I have," Annie said. "It's good. Thank you."

"Dear lady, my thanks go to the three of you for sharing your food and warmth with a stranger. I wish you a safe journey. Perhaps we shall meet again after the winter."

"You never know," Siobhan said. "Thanks for all the Colorado Springs information."

Nick pulled on his fur gloves and clanked southward into the trees.

While Annie could still hear his clamor, she took the lead and set a quick westward pace. They entered a pine and spruce forest. The wide trees crowded out any undergrowth, but the pine duff cushioned her feet. Squirrels scrambled overhead and yellow-bellied sapsuckers beat a contrasting tattoo to their footsteps. The ground angled upward and soon she was panting on the steep slope.

"Annie, what's the hurry?" Siobhan said.

Jack caught her. "Annie, wait up."

She kept moving. "Am I walking too fast?"

Siobhan laughed in between huffs. "I feel like a packhorse on market day. What gives?"

"I needed to get away from him."

"Nick? Why?"

*No reason. He knew that image word the Redeemers said, that's all.* "He scared me last night."

"Last night, when?" Jack gripped her arm and they all stopped. "Did he do anything to you?"

"No, of course not. I can take care of myself against guys with too many hands. Come over here for a minute."

She led them to a fallen pine trunk a few feet ahead and they sat between branches. "He was talking in his sleep and woke me up.

At first it was nothing, but he said that 'image' word."

"Annie…" Siobhan said.

"Don't. I'm not stupid. I know it's a regular word. What he said exactly was, 'conformed to the image.' I recognized that long word, sort of. I can't remember the whole thing, but I know they said it when I was hanging there." She pushed her hands over her face and deliberately slowed her breathing.

"All right." Siobhan reached over a branch and gave her a quick hug. "How could he have known it? And did it sound like he was having a conversation or was it more like a nightmare?"

"Nightmare."

"Is there any way he could've been rescued, like you?" Jack said.

"He didn't hide his hands. I saw them when he put those fur mittens on. No scars."

"What if he saw a Reader, uh, like you were…you know."

"Hung up to die?" Her voice cracked. If she kept obsessing about it she'd shatter like the windows in a pre-Last War building.

"If that's true, he might know something," Siobhan said. "Do you think we should go after him?"

"No!"

They looked at her. She shook herself and attempted the bright smile which meant nothing. "Sorry. He gave me the creeps. I'd rather keep going to Colorado Springs and find him on the way back."

"But he talks a lot. What if he can give us more information about Redeemers and Colorado Springs?" Siobhan said.

"I don't care. He's a distraction I don't want anything to delay getting to Colorado Springs this week."

"No problem," Jack said. "We'll take everything we learn in Colorado Springs and maybe detour to Fountain and surprise him with it. He said he'd be there for a month or so."

Annie cut off the end of his sentence with the fear that had been eating her hollow. "What if he's a Redeemer?"

"Without calling you 'heretic' or trying to stab you with something?" Siobhan said. "Nah. They only have one thing on their minds, and it's not cold feet or iron flowers on fences."

"All right. I know I'm obsessing. Sorry. Sometimes I get these flashes of memory and they crowd out everything else." Annie looked down. Her right hand was rubbing her left wrist. "He spooked me more than I thought."

Jack said, "What do you mean?"

"I worried at the scars like this while I was recovering in Sara's secret cellar room. Her and Max said to quit because the action would draw attention to the scars, so I broke the habit. Usually. It comes back when I'm stressed."

She caught the look Siobhan and Jack gave each other. "Thank you; I know I'm not the ideal type of girl you'd want to bring home to your mother."

Jack punched her arm. "Yes, you are." Then he rubbed the spot he punched. "Annie, did I hurt you? Are you okay?"

She laughed for real. "Jack, I'm not a fragile flower."

He pecked her on the cheek. "Yes, you are. You are as beautiful as a flower. And you're the perfect woman to bring home."

She got off the tree trunk. She'd have to remind him about Eva again soon.

Siobhan stood and looked down at Jack. "Would you like me to tie a handkerchief around your mouth so you stop sticking your foot in it?"

"Maybe. Yeah."

# CHAPTER THIRTY-TWO

"I smell snow," Annie said after clouds and biting wind pummeled them for the rest of that day.

Jack stopped short. "Oh, yes." He bent his head back and inhaled long and deeply. Then his body teetered backwards as well.

"Careful." Siobhan stretched out her hands to block him.

He stumbled and caught himself. "Sorry. Wow. Snow at last."

"We had maybe an inch of it three years ago," Siobhan said. "The sheep looked like giant balls of fluff from the cottonwood trees. But it was way too cold."

Annie smiled. "We woke up to it in Kansas City one morning last January. The whole town skipped work and school. All the shops in the square had a huge snowball fight."

"Did the snow last?" Jack said.

"No. It melted by afternoon. But it was gorgeous. Everything glittered in the sun."

"Bet you'll change your mind about that if we wake up tomorrow morning covered in it," Siobhan said.

"You're a living, breathing Doris the Dismal Donkey," Jack said.

Annie groaned. "Our second-grade teacher read that book to us once a week for months. We used to braid flowers together to put on the head of any donkey we saw, to cheer it up."

Siobhan said, "I hate the cold. Haven't you heard me grumbling for the last several hours?"

Annie looked at Jack. "Oh, yes, we have," they said together.

Siobhan glowered at them. "And if the wind turns we'll get freezing rain."

"Would you rather walk all night instead?" Annie rubbed her gloved hands together and blew on them.

"Redeemers forbid it, no. Why?"

"Colorado Springs can't be that far now. Maybe we could beat the weather."

"I refuse to keep this up all night without a break. That's worse than getting stuck out here in the snow. Can't we look for a fallen tree or a cave or something?"

Annie patted her on the back. "Don't panic. I wasn't serious."

The ground kept its sharp upward slant and the pines crowded out the spruce as the afternoon passed. When they emerged from a dense stand of pines, Siobhan held out her sleeve. "The first flake. We're doomed."

Annie looked up through the trees. Snow drifted through the branches and clung in crystal puffs. "Isn't it pretty?" She tried to catch a flake on her tongue.

Siobhan moaned. "You've lost your mind."

A few minutes later, they walked into a wall of heavy, wet snow driven by a stinging wind. Icy needles covered them in minutes.

Jack pointed. "Clearing on the left."

Annie shielded her face with her arm. "We're right behind you."

They tripped over hidden rocks and roots. When Jack pushed through two trees he showered them all with more snow.

"Sorry. Look. The lowest branches are at least five feet off the ground. We'll fit under them."

Annie wormed her hands under the pine duff. "It's dry underneath." She raked away the top layer.

"Siobhan, get out the blankets while I cut branches," Jack said.

Siobhan covered her feet with the knapsacks and wrapped all three blankets around herself. The trees blocked most of the snow, but the wind kept changing directions and snow sneaked between the trunks to keep pounding them.

Jack returned. "Take these." He handed Siobhan four long branches. "Annie, take these." He gave her five. "We're building a teepee." He cleared away another foot of duff. "Okay, Annie, hand me two."

He laid them on the ground side by side. "Another." He set its tip between the tips of the first two. The wind picked them up and he pushed them down into the duff. "Get my string out of the front pocket of my knapsack." He wound a piece crosswise around the three branch tops, then wound two lengths the opposite way around the string in the gaps on both sides of the center branch.

The wind shook the trees, which dumped yet another layer of snow over everything.

"Stand back." He picked up the branches, bent them at the string, and set them on the ground in a triangle. "Annie, the rest of your branches next." He balanced them on the triangle. "Siobhan, now yours." The triangle became a cone with one open side.

"I'll get some firewood." Annie squirmed under the nearest tree.

"Blankets," Jack said to Siobhan.

When Annie returned, the blankets covered the cone. Only the tips of the branches showed. Siobhan sat inside, shivering.

Annie built a small fire at the opening. Jack crawled around it and sat on Siobhan's left. Annie followed and sat on her right. The fire had already warmed the small space and the smoke rose away from them, out the front.

"Th-thanks," Siobhan said.

"So you don't like the cold, is that it?" Jack said.

"What-what was your first clue?"

The wind shifted again and snow blew across the opening. The fire fluttered.

Annie added more wood. "Jack, where did you learn to make this?"

"Dad taught me. He started taking me on his dye searches when I was five. We went in every kind of weather."

"He sounds like a great guy." Siobhan shivered and inched nearer the fire.

Annie stared at the fire. Snow hissed on its outer edge. "Siobhan, there's something I don't understand."

"About what?"

"About you Readers. If you've always knows about the Redeemers, why haven't you done something?"

Silence. Siobhan turned a twig over and over in her hands. "Blame it on tradition. I don't know how many Readers think things should change, but keeping the secret is pounded into every Reader from their very first meeting."

Annie's mouth twisted. "You're like pill bugs or pine sawflies."

"I know what pill bugs are and you're right," Siobhan said. "We definitely roll up into a ball to protect ourselves. What are pine sawflies?"

"Jack said," They're these little caterpillars. They like to swarm up a pine branch and eat everything on it. If anyone comes near them, they all burst out like flower petals, if flowers ever got roaring mad. It's supposed to scare away anything that wants to eat them." He stared at Annie. "You think Readers attack when they're scared? Oh, wait. I'm from Abilene. I'll shut up now."

Siobhan poked a twig into the pine duff. "Annie, you make us all sound like we're as spineless as earthworms." The twig snapped and she threw the pieces into the fire.

"It's hard to see Readers any other way when they've hounded me, lied to me, tried to kill me—"

"If you mean my family I told you the real story." Siobhan's voice rose.

"I know what you told me. I know you all work from a history of fear. But you said you weren't sure what happens in the abbeys." Annie's matched hers.

Jack said in an even voice, "No, but the rumors are enough to give anyone nightmares."

Siobhan lowered hers to match. "That's why I passed that letter on. I couldn't stomach the thought that even a piece of what Readers have imagined could happen to me."

Annie wiggled her toes in her boots and the scars pulled. "Whatever lets you sleep at night." She swallowed the rest of her invective. *We still have to travel together. My real fight is with the Redeemers.*

"Thanks, Annie." Her voice slowed and slurred. Her head lolled onto Annie's shoulder.

"I'll keep an eye on the fire," Jack said. "My arms can reach the woodpile from here."

\* \* \*

A crow squawked in Annie's ear and she jumped. Jack stopped in mid-snore.

Siobhan yawned. "What's happening?"

Annie stretched one arm. "I think the snow stopped."

Jack unfolded himself and stuck his head out over the dead fire. "Yup."

He crawled out and they followed. They stood in a white, silent world. No other birds called. The clouds above the treetops still looked full of snow.

Annie breathed in the crisp air. "Admit it, Siobhan. It's beautiful."

"Maybe. But it's still too cold."

"Okay." Annie found her matches. "I'll restart the fire."

"Not the same. I want fresh, hot meat."

They were reversing the blankets to dry the outsides when a massive thunderclap rattled the trees. Annie looked up in time for an epic downpour to blind her. The fire sizzled out. She and Siobhan grabbed the blankets and shoved them into their packs while Jack kicked apart the teepee. Annie dumped piles of melting snow on the embers and they tramped west against the wind until they climbed out of the rain.

"Isn't the sun supposed to make things warmer?" Siobhan's teeth chattered.

Annie shivered and wrung out her mittens. "In theory." The wind whipped past her. "Want one of the blankets to wrap around you?"

"I'm cold, but I'm not feeble." Siobhan huddled into her coat collar and walked faster.

The path zigzagged across the steep hillside. The trees thinned. When the sun reached noon, they saw a ridge ahead with a cleft cut into it.

"Someone's keeping this pass repaired," Jack said as they came close enough to make out details.

Thick hedges lined the sides and flat paving stones started several feet before the actual opening. The trimmed, rectangular hedges topped Jack by several inches.

Annie set a foot on the outermost row of paving. "I almost feel like we should wipe our boots."

They reached the other side of the cleft and their feet stopped.

"Did you have any idea it was this big?" Jack whispered.

Annie shook her head. Siobhan's mouth hung open.

Terraced fields covered the other side of the crest. Their slant diminished until, a good quarter-mile down, the valley leveled and Colorado Springs began.

It filled the valley from end to end, at least ten square miles of streets and houses, more streets and more houses. The streets wove across and around each other with no discernible pattern at first. Then Annie's eyes followed a wide spiral that passed through all the streets and ended in the center of town.

"Have you ever seen an abbey that size?" Siobhan whispered as well.

Annie shook her head again. The town resembled a giant spider web, with houses clustered between the strands like building blocks. There was almost nothing green and growing and she couldn't see a single person in the streets. *It looks like one of the pre-Last War cities. But I am not going to be intimidated by a bunch of houses.* "It's just a town. That's just an abbey. Right now, all I want is food in my stomach and a fireplace for my toes. Come on." She set her right foot in front of her left.

The path switchbacked several times as it descended into town. Goats and sheep bleated at them as they passed the farms; cows ignored them. There were no farmers or herders in sight.

The sun vanished behind more thunderclouds as the town enveloped them. The streets were wide but dim, the houses crowding each other for every inch of space. They passed a shuttered bookseller's with a sign tacked to the door: "Vacation— Back on November 14th."

Siobhan pointed. "There's a grocer's at the intersection."

A bell rang as they opened the door. The fuzzy-haired old man inside started. HE was the only one in the large shop.

Annie smiled. "Can you tell us how to get to the inn?"

"There are four. Margaret's is nearest. Go left out the door, left at the first street, then straight past five cross-streets. It has half a block all to itself." He turned his back on them and continued unpacking dried fruit.

Wind and the first drops of rain hit them as they closed the door. They were still the only people in the street.

"This is the middle of the day," Siobhan said. "Where is everybody?"

They turned left again and passed the blacksmith's.

"No smoke from the chimney," Jack said.

They fought the growing storm all the way down the empty sidewalk to the inn. No stream of hungry people crowded the wide steps with them.

"Gotta say it," Jack said. "Have you ever seen an inn this big?"

"Jack," they said.

The wind pushed them inside. Jack pushed back hard to close the door.

"Hello," Siobhan said to the empty hall.

A spiky woman came to the desk, graying braids wrapped

around her head, a flowered apron over her plain brown dress.

"We'd like two rooms, please," Annie said.

"Name your preference." She opened the registration book and faced it toward them. "We're mostly empty these two weeks."

"Second floor near the bathroom, if we can."

"Certainly. For how long?"

Annie looked at Siobhan and Jack. "A week." Siobhan nodded.

"That'll be seven dollars for both rooms, and three-fifty more for meals. These are our bargain weeks."

Annie wrote in their names while Siobhan handed over the money.

"Welcome to my inn. I'm Margaret." She flashed a toothy smile. "Follow me."

She led them up a wide, polished central staircase to the second floor and opened the third door on her left. "This one has room for an extra bed. I'll have my handyman carry it in. The next room is meant for one person and the bathrooms are right here." She tapped on the opposite door.

"Thank you." Annie's stomach growled. "Is there any chance of lunch?"

"Hungry? I'll have the cook put something together for you."

"Thanks," Siobhan said.

"There's a good fire in the living room. You look like you could use it. Go ahead and hang up your coats in there to dry, too."

Margaret went back to the staircase and cupped her hands around her mouth. "Joe! Heat up the soup again, please!"

# Chapter Thirty-three

Annie and Siobhan sat on either side of the hearth, hands and feet stretched out to the generous fire. Jack turned his back to the five-foot wide fireplace and stuck out his rump.

"Jack, what on earth are you doing?" Annie said.

"It's still cold from last night," Jack said.

"I see." Annie pressed her lips together to squash a smile.

The living room, across the entrance hall from the dining room, mirrored the empty streets outside. They stretched their coats across six borrowed dining room chairs. Their boots and socks, hats and gloves steamed on one side of the hearth. A blast of wind drove sheets of rain against the windows.

"You made it inside just in time," Margaret said at the doorway, hands full of cloth and place settings. She nodded at a round table to her left. "Could someone move this over by you?"

Jack left the fire and carried back the table. Margaret followed.

"The only ones here are you three and four little old guests who live here year 'round. I'll save wood if I don't light a fire in the dining room just yet. I hope you don't mind."

"Not at all." Annie took the plates and utensils from her.

Margaret spread a dark red tablecloth, piled the silverware in the center, and set out napkins. "All set, Joe!"

A round young man came in, hefting a tray covered with steaming dishes and pots.

"Vegetable soup—we grow all our own vegetables, of course." Joe ladled soup and Margaret handed them around. "Joe here makes all our bread."

Joe grinned at them and set out butter, salt, and pepper.

"Wednesday is marbled rye day. You're in luck again—no one makes better marbled rye than Joe. My daughters make our butter and cheese and the cherry pie is mine. You'll have to let me know if you can taste my secret ingredient. Eat, eat."

Annie started on the soup. Jack passed the butter to Siobhan. Joe poured hot, spiced wine into their cups.

Siobhan drank. "That hits the spot."

Annie followed. "Nutmeg?"

"Yes." Margaret sliced cheese and arranged it on a plate

She swirled another sip around her mouth. "I've never tried that in wine. I usually put in allspice. This makes it a little sweeter."

"Thank you." She stopped. "Oh, dear, I didn't look at your names."

"Annie Cook."

"I should've guessed. Thank you. I do like it when someone notices the little touches." She poured wine for herself. "And you, my dear?" she said to Siobhan.

Siobhan gulped her soup. "Siobhan Farmer."

Jack stopped his bread halfway to his mouth. "Jack Chandler."

"Please, eat," Margaret said. "And tell me what brings you to Colorado Springs at such an inhospitable time of year."

Annie buttered a slice of bread. "We're looking for work."

"Goodness, dear, everyone's closed for the rest of the week."

"We just heard about the Redeemer reunion a few days ago," Siobhan said. "We've never been this far west before."

Margaret sipped wine and shook her head. "There's no point in you even trying anywhere until the eighteenth. More soup? Jack? Here. Where were you hoping to work?"

"The weaver for me," Siobhan said.

"The one at the far west side of town always needs dyers."

"Why?" Siobhan raised one eyebrow.

"Frankly, because she always makes them work late without warning. Joe is dating her oldest daughter, so I hear about it every time another dyer quits."

"What about the other one?"

"One? There are five altogether."

"What?"

Margaret preened. "Colorado Springs isn't like other towns. Here we have the biggest and best of everything. And the most, too. Ask anyone who's lived here all their lives, like me."

Siobhan made a wry face. "Okay, what about the other four?"

"I haven't heard anything bad about the north side shop. The south side shops work together. One does all the weaving, dyeing, and cutting out. The other does the sewing and fancy work. You know; alterations, lace, embroidery."

Siobhan raised her index finger. "That's the one for me."

Margaret set the wine jug on the table. "Joe, before I forget, bring everything else back to the kitchen, please, and tell Denise there'll be three extra for supper. Now, Jack, what about you?"

"I'm good with herbs and candles."

"Hugh broke his arm last week. He's the doctor's second assistant—the doctor on this side of town. That's perfect for you. Angelo's been over here every other day moaning about how he'll never manage the extra work when everyone opens back up on Friday."

"Is he anywhere near here?'

"Well, in a way. He's only about twenty blocks south. I know the weather's not the best now, but he'll make the walk worth your while." She poured more wine for herself. "He should be here tomorrow or Thursday for supper. I'll introduce you."

Annie ate her first bite of pie. "How many booksellers does Colorado Springs have?"

"Four."

"There are more weavers than booksellers?" Siobhan said.

"You didn't let me finish," Margaret said. "There are only four, but each one has a shop that stretches a full block."

"A block?" Annie's wine went down the wrong pipe. Jack pounded her back until she stopped coughing.

Margaret preened as thought she and not the Redeemers had built Colorado Springs. "I told you. The biggest and the best."

Jack tried the pie. "What do they keep in a shop that big?"

"Everything's divided between them. The north side shop only does schoolbooks. The west side does newspapers. They have several years' worth in storage there. The south side handles paper, pens, ink, and sheet music. The east side has novels and poetry, and supplies multiple copies of plays to theaters from here all the way east to Jefferson City and north to Big Piney."

"Wow," Jack said.

"One of the four must need another pair of hands," Annie said.

Margaret tilted her head like a bird eyeing a worm. "What have you done before?"

"Sorted books, cleaned, made up bills—"

"Bills. You head to the east-side bookseller's right after breakfast on Friday. She can never put her hands on a price list or a piece of paper to write a bill."

The hall clock bonged three times.

Margaret set her cup on the table and stood. "Time to help out with supper. Most of my staff goes away these two weeks as well, so I do a bit of everything. Now, you three stay in here as long as you like. You'll hear a loud bell when supper's ready. My little old people need the extra noise." She crossed into the hall. "Joe, I'm in the cellar getting potatoes and onions!"

Siobhan finished her pie. "That chair by the window has my name on it." She curled up in a deep armchair and wrapped herself in a gold and crimson afghan. "Now that we're finally here, what do we want to do next?"

Annie frowned. "If you can manage to stay awake, we should figure out how to get the information we came all this way for."

"I'm awake." Siobhan's mouth stretched in a yawn.

Jack set down his fork. "Should we go upstairs for this?"

"Even I don't think a few grandmas are," Annie lowered her voice, "Redeemers in disguise."

Siobhan opened her eyes. "Don't tell me you actually considered that."

"I think about it all the time. It wakes me up in the middle of the night." Annie leaned her elbows on the table and put her head in her hands. "How could they have created such a perfect character for themselves? It's better than a play because they're real, not characters, and everyone believes it."

Her scars ached. She rubbed them, stopped, rubbed them again. She didn't care. She was with friends. She pushed up her sleeves and kneaded them.

"Because it's not a part in a play to them?" Jack lowered his voice to match Annie's.

Annie closed her eyes and heard the Redeemers singing. Heard them reciting that image phrase as she hung on the wall. "Because it's really who they are? They redeemed the world only to slaughter people at will?" She clamped her hands over her wrists. "They sang while they did it to me. You sing when you're happy, right?"

No. She must be wrong. Real life wasn't like that. Books and plays meant to give the audience a shiver were one thing. It was fun to jump and squeal knowing everything in your house or just outside the theater is fine. Redeemers were not supposed to be like that. Redeemers were supposed to be comfort and safety and everything that was right with the world.

*Redeemers were like that when I was in school and the teacher taught us the only correct answers for all our questions. I can't go back.*

"Shh." Jack pointed to the farthest window. "I saw something."

Annie couldn't see through the rain. "Are you sure?" She slid out of her chair and ducked under the window nearest her. Inch by inch, she raised her head until it was level with the sill.

She looked over her shoulder at Jack. "See anything now?"

He shook his head.

She held her breath and peeked over.

A pair of eyes surrounded by hood-shaped darkness stared back.

# CHAPTER THIRTY-FOUR

Annie fell backwards.

"What?" Jack said.

"What is it?" Siobhan jumped out of her chair.

Annie crawled sideways and crouched between the windows. "There's only one way out of here."

"What are you talking about?' Siobhan said.

The front door slammed open.

"Margaret!" It was the deepest bass voice Annie had ever heard, easily carrying through the hall and into the living room.

Running footsteps clattered beneath them, then slapped up stone stairs. Another door opened. "Fred!"

Through the doorway, Annie saw Margaret remove a dark green hooded cloak from the newcomer. She draped it over one arm, kissed him, and closed the front door.

"You're letting rain into my hall. And I didn't expect you back 'til tomorrow! What happened? Did you run into trouble? How did the bargaining go?'

"Margaret, I'm soaked and freezing and need some hot wine. And you call yourself a wife and an innkeeper?"

"Oh, Fred." Margaret kissed him again. "Come into the kitchen. Joe has wine mulling. We have three new guests. At this time of year, too. Tell me about your trip. Did you find the hot pepper seeds and the goose feathers?" She led the way to the kitchen, the cloak dripping a trail of puddles behind her. The closed door finally muffled her voice.

Annie stood and walked over to the basket of kindling. She picked up a twig and snapped it in half. Then she snapped those pieces in half and in half again and again until she had two handfuls of minuscule sticks.

"I hate them!" She flung the pieces into the fire. "I hate myself for being such a sniveling coward. I hate most of all how so many people wear dark, hooded cloaks in the fall."

Jack and Siobhan stared at her.

"That didn't make any sense, did it?" She managed a crooked smile. "Sorry. I panicked."

"What did you see?" Jack said.

"That man, Fred, who just came in. He looked in the window when I looked out. He was wearing a dark cloak."

Siobhan settled back into her chair. "You saw a hood."

"And his eyes. Nothing else." She poured herself the last swallow of wine from the jug. "I'm so tired of jumping at every shadow."

Joe poked his head around the doorframe.

"You finished? Great. I'll take the dishes." He piled everything on a different tray and repositioned the logs in the fireplace. "Supper's in a couple hours. Don't worry, you'll hear the bell."

Annie waited for him to leave. "So do we have a plan?"

"I don't think so," Siobhan said. "Not in detail."

Jack stretched out on a couch. "No one's around to ask anyway. How are we going to find out anything before Friday?"

"We can ask the Readers," Annie said.

Siobhan stopped in the middle of another yawn. "Readers?"

"Why not? If Colorado Springs is a beehive of Redeemers, then Readers here should know more about them than Readers anywhere else."

"I suppose so," Jack said.

"No way," Siobhan said.

"Why not?"

"You said why not earlier," Siobhan said. "If there are any Readers in this town, they're all rolled up like pill bugs until the danger passes."

Annie rolled her eyes. "Why do you keep your little groups together if being a Reader is such a waking nightmare? Don't answer that. Siobhan, there must be some Readers who have an ounce of curiosity. Like that guy who wrote the letter about the abbey here. How do we find them?"

"We don't. You have to know one. Or someone in your family has to be one."

"For crying out loud, I'm not trying to steal a shop's money on payday. I just want information." She picked up her hat to check the level of dampness.

"Payday is nothing compared to being a Reader," Siobhan said. "The wrong people can't be allowed to learn our secrets. We can't take any risks."

"Actually, Siobhan," Jack said, "my dad told me a way he used once or twice to find Readers."

Annie stopped with her hand inside one of the boots. "What is it?"

"It's kind of obvious, if you think about it. You find some dirt or dust, like on a table. Then you draw this."

He went to the window fogged the most from the heat of the fireplace and sketched      with a fingertip. "Get it? It's an open book." He erased it with the side of his fist and checked the cleared area before he turned back to them. "If you ever write it, clean it off right away and always make sure there's no trace left."

"Watch this." Siobhan went to the window and breathed on the same spot. The outline of Jack's symbol reappeared.

"Matthew's balls. I had no idea that would happen."

"One winter when I was ten, Padraig and I traded insults on the kitchen windows. When they fogged up again Mom saw everything we'd written. She whipped both our butts with a spatula and made us clean every window in the house once a week for a month. Next time we felt like ragging on each other, we got rid of the evidence. Like this." She scribbled out the sign with her index finger, breathed on it again, and only the scribbles showed.

Annie took Siobhan's place at the window and traced the symbol, then scribbled over it. "Jack, did your father ever really use that to find Readers? It sounds too easy."

"Too hard is more like it. We have to be extra-careful where we write it."

"Then how can it work?"

"Once Dad was selling bottles of dye to the chandler in Grand Junction. While she wrote his receipt, she said a phrase Dad recognized from one of his Pages. He took the pen out of her hand and drew the open book really small in a corner of the paper. She stopped talking. Dad covered the corner with ink and gave her a lecture about watching her mouth." He smiled. "Dad could lecture like a crabby schoolteacher."

"Did he use it any other times?" Annie chewed the inside of her cheek.

"None he told me."

"Well, I'm willing to risk it. We're in Colorado Springs during the week the Redeemers apparently don't come out of their abbey"

Siobhan returned to her chair. "Margaret talks enough. Let's see if she drops a phrase."

"We can listen at our new jobs, after the town comes out of its shell." Jack flopped onto the couch again. "We can't do much 'til then. I didn't think the town would be closed up and locked like this, no matter what Nick the tinker said."

Annie said with as much calm as she could muster, "We didn't come all this way to slug around the fire."

"What else can we do?" Siobhan snuggled into the afghan and closed her eyes. "The town's empty. The shops are closed. I say we read a book, do a puzzle, and enjoy dry feet until the fourteenth at least."

*Who needs these Readers, anyway?* Annie stood and walked toward the hall. "This town was made for you two. Enjoy your vacation. I have work to do."

Jack threw an arm over the back of the couch. "Annie, wait."

Siobhan began to braid her hair. "Speaking of crabby teachers who like to order everyone around..."

"Siobhan," Jack said.

*Oh, yes. Traveling with Readers has been such a great idea.* "I'm so sorry my plans aren't in perfect harmony with yours, Siobhan. When we get what we came for, maybe you can teach me how to relax."

"Annie, you're rubbing your wrists again," Jack said.

She looked down, flung her hands apart, and left.

\* \* \*

At supper, they sat two tables over from the permanent guests so Joe wouldn't have to walk the length of the dining room. The old people spoke at top volume to each other, but Annie was still worried about other possible listeners.

Jack buttered rye bread. "I checked our stuff before supper. Everything's dry except the boots."

"Give me your extra socks tomorrow morning, Jack," Siobhan

said. "Yours too, Annie. I'll darn the thin spots."

"I'm going to find a book and head to bed early," Annie said after dessert.

"I saw a shelf of jigsaw puzzles in the living room," Siobhan said. "That's where I'll be."

"Want some help?" Jack said.

Annie finished her coffee. "I miss this when we're on the road."

"You know what I like about any inn," Siobhan said.

"Someone else guts the fish," Annie said.

Siobhan went straight to a puzzle labeled "Mountain Sunrise" and emptied the box on a corner table. Jack sat opposite her and started turning pieces color side up.

Annie stared at the bookshelf. "Something mindless. A fluffy romance would do it. How does 'Sailing Happily Ever After' sound?"

Jack grimaced. "How can you women read that stuff?"

"Because it's what we want in life. Besides. any title that could give a man heartburn is the one for me." She pulled out a thin pink-and-blue book. "I'll take the coats and everything on my way up."

"Thanks," Jack said.

"Goodnight." Siobhan plucked a piece from Jack's hand and snapped it into the bottom row.

Annie put everyone's clothes on their beds. *A romance. Right. As though I care about this undertaking as little as they apparently do.* She tossed the book on the dresser and closed the curtains.

*Boots, coat, hat, gloves. Ready.*

She had to do something. Not sit and devise plan number five or listen to Siobhan hint about Readers or avoid Jack's yearning eyes. *I didn't claw my way back from that wall of skeletons just to play at solving mysteries for the rest of my life. Siobhan will say I don't have the brains of a sheep for going out tonight. What she really means is she wants to make sure I don't slip out of her leash. Well, I'm eighteen and married. Was married. I ran my own business. I am more than able to map out the center of Colorado Springs leading to the abbey without a snake of a babysitter and a lovesick overprotector. And I'll do it without getting caught.*

She tiptoed into the hall. The lamp at the head of the back stairs lit her down to the outside door.

A crescent moon tried to shine through the skirts of the thunderstorm. Annie picked her way through the withered pumpkin vines and paused at the end of the gardens.

Nobody up the street. Nobody around the corner.

She glanced back at the inn. All the curtains were drawn. She turned to her right into the spiderwebbed streets, toward the center of town and the abbey.

# CHAPTER THIRTY-FIVE

Ten rights and eleven lefts and she stepped into the town square. Every single shop and house was dark. Of course. No one was home anywhere in Colorado Springs this week.

*I can't take more than an hour for this. Siobhan might get tired of playing with her puzzles.*

Left at the next corner, right, then left.

The abbey.

Its black mass loomed over her. She bent her neck until her face was parallel with the sky and tried to see its roof. When she crossed the street, she stopped at the circular paving around the building. Yes, those were the front doors.

Another right to walk around the abbey's long side. The first floor was dark, but lamplight shone through several windows on the top two floors.

Four floors could hold a hundred Redeemers. She came closer and touched the stone wall. Stability. Security. She turned the corner of the building. No doorknob on the back door. How was she going to get in there?

She smothered a giggle. *Knock, knock. Good evening, Redeemers. I'd like to ask you a few questions.*

"Shit!"

Annie jumped.

"Whisper, dummy!"

"I know. I slipped."

She followed the voices around the corner to the fourth side. A dark body hung from a fourth-floor window ledge. Two black shapes watched the climber from below.

"Susan," one whispered, "there's a stone sticking out by your left foot. You can reach it. Another inch. There."

"Now feel six inches down on your right," the other one whispered.

Susan eased her foot down. "Got it," she whispered. "I'm coming down."

Annie circled behind the two on the paving. Schoolboys; younger than Jack.

Susan checked the distance and jumped the last three feet. Together all three turned away from the wall.

"Good evening," Annie said.

They stood like three rabbits confronted by a snake. What Annie could see of them beneath the black clothes in the fitful moonlight showed her that two were tall and brown, and the other shorter, stocky, and blond.

Annie arched her eyebrows in her best schoolteacher imitation. "Your mouths are open."

Three sets of teeth clicked together. The shorter, darker boy on the left took a step sideways.

Annie held up a hand. "Don't even think about it."

The tall boy on the right stepped out in front of the others. "I take responsibility for our actions, Redeemer."

"Ben, don't." Susan said.

Ben pushed his hand backwards at her. "Please do not hold my companions accountable."

Annie smiled. The hand he'd gestured with was trembling, but his voice had only cracked once. "I'm not a Redeemer."

"You're not?" Susan said.

"Shh." Ben jerked his head toward her.

"But I think you have some explaining to do," Annie said.

"Wait a minute," the other boy said. "What are you doing here?"

"George," Susan said, "we don't know—"

"Right," George said. "We don't know her and she doesn't know us." He crossed his arms. "We'll explain if you do."

Annie's smile returned. "Deal. But how about someplace else? I don't like those lighted windows."

Ben, George, and Susan looked over their shoulders.

"I'm at the inn," Annie said

"Our house is right near there," Susan said.

George moved to Annie's left and Susan to her right. Ben stayed next to Susan and they walked through the streets of empty, unlit shops and houses.

"I'm Susan. That's George next to you and Ben next to me. Our grandmother is Colorado Springs' head carpenter."

"I'm Annie. My friends and I came here today looking for work."

"In November?" Ben said.

"Everyone says that." Annie pointed back toward Plainville. "Someone should post a sign at the pass in big red letters that says if you're reading this between November first and fourteenth, turn around and come back on the fifteenth."

Susan giggled.

"Now, what's behind the wall-climbing expedition?"

"No," George said. "You're the stranger here. Why are you snooping around the abbey the only time it's guaranteed the Redeemers won't come out?"

"I want information, and the only place to get it is inside."

"See, Ben, I told you we're not the only ones," Susan said.

"I told you that. Getting someone to admit it is the problem."

Annie nodded. "I know." *These three make me feel even older than Jack does. If any of them have turned thirteen yet, I'll eat my knapsack for breakfast.*

"What information?" George said.

"Let me ask you a question first. Have any of the Readers here ever disappeared?"

"Three a year, every November," George said.

Annie stopped. "Three every year? Matthew's hairy ass."

They all burst out laughing and a second later clapped their hands over their mouths in perfect unison.

"Shh," Ben said. "One of our customers vanished this year. So we decided it was now or never."

"Now or never what, exactly?"

"Ages ago one November tenth, Grandma's sister disappeared," Susan said. "We overheard Grandma and Grandpa talking a couple years ago, before Grandpa died. Her older brother saw them take her into the abbey. He climbed into it on the thirteenth."

"Why did he wait so long?"

"Great-Grandpa made the whole family hide and he couldn't sneak out before then. Nobody knows what he saw, but they killed her."

Annie stopped walking. *Three days. Wasn't that how long they kept me in the cell?*

"This is our street," Ben said. "Turn here."

When Annie didn't move, he pulled her around the corner and they stopped under a wall lined with dark windows.

"Do your wrists hurt?" Susan said.

Annie didn't have to look at what her hands were doing. She pulled her right hand away from her left wrist and shoved both hands into her coat pockets. "Sorry. Let's go."

Ben and Susan whispered to each other. George kept looking sideways at her. When they turned a corner and saw the inn's front porch, Susan elbowed Ben.

"Why do you want to know what goes on in there?" Susan said.

"I wish I didn't."

"Huh?"

"I already know." *I wish I was still ignorant, happy, and pregnant in Kansas City. And as long as I'm wishing, I'd like to sprout wings to fly into the abbey, snatch their history books, and fly out again before anyone saw me.*

George spun around and blocked her path. "If you know what happens, you don't need information from us. What game are you playing? Are you really a Redeemer in disguise?"

Annie shook her head. "The last thing I could be is a Redeemer. And I'm not playing any game. I don't know anything about the annual Redeemer meeting, but I know what happens to kidnapped Readers in Kansas City, at least. Probably in all the other towns, too."

"You do? Tell us." Susan said.

"How do you know?" George said.

"I don't want to get into it out here in the open "

"Come home with us," Ben said. "You can tell our folks."

"So you won't get into trouble?"

"Sort of," George said.

"Not tonight. My friends don't know I snuck out, either. I don't want to worry them."

"So you're going to be in trouble too," Susan said.

"We're all adults. We might just—discuss it."

Ben snorted. "Like Mom and Dad have 'discussions.' We've heard some of those."

Susan said, "Come for supper tomorrow. Bring your friends,

too. Right, George? Right, Ben? We'll work on Grandma and our folks. When the babies are in bed after supper, you can tell all of us what you know." She elbowed Ben. "I told you we'd be in luck tonight."

"Okay, I'll bargain with you. I'll tell you what I know about abbeys if you tell me how you learned the best place to climb up the abbey wall." *So much for Siobhan and Jack insisting we can't do anything until the fourteenth.*

"Seven o'clock," Susan said. "Go to the end of the block and turn right. We take up the whole second half of that street."

George held out his hand. "Sorry I was a jerk back there. We were kinda nervous."

Annie shook it. "I completely understand."

"See you tomorrow," Ben said.

They ran to the end of the street and turned the corner, their black clothes nearly invisible in the now-hazy moonlight.

Annie let herself in the garden door and tiptoed up the empty stairs and down the silent hall. She slipped into her room without a noise.

Two hands grabbed her.

# CHAPTER THIRTY-SIX

"Where have you been?" Siobhan shouted.

"Out," Annie tried to say as her head wobbled from Siobhan's shaking.

"What do you mean, 'Out?' Jack is scouring the cellars for you. I was just about to comb the neighborhood. What's the matter with you?"

"I didn't think I'd be this long."

The door opened. "She's not down there," Jack said. Then he saw her. "Annie." He pulled her away from Siobhan and engulfed her in a hug. Then he grabbed her arms and shook her, too. "Where have you been?"

She jerked out of his hold. "Let go." She took off her hat and gloves and unbuttoned her coat. "I walked to the abbey."

"What?" they said together.

"Wait a minute. Why were you looking for me in the cellars?"

I thought Fred in the window might still be giving you the creeps, and maybe you'd try to hide down there," Jack said.

"Okay..."

"Hey, it was all I could think of. We came upstairs and you weren't here. We thought there were only two possibilities: You were hiding or they took you."

Siobhan waved a hand at him. "Don't change the subject." She pointed her finger at Annie. "What do you mean, you went to the abbey?"

"I was annoyed because you two were willing to wait here for things to start up again. So I did a little research."

"Redeemers help us all. Annie, would you please try to think of someone besides yourself?"

Annie sat on her bed, took off her boots, and rubbed her feet. "I planned to get back while you were still downstairs with the puzzle."

"The puzzle was an insult to any adult's intelligence. We finished it in less than an hour." She shook her head. "Hanging around the abbey. Sometimes I think you've lost your mind."

"Thanks. Want to know what I found out?'

Siobhan sighed. "Of course we do." She sat next to Annie and Jack leaned against the closed door.

"A kid was hanging from a fourth-floor abbey window ledge."

"What?" Jack said.

"Her cousins, I guess, were on the ground, giving her directions. I scared them out of a few years' growth."

"What were they doing?" Siobhan said.

"Trying to find out what happens to the Readers who get taken there."

"And no Redeemers saw them?" Siobhan said.

"My new friends told me that the Redeemers never come out of the abbey at this time of year." She rubbed the scars on the feet through her socks. "They said that The Redeemers took their great-aunt years ago, and their great-uncle climbed in to get her."

Siobhan said. "He climbed in? Did he rescue her?"

"No. She died."

"Like you? I mean, that is, like you almost died?"

"Why now?" Jack said. "I mean, why were they climbing in tonight?"

"One of their customers—they're the carpenters here—disappeared this week." Annie stared at her hands. "They said three Readers disappear this same week every year."

"Three," Siobhan said.

"Every single year?" Jack turned green. "No wonder everyone hides."

"I told them I know what happens to Readers in there. So we're all invited to supper tomorrow to pool our knowledge."

"Just like that?" Siobhan said.

"How come they trusted you so soon?" Jack said.

"My charming personality?" Annie arched her eyebrows.

"They're twelve or thirteen at the most, trying to be adults, but scared. Along comes an actual adult who not only agrees with them, but who they could sweet-talk into being a buffer between them and their parents."

"You were perfect for them," Siobhan said.

"Thank you. I'll refrain from saying 'I told you so' more than five times."

"If we're not here for supper tomorrow, we'll have to make up a story for Margaret," Jack said. "I wonder if she's this nosy when it's crowded here."

"What if we tell her I'm related to the carpenter?" Annie said. "A cousin, maybe."

"Okay, let me think: Siobhan said. "How about this? Your cousin headed west when you were little. She made you...a favorite doll before she left?"

"A puppet, the kind on strings," Jack said. "They're always made from wood."

"Yeah. She sent you a letter from here a couple years ago, so before you start your new job, you want to see if she still lives here."

"Why didn't we ask Margaret about them right away then?" Annie said.

Jack said, "We were so concerned with trying to find jobs that we didn't think of it until Margaret went to look after her husband?"

"Not bad," Annie said. "I'll pretend I don't know where the carpenter's is get directions from Margaret after breakfast, head over there to make sure we'll be welcome, and come back with our invitation to supper."

\* \* \*

"That's horseradish in front of you, Annie, or cheese sauce next to it if you want something milder," Susan said the next night at supper.

Sixteen people sat at two tables in the carpenter's enormous kitchen. Shutters covered all the windows, but a dozen lamps cheered up the room. Paintings of summer meadows and spring flowers hung on the walls. Annie knew Susan across from her and Susan's little brother Alex at the corner, but she was still sorting the rest of the family's names.

"I love horseradish." She stabbed a slice of roast beef and passed the platter to Siobhan on her right.

Siobhan took meat, passed the dish to Jack, and spooned

cheese sauce onto her plate. "I love beef and cheese." She smiled at Susan.

Annie handed the basket of rolls to Bess, the adventurers' grandmother, on her left at the head of the table. At the other end, Jack and Bess' son Luke debated arrow-fletching techniques. Across from Jack, Luke's wife Erin cut up little Alex's meat and buttered his roll.

Ben kept grinning at Annie from the other table. George nodded at her once, then paid attention to supper and Lucy, his older sister. Thomas and Eleanor, Ben's parents, discussed the annual shop inventory throughout the meal.

"Bess, the pickles are terrific." Annie leaned back from her empty plate a while later.

"So is the cheese," Siobhan said.

Bess laughed. "I can't take credit for them. I didn't grow the cucumbers or milk the cows. The grocers here stock most things that people make for themselves in other towns. No one in Colorado Springs has enough land."

"We have the apple tree and the horseradish patch, Grandma," Susan said.

"I stand corrected." Bess smiled at her. "Susan, everyone seems to be done. Would you and George collect the plates? Ben," she looked across the other table, "would you and Lucy bring in dessert?"

Erin took the kettle off the hob and added tea. "I'm afraid we're out of coffee. We can't get any more until the fourteenth, of course. I hope you don't mind."

"Of course not."

Siobhan kicked Annie's ankle. Annie kept her face neutral as she kicked her in return.

Ben set a tray on the table and passed out baked apples in deep bowls. Then he handed Annie a larger, steaming bowl with a small ladle in it. "Caramel sauce."

She inhaled with relish. "This is my one cooking failure—I always burn it. If we stay here as long as we hope, could you teach me how to make this?"

"Of course. George is about ready for it too. You can learn together."

George shot an annoyed look at Bess.

"The family hardhead has a soft side, Annie," Susan said.

George scowled at her.

"Joe at the inn is a good cook, Bess," Siobhan said, "but you have it all over him."

"Thank you, dear, but Joe's marbled rye beats ours every time."

"I volunteer to test your next batch," Jack said.

Bess and Susan laughed.

Annie scooped up more dessert. *This family is all I wanted once. Hank and a baby, friends, good food, laughter.* The sweet sauce threatened to curdle in her mouth. *Now I have hate and nightmares and revenge. Revenge helps.* She ignored the ghost echoes from her empty womb.

\* \* \*

Susan took Annie's arm after Ben and George collected the dishes. "Come on, Annie. I'll show you the house."

"Jack and I will be in the small workshop with those new arrows," Luke said.

"Siobhan, could you show me your cattail pattern?" Lucy said. "I heard you and Grandma talking about it."

"I'll mull some wine," Ben's older brother Richard said.

"Put on more water for tea, please, Richard," Bess said.

"George and I need to clean a mess we left in our room," Ben said.

"We'll call when the wine is ready," Bess said.

"Say goodnight, Alex," Erin said.

Annie's head ached from trying to match all the new faces with their names. Susan led her on a cursory tour, adding multiple room locations to the list. It didn't help.

"Living room, office, big workshop, small workshop, storage." She pulled Annie upstairs and pointed at each door. "Mom and Dad's room, Grandma's room, Thomas and Eleanor, James and Katherine, Alex, Ben and George, Richard." She walked faster. "Here's Lucy's and my room." Susan opened the door and pushed Annie inside.

"Hi," Ben said from the floor.

"Hi," George said, next to him.

Susan closed the door and wedged a chair under the knob. Then she sat on the throw rug.

"We didn't get into too much trouble last night," Ben said. "We only told Grandma, though."

Annie sat next to Susan. "What exactly did you say?"

"Just that we went exploring because we wanted to find things out for ourselves," George said. "And that we met you, and you knew something."

"So Grandma said we should invite you to supper to apologize for how we must've startled you," Susan said. "We told her it was the other way around."

"And then we told her we'd already invited you."

"Then you came this morning and took care of all that."

"We have to tell you what we were doing last night before the meeting starts downstairs," Ben said.

*They're cute. And they'd groan at me for thinking that.* "You were climbing the abbey wall."

George arched his brows. "Not just climbing. Getting inside."

*Maybe I've underestimated them.* "Inside? How? Was the window open?" *I—we—could use their footholds.*

"Closed but not locked," Susan said. "I went first because I'm the smallest and lightest."

"What were you going to do when you got in?"

George puffed out his chest. "Rescue Helen. Our customer."

*Rescue. Of course. Could I—could we— do it without pliers? Or would the Redeemers' tools be easy to find? If they keep their tools ready to use.*

"We know Grandma's brother got inside years and years ago," Susan said, "so we made our own way up."

Their voices overlapped with enthusiasm.

"There's a broken stone a foot off the ground—"

"One place where two stones don't quite meet—"

"Three small stones we took out of the second story—"

"Wait." Annie held up her hands. "You made your own ladder?"

"On the outside of the abbey," George said.

"Exactly," Susan and Ben said.

"After we overheard Grandma and Grandpa talking," Ben said, "we decided that being a Reader ought to mean more than going to secret meetings a few times a year."

"So this year when we had some free time after work, we started making plans," Susan said.

"It was easier in the spring and fall when nights are longer. We'd wait for a new moon or a cloudy night, dress all in black, and poke around the abbey walls."

"On a side without a door, of course."

"Don't you think Annie would know that?" Ben said. "Anyway, we found spots where the stones were cracked, and we sort of helped them along."

"Now we have hand—and footholds all the way to the fourth floor windows."

"We got together last night to decide what to do next." Susan brought out a box from under her bed. She unlocked it and held up a length of thick rope double-knotted every foot or so.

Annie looked from Susan to the rope and back. What was she supposed to say?

"Don't you see?" Susan stepped on a knot. "It's the escape ladder."

"Ben got the rope this summer when he had to go to Cheyenne Wells," George said.

"We put the knots close together so they could be used for hands or feet," Ben said.

"Last night was our trial run," Susan said. "We thought it'd be too hard to climb down the same way we climbed up, and we were right."

"If Susan couldn't do it fast, then we knew someone bigger and older, like Helen, couldn't either. We planned to tie this under the window and use it to climb down."

Annie looked hard at them. "But there's a problem."

Their excitement vanished.

"Our parents made us promise to stay in the house until November fifteenth." George pounded his fist into his open hand. "They know Helen is in there. We told them."

"We said we had to get her out," Susan said.

"They told us they know what a Reader is supposed to do and to forget everything we saw," Ben said. "How can we forget?"

"We can't just turn our backs on Helen and pretend she doesn't exist," Susan said.

"No, you can't." Annie held out her hands. *I can do this. I can save someone from the Reedemers. That is my revenge.*

Susan gave her the rope. "You're going to do it?"

"Yes."

"Alone?"

"Yes. It's too dangerous to involve my friends. It's too dangerous for you."

"But—"

"Wait—"

"You—"

Annie held up her left hand. "Trust me. I know what I'm talking about."

George stood. "You're acting just like our parents. All they talk about is tradition and being safe. Why should we listen to the same speeches from a stranger?"

Annie shook her head. "I don't care about anything Readers do or say. I don't care what you three think of me. But I do want you to be safe. You don't know what happens in there. I do."

"We're practically adults," Ben said. "We deserve answers."

George stepped closer and towered over her. "We won't let you out of here with our ladder without an explanation."

"You have an explanation, right, Annie?" Susan said.

*I'll have to show them. Can they take it?* "Please sit down, George. I do have an explanation, but I have to show it to you."

George sat.

*Lead up to it slowly. Remember they're still in school no matter how adult they act.*

A woman's voice called from downstairs. "Ben? George? Susan?"

Susan jumped. "That's Mom. We have to go or we'll get in more trouble."

*So much for slow and easy.* "Listen. The Redeemers took me last spring and tried to kill me. Some Readers rescued me. That's why I'm here tonight." She unbuttoned her cuffs and held out her wrists. "This is why I'm going in and not you."

Ben and Susan gasped.

"A nail did that," George the carpenter said. He looked up at her, his face drawn. "Nails through your wrists?"

"Yes. I won't show you my feet."

"Your feet, too?" Ben said, eyes big as plates.

Annie nodded and fastened her buttons. *There. I survived. Good thing it was just for these three because I feel naked and sick to my stomach.* "You and my friends are the only Readers who aren't obsessed with digging a deeper and better hole to hide in. I'll bring all three of them out of the abbey and we'll expose the Redeemers for what they really are."

"Give me the ladder," George said. "I'll hide it in your coat."

Susan moved the chair away from the door as Erin called again.

"Susan! Ben! George! Where have you hidden Annie?"

# CHAPTER THIRTY-SEVEN

Annie sipped from a flowered cup. "Bess, what's in this tea?"

"Make Grandma happy and tell her you've never tasted anything like it before," Susan said.

"I haven't. Does it have a name?"

"The kids called it Honey Tea when they were little," Bess said. "My grandmother used to make it on New Year's when I was too young to drink eggnog because of the whisky."

Annie drank again, raising her eyebrows over the rim. "And?"

Bess laughed. "Honey, allspice, ginger, milk, and pepper. You have to brew the tea quite strong to stand up to the other ingredients."

"Annie, if you start comparing recipes, we won't get back to the inn until midnight," Siobhan said.

Annie stuck out her tongue at Siobhan. "Fine. Spoil my fun."

"I'll give you the recipe tomorrow," Bess said.

"At least Bess understands me." *Redeemers be thanked for light humor and good food.*

Siobhan groaned.

George came into the living room carrying paper, a pen, and a bottle of ink. "Siobhan, you said you'd write out your mother's apple cake recipe for me."

"You weasel," Annie said.

Siobhan covered her face with the paper.

"I think we're ready now," Bess said.

Annie clutched her teacup tighter and squeezed into the couch corner. Farthest from the fireplace, it kept her face in shadow.

Jack sat at the other end with a tall, thin glass. "Aren't you cold?"

"No." She avoided his eyes.

Couches paired with tall chairs and short, round tables in several groups around the living room. Lamps hung from the ceiling over the tables, raised and lowered by chains hooked to the walls. The long fireplace took up most of the wall between the living room and the kitchen.

"Who would like to start?" Bess said.

Ben, Susan, and George looked at Annie. She looked at the fire.

George cleared his throat. "Grandma already knows this. Last night we went to the abbey to try and see inside."

"What?" Katherine said. "We told you never to go there, especially at this time of year."

"Mom, it's okay."

"It is not," James said. "You deliberately disobeyed us. You're thirteen. You won't have the privileges of an adult for three more years."

"You certainly don't have anything like the common sense of an adult," Thomas said. "Ben, your mother and I told you the exact same thing."

"Susan, were you part of this nonsense?" Luke said.

"Yes, Dad."

"What were the three of you thinking?" Erin said.

"We were thinking about Helen," Susan said.

"Not again," Erin said. "I know you and Helen's daughter are friends, Susan, but you have to learn where to draw the line."

"Mom, what if you were the one missing?" Susan said. "You'd want me to find you."

"No. I'd want you to stay safe."

Susan's eyes got very wide.

"You don't mean that, Aunt Erin," Ben said.

"Yes, she does," Luke said.

"Luke's right," Thomas said. "If you only learn one lesson from us, this is the one: Be afraid. Keep hidden. No matter what, stay safe."

Annie sipped tea to hide her facial expression. *I hate these people. And just a minute ago I was envying them their happy life.*

*They're like inside-out Halloween costumes: Sweet on the outside, scary when they show their real selves.*

"We read you that new letter the week before last," Bess said. "It confirmed that we can never be too careful."

Ben, George, and Susan slumped down on their couch.

Siobhan cleared her throat. "What letter?"

"You three have been on the road for awhile, haven't you? Luke, would you bring it in?"

"Sure, Mom." He ran upstairs and down within a minute. "Want me to read it?"

Annie kept up her flimsy teacup shield. *It has to be the letter about me. I never thought I'd miss being plain old Annie, whose only claim to fame is a knack for piecrust.*

Luke leaned next to the lamp over the table at his right and read: "Watch for a short woman with red hair. She's young, but her hair has white streaks. Her wrists and feet will always be covered, no matter what the weather is like."

Siobhan glanced at Annie. "We did have a chance to hear that letter in Abilene."

"Then, Annie, I don't understand why you were at the abbey last night," Bess said. "My grandchildren said you knew something. You must know the importance of safety above everything."

*I will get what I came here for tonight any way I have to.*

"No, Bess, I don't." She stood, still in shadow. "I was exploring the outside of the abbey because it's the reason I'm—we're—in Colorado Springs."

She looked down at Susan and smiled, then turned her gaze on everyone else in the room. Three sets of worried parents and all the other faces filled with concern or annoyance.

She spoke to the annoyance. "I'm not willing to crawl into bed and pull the covers over my head anymore."

"Annie, stop." Siobhan said.

"Why?"

"They might not be ready."

"How long should I wait? A year? Five years? Will they be ready then? Will any of you ever be ready?" She faced Bess again. "It's time for action. George told me yesterday that you lose three Readers every year."

"Yes."

"Why haven't you tried to do something about it?"

"It's the price of being a Reader in Colorado Springs," Luke said. "We've all learned to accept it."

"Accept it?" Jack clunked his glass on the table. "Do you have any idea what happens in there?"

"Not exactly," Bess said.

"Grandma," Susan said. "You do too know, sort of. You read that other letter to us every year."

"Susan, don't sass your grandmother," Erin said.

Bess nodded. "Susan is right, as far as she knows. There is a letter about things happening to Readers in the abbey."

"Do you mean the one that the Readers in Cheyenne Wells have a copy of?" Siobhan said. "I was there a few years ago and heard them read it."

"Then you should understand," Thomas said. "We keep ourselves hidden and we keep our families safe."

Annie dug her nails into her palms. *I will never understand these people.* "You are not safe." She bent over Thomas. "Do you know how they choose the ones they take? No." She turned toward Bess and Luke. "You have to learn how and why they do things before you can stop them."

"Stop the Redeemers?" Luke said. "Impossible. The only answer is secrecy."

"The only answer is knowledge. Or are you too afraid to learn what happens in there?"

"That is a pointless question," Bess said. "There's no way to find out. The letter was written decades ago."

Annie moved closer to the fire, chilled despite the warm room. She had to wake them up. To shock them out of their complacency.

Susan said, "Annie?"

*I know. If I'd been honest with myself, I'd have known all along things would reach this point. If the daring schoolkids needed physical proof, of course their cowering parents would.* She caught Susan's eye and gave her a half-smile. "Plain old Annie Cook, upsetting Readers wherever she goes." She turned back to Bess. "I'm that Annie."

"I beg your pardon?" Bess said.

Luke gaped. "She means the one in this letter. The Redeemers are looking for you? Now?"

"Why?" Thomas said.

*Here it comes.* "What exactly does the old letter say?"

"Why?" Bess said.

"Because it's all connected."

Bess shook her head. "Just a moment. I paid attention to the new letter, if the rest of my family did not. It said you aren't one of us. Tell me why we should trust you or your friends?"

"Because they are Readers and they trust me."

Eleanor moved next to Ben. "That's not good enough. My son seems to have been taken in by you, but he doesn't have the people experience I do. You have to prove you're not spying for the Redeemers."

Erin started and knelt in front of Susan. Katherine moved toward George, but he frowned at her and shook his head.

Annie closed her eyes. Readers were hopeless. All these years of wondering who would vanish next, and the best they could come up with was bolt the doors and pretend reading a few crumbling scraps of paper made a difference. "Read me the third line of that letter,"

Luke switched his scowl from her face to his hand, surprise taking its place as he saw the crumpled paper in his fist. He smoothed it out on his chest. "Her wrists and feet will always be covered."

*Deep breath. Unbutton the cuffs.* "You can trust me because of these." She folded up her sleeves and held out her hands to Bess and Luke. "This is what happens to Readers inside the abbey. It happened to me in Kansas City. I'm alive because the Readers there were different, to a point. They risked going into the abbey to rescue me." *Sara, you're a lying, spineless sheep but I'm giving you credit. It's the last acknowledgement you'll ever get from me.*

George said, "Nails made those scars, Uncle Luke."

Someone whimpered, possibly Eleanor. Two or three gasped. Luke looked down at the letter, up at Annie, and down again.

Bess pushed out of her chair, took hold of both Annie's hands, and touched the scars. Her thumbs jerked up a second later, as though the scars were open flames.

Their eyes met.

"Kathleen."

# CHAPTER THIRTY-EIGHT

Bess transformed in front of Annie from a frightened and suspicious mother hen into a troubled girl. The moment passed in the time it took her to see it, and the strong old woman returned.

Annie hadn't expected this. "Who's Kathleen?"

Bess sat Annie down on the hearth.

"I'm so sorry. We're only trying to protect the family. I was sure you were an honest person after what the grandkids said about you last night." She looked at the wrinkled letter in Luke's hand. "But we're steeped in the tradition of silence."

"Mom?" Katherine said. "Do you mean your sister Kathleen?"

"The one who died when you were little?" Luke said. "What does she have to do with this?"

"A lot." Bess plucked a mug from the tray on the table next to her chair, filled it with mulled wine, and drank. "Sit down, Luke. Everyone sit. I've kept this secret all my life. Only your grandfather knew, and I didn't tell him until Luke was old enough to be a Reader."

Annie started to roll down her sleeves, but Bess put a hand on her arm.

"Please don't do that yet. I might need your help."

*I might as well be a Carnival decoration. I'm certainly spending enough time on display.* "All right." She sneaked a look at Siobhan, who shrugged her shoulders.

Bess licked her lips. "This happened when I was eleven, Kathleen was eighteen, and my brother Samuel was twenty. You might remember Samuel, George—you were five the last time he came for a visit."

"Bushy gray beard, long fingers? He carved me a boat with oars and everything."

"He loved making toys. I haven't heard from him since then." She picked at her cup with her fingers. "I should've told you all this sooner."

Annie's voice filled with defeat. "But you were afraid."

"Always. The day Sam left, I heard him moving around in his room an hour or so after sunrise. Everyone else was sleeping in because it was November twenty-eighth. I was a nosy baby sister, and I had to see what was going on. He was packing. He tried to send me back to bed, but I was sure he was eloping with his latest girlfriend and I refused to leave until he told me everything."

Bess held out her hand. Annie laid her right one in it, and Bess put her fingers over the scars and kept them there. "He sat me down next to him on the bed and put his hand over my mouth. Then he told me Kathleen was dead. I would've shrieked if he hadn't stopped me. Kathleen was my favorite person in the world. He let me cry a little then shook me and said he had to talk to me."

"Grandma, that was something like forty years ago," Ben said. "How come you remember it so well?"

"I wrote it all down and kept it with my Page so I would never forget. Sam told me that the Redeemers had killed her. He wouldn't say how. She'd disappeared three days earlier and our parents locked the house and kept us away from the windows. It took him all that time to plan a way out."

"And we think they're strict now," Susan whispered to Ben.

Bess smiled at Susan. "Sam made me promise not to tell anyone why he was leaving. He'd written a note to our parents that said he had a lead on opening up his own business out east and he didn't like weepy goodbyes."

"Mom, why didn't you ever tell us?" Eleanor said.

"We have families of our own," Luke said. "It's our responsibility to protect them."

"I've taught you everything you need," Bess said. "You know no one is safe the first two weeks of November. You know to keep hidden. Why clutter your lives up with useless speculation and nightmares?"

"What nightmares, Mom?" Erin said.

"Sam was a sweet, easygoing big brother. He liked to carve little animals out of scrap wood and hide them in my room." Bess's hand tightened on Annie's. "That November thirteenth, he was so scared his hands shook when he tied up his knapsack. I wondered what could've done that to him, and I had a vivid imagination. We went to Denver to stay with cousins for the first two weeks of November every year after that." She turned to Annie. "Tell me what happened to Kathleen."

Everyone stared at Annie like marionettes whose strings had been yanked.

*They need to be shocked. It'll scare Susan and George and Ben, but if it keeps them safe and away from the abbey, it'll be worth it. The adults can rot and die in their safe holes, but the kids deserve a chance.*

She took a deep breath and released it. "The Redeemers nailed your sister's hands and feet to two crossed boards, hung her on a wall, and left her there to die." She removed her hands from Bess', stood, and caught Luke's eyes. "You have to stop it."

Eleanor's eyes. "The way to do it is what Sam tried to do."

Erin's. "Get into the abbey."

Thomas's. "Rescue the Readers."

James's. "Find out what's behind November thirteenth."

"Go inside?"

"While they're all in there?"

"No, no."

"Yes," George said. "We can get in. We can do it."

"I forbid it." James's voice, an octave lower than anyone else's in the room, cut through the babble and shut everyone up.

"But, Dad—"

"I will not repeat myself."

"James is right," Thomas said. "You three will not set foot out of this house before November fifteenth."

"Dad—" Ben said.

"We will lock you in your rooms if that's what it takes," Luke said.

"Dad, you don't—"

"Susan, be quiet," Luke said. "The subject is closed."

"After the fifteenth," Bess said, "we will ask Annie and her friends to tell us everything they know. Then you can tell us what you thought you wanted to do."

"We didn't just think about it. We did it," George said. "We climbed the abbey wall and opened a window."

"George, shut up," Ben said.

"We can go in there tonight. We can get Helen and the others out." George jumped up. "We can't wait until next year. We can't leave them in the abbey."

"We can and we will," Luke said. "If we ever reach the time when a rescue is possible, that time is certainly not tonight."

Susan squirmed out of her mother's hold and stood. "I'm going to Abby's house. She'll come with us to rescue her mom. Her dad will help if you won't."

Erin stood and loomed over Susan. "You will not and he will not. Abby's father's job is not to save Helen. It's to keep Abby safe." When Susan opened her mouth, Erin cut her off. "We will keep you safe in this house by any means necessary whether or not you agree or cooperate."

Annie turned her face to the fire to hide her expression again. *So that's that. Fear beats courage. Tradition defeats the only right thing to do.* She buttoned her cuffs.

When she turned around, she wore a mask of politeness. "I think we'd better get going."

"I didn't plan for the evening to end this way," Bess said. "These three are always getting into trouble. You understand why we have to be so strict."

"Completely. Whatever you decide to do, you'll keep them away from the abbey?"

"But—"

"Annie—"

"You said—"

Bess glared at them. "Of course. Come back tomorrow. We like to do something all together most of the day. I'll make it a cooking lesson."

"Sure," George said. "Nothing is happening tomorrow that we need to care about. Cooking is exactly what we should be doing."

"George, get their coats, please," James said.

Luke and Thomas already flanked the kids' couch like sheepdogs.

"Goodnight," Annie said to the three of them. Ben turned his back. Susan whispered, "Traitor." Only George was looking when Annie patted the hidden rope.

# CHAPTER THIRTY-NINE

"That could've gone better." Annie squirmed in her coat. It wasn't meant to hold one person plus a thick, knotted rope.

It started to sprinkle when they reached the corner.

"I felt sorry for Ben and George," Jack said.

"Especially Susan," Annie said.

"Yeah. Getting bawled out in front of your whole family plus three strangers. Rough."

"They deserved it. They're old enough to have some sense." Siobhan lowered her voice. "They should've known what a bone-headed idea it was to sneak around the abbey when every Redeemer in the world is inside. Like someone else I could mention."

Annie swallowed before she trusted herself to speak. "Point taken. But I do like them."

"So do I. And I like even more knowing their parents will keep them inside 'til the fifteenth."

Annie opened the inn door. A single lamp sat on the front desk; the rest of the first floor was dark.

Siobhan unbuttoned her coat. "How late is it?"

Jack picked up the lamp and brought it to the hall clock. "Eleven-twenty."

"Just a second." Annie went into the living room, where the banked fire gave her enough light to see the paper box on the bookshelf. She took two sheets, a pen, and an inkbottle and came back to the hall. "Jack, can you come to our room for a minute? I want to get everything written down while it's fresh."

They climbed the stairs with only a few creaks and rustles. Annie faced the wall when she removed her coat and folded it to hide the rope before standing at the dresser. Jack and Siobhan sat on the beds.

"First." She yawned. "Sorry. First Ben and Susan and George told me their way up the abbey wall will work going up or down. No need to hide a ladder or anything."

*Lie number one, exactly like a Reader.*

Jack said, "James was telling me that even though most of the Redeemers leave on the fourteenth, he's seen some appear as late as the sixteenth. So second on the list should be our waiting time. I vote for a delay of at least two weeks before we check out the wall they said they climbed up." He yawned. "Anyone know when the next quarter-moon is?"

"Not me," Siobhan said. "Third. When we get inside we need to find their schoolroom or apprentice section. Or whatever Redeemers-in-training are called. If we go by that letter we have at home, it'll be in the cellar."

"Do we assume the Redeemers train apprentices like every other job?" Jack said. "What makes someone a Redeemer? Or are they one big family?"

"A family..." Annie doodled on the paper. "Do they marry each other? Or do they...no."

*Redeemers help us. Not that.*

"What?" Siobhan said.

"What if they don't kill every Reader they take? What if they marry some and have kids with them?"

"Marry?" Siobhan said. "Married to a Redeemer? First someone has to prove Redeemers are regular people."

"Of course they are," Jack said. "What else could they be?"

"People, but not regular people." Annie shuddered. "Forget I said anything. They have to sleep and eat, but on what schedule? When should we sneak in?"

"We'll have to take a calculated risk," Siobhan said. "Midnight?"

"Too obvious. An hour before sunrise?"

"What if they're 'up with the sun' types?" Siobhan said.

"Three a.m.," Jack said. "The night owls give up around two, and the early risers wait until an hour before dawn."

"How do you know?"

"When I traveled with Dad, we learned the patterns of the customers who kept odd hours. The three a.m. or dawn thing repeated everywhere."

"You're the expert," Siobhan said. "And it's fall, so sunrise is later. One element works in our favor."

"Three a.m. it is." Annie wrote. "Fourth. Do we grab what we can and hope they don't notice anything missing?"

"If it's a Redeemer school, they'll have lots of copies of everything," Jack said. "They won't miss one."

"Probably."

"Fifth?" Jack said.

"Do we have a fifth?" Annie said.

Siobhan yawned. "Fifth is we borrow Luke's idea. Annie, if you even think about climbing in there tomorrow, we'll lock you in this room and guard the door and the window all day."

Annie capped the inkbottle and wiped the pen on a corner of the paper. "Whatever you say."

"There's nothing else we can do," Siobhan said. "We can't get into an abbey packed top to bottom with Redeemers, let alone find the Readers and get them and ourselves back out safely."

"Besides," Jack said, "what if your idea was right? The three Readers could be forced into marriage instead."

"And that's okay?"

"No, it's not okay, but—"

"But there-is-nothing-we-can-do-about-it." Siobhan shook a finger at Annie with every clipped word. "We absolutely cannot barge in there like heroes in a romance."

Jack said, "Remember what that tinker told us. There could be a hundred Redeemers in there, and they know their own house. We don't. If they saw us, they'd cut off our escape right away. What good would we be able to do then?"

"Exactly," Siobhan said. "We want to do the most good. We can't do that if we're stumbling around the abbey looking for a schoolroom and trying to avoid every Redeemer on the planet at the same time."

Annie maintained her expressionless mask.

"We need to save Readers everywhere. In every town," Jack said. "We have to look at the finish line. Like a race."

"Right," Siobhan said. "We set up our strategy and pace ourselves."

Annie seriously considered throwing the inkwell at them. "It's too bad for the three inside there tonight? I guess they're like the old shoes you toss away because they won't help you win that race."

"That's not what I meant," Jack said.

"If we had arrived in town on the fifteenth, we wouldn't be having this discussion," Siobhan said. "We need to treat the current situation in that way. It's over and we move on."

Annie fumbled with her trouser pocket and pulled the end of the inner bow. She yanked out the leather-covered paper, and with a muffled shout flung it across the room. It bounced off the door and landed at Jack's feet.

He bent over and picked it up. "What's this?"

"A Page." She didn't bother to keep the contempt out of her voice.

Siobhan leapt to Jack's side. "You have a Page? Where'd you find it? Why didn't you tell me?" She hovered over Jack as he untied the ribbon. "What's it say?"

"This is a page from a novel." Jack read further. "Wait. Here, Siobhan, look at this."

"I am the Resurrection and the Life? Sheep on toast, Annie, that's one of *the* words. What book is this from?" She pulled Jack and the Page off her bed and dragged him to the lamp, shoving Annie aside. "*A Tale of Two Cities*. The Redeemers must've missed this. They'd never let that word out in the open."

Annie wiped the pen on her handkerchief. "Who cares?"

Their heads turned to her like marionettes on strings, the way Bess' family did earlier. *Must be a Reader thing.*

Siobhan's eyes never blinked. "What did you say?"

"I said," Annie mouthed each word with deliberation, "who—cares?"

Jack did blink. Several times. "You have to treat this with respect."

"I refuse to respect a piece of paper."

"I thought you understood about Pages," Siobhan said.

"You people don't understand about your Pages," Annie said. "Jack, you said you and your father tried to figure out what they meant and failed, remember?"

"Yes," he said.

"Then until any of you can give me a clear answer about why you're allowing these old pieces of paper to run your lives, I'm done with them." She pushed the deep blue leather against Jack's chest.

*I'm going to say something we'll all regret in another minute.* "I'm really tired. Good night."

"Annie, you don't really mean I should keep this."

"I do. Enjoy it."

He hesitated for a heartbeat, then pulled her against him with his free arm and kissed her the way Hank used to.

*He loves that piece of paper more than me. Well, I wanted him to stop thinking I'm all he ever wanted.*

This time it was Jack who broke the embrace. "Good night," he said in a husky voice, and left.

* * *

*She wanders through dark, cold halls. She holds a long candle. Its light reaches only a few inches beyond her feet. She hears water drip from her soaked clothing. She walks for an endless time, listening for voices.*

*I'm inside the abbey. Where are all the Redeemers?*

*She enters an open space on her right. The drips from her clothes set off a handful of echoes. She holds up the candle. Something catches her eye. She walks forward, slips, and lands on one knee and one hand.*

*Thick liquid covers her hand. The liquid shines dark red in the candlelight.*

*The dripping echoes continue. Her heart pounds. A drop falls on her hair. She looks up. In front of her nose is a pair of feet, perfectly still. She stands, one trouser leg sodden with the red liquid. She raises the candle.*

*Siobhan and Jack hang from the wall, nailed to crosses. She calls their names. They're dead. A third body hangs next to them. Hers. She drops the candle.*

*In its guttering light she sees the red eyes of hundreds of rats. The leaders lift their snouts, sniffing the air. She looks down at her blood-soaked trousers and backs away. The nearest one leaps for her.*

* * *

Annie listened for a minute after she woke. Siobhan breathed in an even rhythm. She unwound herself from the corkscrew she'd made of her blanket and slipped out of bed. The half moon illuminated the door. Siobhan hadn't set a noise trap on it.

"I'm not asleep," Siobhan said from the other side of the narrow room.

Annie returned to her bed without comment and waited. And waited. The moon inched down. When it touched the top of the nearest building, Siobhan began to snore. Annie waited a few minutes longer. Without making a sound, she slipped the knotted rope over her left shoulder and picked up her boots in one hand. Siobhan kept snoring. Annie turned the doorknob slow enough to make her doubt she was moving it at all. At last the door came free. She looked over her shoulder. Siobhan's eyes were closed and the snores continued without interruption. She opened the door a few more inches and saw a dark string pulled taut across the doorway six inches from the floor.

She stepped over it and closed the door with the same exaggerated slowness. The hall was too dark to see the trap with clarity, but Annie guessed twine rather than fishing string. Siobhan's plate and cup from her backpack might be the noisemakers this time. She must have been desperate to set something so simple.

Free, Annie crept downstairs to the warmth of the banked fire in the living room.

The clock bonged four a.m. She sat on the hearthstones until her teeth stopped chattering. When her feet thawed, she went to the window and pulled aside the curtain. Rain.

*Someone has to save the Readers.*

A piece of wood cracked and sent out a puff of heat. She heard nails ripping holes in her body. She stamped the memory down but the locks on her imaginary door were working themselves loose.

*What if it happens as early as sunrise? Bess said she heard her brother packing soon after dawn.*

The rain clouds started to change from one huge black lump into smaller charcoal-gray blobs.

*Readers are big on tradition. Act a certain way, teach a certain way, be a Reader a certain way. Are the Redeemers also ruled by tradition? Probably. They seem to be exactly like Readers. Siobhan would screech in protest at the idea, but it makes the most sense.*

The clock chimed twice for four-thirty. Sunrise in an hour and a half.

*Time to be a hero.*

She slipped her bare feet into her boots, head pounding. Mallets and nails. She closed her eyes and pulled the top bolt on the stone cell in her head to open the door and throw them in.

*Bang. Bang. Bang.* The pounding came from inside the cell.

The five other bolts rattled. Pieces of stone flaked off the walls and door. The piles of wood and hammers and nails and dead rats and buckets of blood she'd stuffed in there were trying to get out.

*I'm losing my grip. I have to find something practical to do.* She wrapped it around her as a lumpy belt. *My coat would slow me down anyway. So I'll get wet. I won't melt.*

She opened the front door as little as possible, squeezed through sideways, and dived into the rain.

# CHAPTER FORTY

Every stitch on Annie's body was soaked by the time she reached the abbey. When she found the first foothold on the wall, she took off her boots and left them on the pavement.

The climb wasn't as bad as she'd feared. The gaps and cracks zigzagged up the wall in easy intervals.

*Slippery. Watch it. Grab that stone with your toes.*

Finally she pulled herself onto the same window ledge Susan had dangled from. The window opened in the middle like a double door, and she jumped down a few feet into a long stone hallway. The walls were bare except for hanging lamps on alternate sides every twenty feet. She looked at the ceiling and breathed easier when she didn't see wood eaten by termites.

*Stop it. I'm not in Kansas City. This isn't about me. Find them.*

She unwound the rope from her waist. *No place to hide it, and we may need it in a hurry.* In the end she tied the end to the lamp hook nearest the window and coiled it on the floor.

*Pick a hall. Eeny, meeny, miney, moe. Right it is.*

She passed narrow, closed doors on both sides. A small side-hall with more closed doors opened off the right just before the stairs. On the left, too. Annie closed her eyes. She knew that shape... her arms rose up as the image grew clearer...

Her eyes snapped open. A *T.* Her arms dropped.

*Stop taking things to extremes. Focus.*

If these were Redeemer bedrooms they must be skinnier than the narrow rooms at the Topeka inn. She'd really think the walls were closing in on her if she lived here.

*Live here? Pigs really will dance on stage before that happens.*

When she reached the staircase, she looked behind her. A clear trail of wet footprints and water drops shimmered in the lamplight. Shrugging her shoulders, she descended and walked through another hallway. More closed doors. *If three or four Redeemers lived in every town, dozens must live here permanently. What do they all do? Besides clean this huge place, that is.*

The stone floor sent chills from her wet feet through her legs and into her back and shoulders. She sneezed into her sleeve. Was she just cold, or cold and afraid?

*Don't think. Keep walking.*

Wider doors spaced farther apart lined on the outer wall of the second floor, but the long, blank inner wall was broken only by a single doorway in the middle. The short hall also had wide doors on either side, all closed.

Bedrooms for important Redeemers? Classrooms? Why on the arms of the *T*?

*Thump.*

Annie flattened herself against the wall. No one behind her. She ran back around the corner. Another thump. Now she placed it: Behind the door on the inner wall.

*Get out of here before the door opens.*

She ran on tiptoe down the next flight of stairs and stuck her head around the doorway. The first floor layout followed the floor above. A basement stairwell opened just beyond the double doors that led to the outside. A lamp above the top step lit a railing on the wall. She looked over her shoulder as a high voice behind the inner wall started to sing warm-up scales.

*Get to business.*

Annie walked down ten stone steps. Another lamp hung at the bottom. She walked three more paces, following the stone wall as it curved left.

She expected a room as wide as the entire abbey, like the cellars beneath any inn. Instead, she stood in an average-sized classroom. Lamps burned in between each of three shelves built onto the left—and right-hand walls. Four tables with a wide aisle in the center and a tall lecture stand at the head of the center aisle. Paper, pens, and bottles of ink packed one shelf on the right, and then the books began. Basic schoolbooks at first: A-B-Cs, First Grade Math. Second Grade English. Fifth Grade History. Eighth Grade Science. Then instruction books for every kind of trade: Farms. Winemaking. Orchards. Paper and ink. Metalworking. Leathercraft. Candles. Soap. Spinning and Weaving.

Copies of one book, *The Vision of Matthew: Redeem the World,* filled an entire top shelf on Annie's right. She pulled one out and opened it.

And lo, the people of the world waxed mighty in evil thoughts and deeds.

*Why, that sounds like a Page. Annie wins: Redeemers and Readers are connected through the Pages.*

Another chapter began: The bomb gave a great light, as though the world had leapt into the sun itself. And the Christ appeared to Matthew out of the light, and said, "I have a Great Commission for you, Matthew. Redeem the world in My name."

*That name. Was it on Hank's Page? I can't remember.*

She'd have to take one. If they could figure out how to decipher the Page-sounding language, she'd bet they'd have the key to the Redeemers.

A set of double doors stood open at the far end of the room. First Annie went back to the bottom of the stairs and listened. Still no Redeemers walking around; she couldn't hear the singer anymore, either. She walked up the aisle and through the doors into another brightly lit room.

*A Redeemer—no, no. It's a statue.* She moved closer. The artist had carved and painted a block of stone to look just like a Redeemer. She looked up at least a foot into its brown hood.

*What's wrong with his eyes?* Fine red veins covered them, leaving only the suggestion of blue irises.

Who was he? She'd never seen a blind Redeemer, if that's what those eyes meant. She crouched to read the carving on the marrow pedestal. 'The first Matthew, blessed with the Vision.'

*Whatever that means. I'm wasting time. Check out the paintings on the walls and see what's in that last room at the end. Move yourself.*

Annie turned her back to the statue and tried not to feel those eyes on her. *They can't see. It's only a statue. Shake it off.*

A group of four paintings in a diamond pattern hung to the right of the doors as she'd come in, one for each season. Black ink on a painted white square on the wall next to them read, 'The Abbey

Before.' Redeemers living high in the mountains planted gardens, hoed fields, and milked cows in the top one. A wooden building like a small abbey dominated the ground and sky. In the right painting, wheat blossomed, fruit covered the trees, and flowers bloomed. On the bottom, harvest. On the left, several scenes inside the small abbey. Classes, winemaking, cooking, and everyone kneeling in a big room with colorful windows, holding books.

Next to these hung a single rectangular painting, five feet tall and three wide. The gardens had withered and the abbey was burning. Redeemers were falling or face down on the ground, fear on the faces of the falling ones. *Redeemers afraid?* Beyond the mountains a tall white cloud rose into the sky, its top spread like an umbrella.

'The Last War.' Of course. That wasn't a normal cloud. Someone had thrown a bomb at the Redeemers. *Incredible.*

In the last painting on this wall, 'Rebuilding,' piles of shriveled plants and trees were stacked to one side as Redeemers planted seeds and saplings. There was no indication of how much time had passed.

She tried to remember Last War history. Had it been ten years from the end of the war until the Redeemers appeared? No, not that long. But more than a few months. She leaned closer to see the dead trees. The leaves had crumbled to ash on the ground and the bark was brittle and falling off. One or two years, maybe, since the first floor of a new abbey was already in place. They'd have rebuilt themselves before coming down to rebuild everything else. At the top of the painting, a single Redeemer sat on a flat rock, his hood off and a bandage around his eyes.

Annie looked over her shoulder at the statue and crossed to the other side of the room.

Three long, narrow paintings, one foot high and four wide, hung one above the other. The top one, 'In the World,' showed several Redeemers standing in the middle of a field. A ruined town stood a ways behind them. All the buildings were burned or broken and dark clouds filled the sky. A group of sickly people in rags faced the Redeemers.

A single Redeemer with upraised arms stood before a group of people in the middle painting, 'Matthew Calls the People.' A spiderweb of red veins surrounded his bluish-white eyes. He gave her goosebumps. She looked behind her again. The stone hood blocked the eyes at this angle. *Good.* She returned to the painting.

The raggedy people and the other Redeemers knelt before him. The Redeemers' faces were hidden, of course, but the others stared up at Matthew like he'd offered them the sun and moon and stars.

The people in the bottom painting, 'The Beginning,' were still unhealthy, but they all wore new clothes. Some built houses using stones from the ruined ones. Some prepared fields for planting. Some sat at the feet of the Redeemers. And some women followed a group of Redeemers toward the mountains.

*They did take women and marry them. Back then, anyway. What if this tradition still exists?* She put her nose right up against the painting. The women as happy as though they had been given a gift. Annie couldn't fathom it.

'Building the Vision' took up the rest of the wall. It showed an early version of Colorado Springs: She recognized the shape of the valley and the mountains. The abbey had two completed floors and the first streets radiated from it. Men, women, and children built houses as wagons unloaded timber and bricks. Farms covered the outlying ground. Women Redeemers, hoods off, sat near the abbey and played with children and babies, so at least five more years had passed. Everyone looked healthier. A tiny break in the clouds over the mountains showed a glimpse of sun. The pale-eyed Redeemer stood in front of the abbey doors with arms open, like a father welcoming everyone home.

*Anyone would've felt at home. Order. Sanity. Peace. Two hundred and three years of it.*

Annie sneezed and looked behind her again. *My luck's going to run out soon. There's an awful lot of lamps burning for this room to stay empty long.* When no one came through the doorway, she turned back to the last painting. It was so vivid, she could almost smell the fresh-cut wood. In the bottom left corner was a red poppy and 'Clare.'

*Will you focus? See what's in this last room and head back upstairs.*

She skirted the statue and headed to the back of the room to open the last set of doors.

This room was longer than the others and it had no second exit. At the far end, a single lamp hung over a carved and polished wood lecture stand. Annie blinked several times to get used to the dimness. A dozen chairs lined the back wall. There was no other furniture. The stone floor was covered with rows of oval indents, smooth and slightly shiny, like they'd been worn away over hundreds of years.

*So what if it's a dark, creepy room? Toughen up.*

She navigated between the hollow indents to the lecture stand. It held a book barely an inch thick, but a foot high and wide, with 'Holy Bible' hand-lettered in gold ink on the cover.

She set the Matthew book on the floor and opened the Bible book. *These letters must be something like three times the size of regular book type.* She touched the text. *Done by hand, too. Wow.*

She grinned at the empty room. *I sound like Jack.*

The first page read 'The Gospel of Jesus Christ According to Matthew.' *Not the same Matthew. Of course not. Can't be.*

But they answering, said: He is guilty of death. Then did they spit in his face and buffeted him. And others struck his face with the palms of their hands, Saying: Prophesy unto us, O Christ. Who is he that struck thee?

*Prophesy? What did that mean? Page-talk annoys me worse than mosquito bites. Talk like human beings, people.*

Three pages later: 'The Gospel of Jesus Christ According to Mark.' *Already? The story sure is short.*

And the soldiers led him away into the court of the palace: and they called together the whole band. And they clothed him with purple: and, platting a crown of thorns, they put it upon him.

*This makes no sense. Now I understand why Jack and his father spent years trying to figure out what their Pages meant.*

You serpents, generation of vipers, how will you flee from the judgment of Hell?

*Serpents I understand. That's one word.*

She flipped forward until she found another page headed 'gospel,' this one by someone named John.

They crucified him with two others, and Jesus in their midst. The soldiers therefore, when they had crucified him, took his garments, and they made four parts, to every soldier a part.

The lamplight vanished. In the darkness in Annie's head, she heard the Redeemer's voice reciting those exact words.

*He's going to slash my clothes and rip them off and take the nails and—*

*No!*

The room reappeared. She'd crumpled the top of the page in her fist. She snatched her hand away, slammed the book shut, and ran out of there, past the statue and down the classroom aisle. At the foot of the stairs, she stopped, gasping. Her hand shook when she leaned it on the wall.

*Think about it later. Find the Readers. That's why I'm here. Find the Readers. Grab the books and go.*

Annie slowed her breathing. She clenched and released her hands several times, digging in her fingernails, until they trembled less. No footsteps or voices reached her ears.

*Go. Now.*

She walked back through all three rooms, step by deliberate step, until she stood before the book of Pages. *No guilt. Take it. This is what you need to break the Redeemers.*

The heavy cover resisted Annie until she saw that it was simply slotted into the lecture stand's flat top. When she angled the stand toward her, the book came free without a sound. She picked up the Matthew textbook she'd left on the floor and shoved both into the back waistband of her trousers.

*Don't stop here. Check the classroom again. You can fit a couple more books down your pants.*

Annie strode past the Matthew statue with head averted. Those blind, painted eyes still burned into her neck. The empty classroom absorbed her soft footsteps as she scrutinized each set of shelves.

*Standard textbooks. Nothing different from what I shelved in Topeka. Basic skills for living and working. Redeemers learn all the trades, then. That would explain why the Redeemers in other towns don't farm or buy food or clothes. They're self-sufficient.*

Still no sign of the book she really wanted, besides the books already in her trousers. *No, not on this shelf either. Come on, Redeemer teachers, you must have a Redeemer How-To Manual."*

At the end of the last shelf, she looked around again for hiding places, although everything seemed to be out in the open here.

*The lecture stand. Maybe it's the kind with a nook for supplies.* But the nook was empty as well.

*I'm not going to get a chance like this again.* Annie pictured the layout of the floors above. The rooms on the arms of the *t* had bigger doors. That Cheyenne Wells letter had said something about kitchen and dining room, but didn't mention a living room. Yet every house had one. *That's where the books for adults will be. Don't think too long. You're supposed to be tough as shoe leather. Get upstairs and open those doors and rescue the Readers.*

Annie still heard no sounds from the rest of the abbey. With this many Redeemers in the place, she should be deafened by footsteps and voices. She should be worried that at least one Redeemer would come down here to look at the paintings, otherwise why would so many lamps be lit?

*It must be nearly dawn. Maybe they're all preparing for... Take the books and get the Readers. Now.*

One hand on the books in her trousers, Annie followed the curved wall back to the stairs. Three steps from the top, she heard the screams.

# CHAPTER FORTY-ONE

*I'm too late.*

Annie ran up the stairs and down the hall. More screams. She reached the end before she remembered the doorway back near the cellar stairs.

*There's another one on the second floor.*

She took the stairs two at a time. Halfway up, the books fell out of her trousers.

*Matthew's balls.* She slipped down a step, caught herself, scooped up the books, and kept running. The deep sound of many voices talking at once filled the upstairs hall. Then silence. Annie forced herself to slow down just enough so her feet wouldn't slap on the stone floor.

A different voice screamed.

*No. No. No.*

Annie skidded to a stop before the single door on the inner wall. *Please be unlocked.* Holding her breath, she lifted the latch and the door swung in without a sound.

Somewhere below her, a hammer hit a nail with a *clang*. The shriek that followed drowned out the other blows. She knew there were more. It had taken three to fasten her arms to the wood.

The balcony Annie stood on ended in a half-wall four feet in front of her. She had to walk forward. She had to see what was happening. The books in her arms weighed a hundred pounds. Her legs turned into trees; her feet their roots. She had to see.

*What if I can still stop it? What if I can save even one?*

Annie set the books on the polished wood floor before dropping to her knees and shuffling forward. *A Redeemer may be looking up here. Can't let any of them see me.* Her knees hit the wall. Her curly hair topped the oval railing, but before she crouched to hide it, she raised herself until she could see everything.

Redeemers. Twenty feet below her, row upon row of brown hooded robes stood at long bench seats, like sofas without cushions. Their hands gripped the back of the bench in front of them. They leaned forward, hoods facing straight ahead. She raised her head to see.

A naked, withered old man hung from t-shaped boards attached to a curved back wall. Vomit dribbled from his mouth, and as he tried to push himself up—to breathe, she remembered—a splinter of bone erupted from his left foot and he collapsed, gagging.

In the center of a raised stage, four Redeemers lifted another set of boards from a wide, red-spattered table. The younger man impaled on them screamed and writhed. When the Redeemers dropped the boards into brackets on the wall, his wrists ripped away from the oversized nails and bright red blood poured from the enlarged holes like water from faucets.

Dozens of lamps lit the room as bright as noon, but Annie went blind at that moment. The cell door in her head burst. Every horror she'd crammed inside spewed into her brain and she was back in the first dark, empty abbey.

*The rats. They're drinking my blood. No. Listen. The Redeemers are talking. You're in Colorado Springs.*

She wrenched herself into the present. Her hands still clutched the railing. Somehow she'd stayed upright. *I have to ignore it. I have to save the Readers. Get down there. Help them escape.*

*Clang.* A woman's high-pitched scream this time.

Annie squeezed shut her eyes and opened them again. The Redeemer pounded the last nail into a tall, plump woman, breaking her left foot.

*The Readers are dead. You failed. You useless sack of pig shit. You were their only hope, and you wandered the cellars admiring paintings instead. You should be hanging there, not that woman. Helen. Her name is Helen.*

Annie slid to the floor. Her hands found her hair, streaked white from the same terror she'd left the three below to, and yanked. With her face smashed against the base of the wall, she tugged and pulled and yanked some more, biting her cheeks to hold in the sobs, trying somehow to mask the Readers' screams and moans piercing her ears.

The Redeemers began some kind of call-and-response. One strong voice followed by many, repeated several times.

Then the lights went out.

Annie opened blurry, wet eyes all the way. *I'm not in Kansas City. I'm not hanging on that wall. Light the lamps. Please, Redeemers, light the lamps again.*

And they did.

"Let us proclaim the mystery of faith." One voice.

All the Redeemers said in unison, "For those whom he did foreknow, he also did predestinate to be conformed into the image of his son."

*That's it. That's the sentence I couldn't remember. Why is it so important?*

Her hands ached. She couldn't breathe. It was because of her stuffed nose, not because she was hanging on the wall with the Readers. She wasn't. She was crouched on a balcony in the Colorado Springs abbey, listening to three people die in horrific agony.

*Your scars don't ache. You're imagining it.* She massaged her insteps anyway. *They are throbbing. What's happening to me? Breathe. It's only snot. Breathe.*

She wiped her nose on her sleeve, not daring to make a noise now that the Redeemers were silent below her.

*Why aren't they talking?*

Annie pulled herself up by the balcony railing. She had to see. It was her obligation. Even if the Readers didn't know she was up here, she had to watch them to the end. *You're not alone. I'm sorry. I'm so sorry. I should have saved you. Can you hear me? Do you know I'm up here? Look up. You can see me if you look up. I'm here.*

Nine Redeemers stooped in front of the three Readers. When they stood, they each held a gold wineglass. With careful steps, they moved to the table, and poured the blood from their wineglasses into dozens of miniature gold cups. When they all were filled, three Redeemers took the trays into the main group. Everyone took a cup.

"This do in remembrance of him," the Redeemer who wielded the hammer said. He raised his cup.

"Lord, I am not worthy to receive you," the Redeemers said, "but only say the word and I shall be healed."

They drank.

One of the dying Readers laughed. In the silence Annie could hear his rasping voice. "Drink it—all—down."

She followed his gaze. The Redeemers upended their cups to catch the last drops on their tongues. Their hoods fell backward, revealing their faces.

In the moment before she ducked behind the wall, she saw the Redeemers' faces full-on.

A different memory slammed into her but another thought shoved it aside and Annie scrambled out the doorway. She made it a few inches down the hall before she puked her guts up.

*They drank the Readers' blood. They drank their blood.* Her stomach heaved again and the rest of last night's wine and dessert splattered the stone floor.

*Get back inside. That was Jacob down there. I saw Zachary too. Jacob drinking blood. Why is Jacob down there? He's too frail to walk from Kansas City to Colorado Springs. Why is her here in Colorado Springs, here in the abbey?*

Annie wiped her mouth on her sleeve and crawled back to the balcony. One of the Readers had sunk to the bottom of the wood and didn't move. The woman in the middle was gasping and trying to force her shuddering legs upward. The old man was still breathing shallow, groaning breaths. Their blood had merged into one irregular puddle and spread over the floor beneath them.

The Redeemers sat on the benches now, hoods still off, watching the Readers.

*They're watching them die. This is how Redeemers celebrate their family reunion.* Annie's stomach clenched, but she forced down the bile.

A female Redeemer stood and sang in a clear, sweet soprano: "Tenebrae factae sunt, dum crucifixissent Jesus."

A strong hand clapped over Annie's mouth. She stiffened for only an instant, then jammed her elbow backwards. A soft grunt sounded in her ear, then a whisper. "It's us."

Siobhan knelt next to Annie, a finger on her lips. The hand removed itself from Annie's mouth and Jack's arm came around her.

"...exclamavit Jesus voce magna..." The space magnified the beauty of the Redeemer's voice.

Siobhan and Jack stared at the balcony wall like they could see through it. Annie shook off Jack's arm and dragged herself up to see the show. *I have to watch them.*

The woman was dead. The old man's chest heaved.

The body of Redeemers sang in turn, "Et inclinato capite, emisit spiritum."

When the echoes faded, the old man's voice cracked once as he tried to say something. He collapsed like the others before any words came out.

*They're dead. I could've saved them. I should have saved them. I'm useless. Why am I still alive?* Annie crumpled against the wall and clawed at her hair. It hurt, but that small pain was nothing compared to the remembered agony pulsing through her scars, ripping through her womb. *I forgot. I'm dead. Like little Hank. Like the three down there, bleeding onto the floor, rotting into skeletons.* She kept tearing at her hair, swallowing the wails that filled her throat.

Jack bent down next to her. "We have to get out of here."

Siobhan pulled her up, hands gentle but firm. She didn't speak.

Jack's hands wormed underneath Annie's and tried to pull them off her head. "Annie, let go. Come on." He pulled harder.

Annie's hands came free and landed in her lap. Tufts of hair tangled in her fingers. Her scalp stung. *How can a dead person's scalp hurt? Why hasn't all my hair rotted off by now? It's been months since they hung me on their wall.*

The Redeemers said something else, all together, and the noise of many footsteps filled the open space.

Jack tugged Annie toward the door.

*The books.* Annie pulled out of his hold and felt for them; her eyes didn't seem to work properly. *There. The Matthew book. There. The Page book.* She reached for Jack and followed him to the hall.

All three of them stood. Annie gagged at the stench of her vomit; Siobhan coughed. Jack led the way to the stairs at the end of the hall. In silence they climbed the flights of stairs and retraced the path to the window with the rope.

The rain had stopped. The day was brightening. Siobhan opened the window and looked out. "Empty streets," she whispered. She let down the rope and climbed through first.

Annie fumbled the books into her front waistband. Jack urged her through while Siobhan held the other end. Her foot slipped on the first knot, and her hands tightened on the rope without thinking. When she was on the ground, Jack untied the rope and tossed it to Siobhan. Then he climbed down by the handholds in the wall, slipping a few times on the wet stones.

When he hit the ground, Siobhan tossed his boots at him. She already held her own and Annie's. They ran barefoot through the muddy streets, Jack's hand on Annie's free arm. She clutched the books in the other. When they reached the carpenter's block, Jack stopped them.

"We can't go back to the inn. Margaret will have a hundred questions."

"What about the carpenter's?" Siobhan said.

"Good. Yes. Let's go."

They ran the length of the block to the house's front door with the stairs that wrapped around the corner. No one answered.

"Where's the back door?" Jack said. "We have to get off the street."

"Behind the workshop, maybe." Siobhan led them around the house through a wide, unlatched gate and across a yard crowded with covered stacks of lumber. She knocked on the door. Nothing. She knocked harder.

The rain started again.

Jack put his mouth to the keyhole. "Luke!"

Still nothing.

"Luke!"

Running footsteps. The door opened.

"Jack?" Luke said. "What's going on?"

"Please let us in," Siobhan said.

"Sure." He opened the door wider and moved aside.

"Luke?" Erin called from the hall. "Was someone at the door?"

"Yeah, honey. Can you get Mom?" He closed and locked the door again.

"What is it, Luke?" Bess came into the workroom. She frowned. "Annie? What's wrong?"

Susan joined Bess, a wet coffee cup in one hand and a dishtowel in the other. "Siobhan? Hi, Jack. Hi, Annie." She stopped. "Annie? What's the matter?"

"She's dead." Annie's voice cracked and tears ran down her cheeks. "Annie's dead and rotting in the abbey. Like the Readers."

Jack gathered Annie into his arms and stood there, rocking her.

"Come into the living room, all of you," Bess said. "The fireplace is lit. You'll warm up faster."

Erin took Susan's arm. "I'll tell Ben to make more tea."

"Come and get dry," Bess said to Siobhan.

"Come on," Jack whispered to Annie. He led her into the living room.

Susan was already at the foot of the stairs. She called, "George!" as Jack eased Annie into a chair.

Annie folded over herself, the sharp edges of the books digging into her ribs. *I'm dead. I shouldn't feel anything. These books shouldn't hurt.*

Annie sat up. *Books.* Her eyes cleared and she saw Susan and George facing her on the couch. Siobhan paced the floor next to Annie. Jack stood behind her, his hands on her shoulders.

She eased the books away from her chest. "Readers and Redeemers are connected." The two books shook in her hands. "Your Pages are what connects you."

Bess sat down hard in the nearest chair. Luke entered. "What?"

"Connected," Annie said. Her voice sounded as flat and lifeless as she felt. "I stole these from the Redeemer's cellar. Read it. It sounds like your Pages." She handed the Bible book to Siobhan.

Siobhan opened it. "Matthew's balls. Jack, look at this."

Jack's hands left Annie's shoulders and everyone gathered around Annie's prize. Several different voices murmured sentences, concentrating on the odd-sounding names.

Annie stared at them. *I should care. It's what's going to help me understand the Redeemers. But it doesn't matter. All that matters is the Readers are dead and I should've saved them. These people should've helped. Look how they drool over a bunch of their precious Pages. Spineless bastards.*

Annie flung the Matthew book across the room. George picked it up off the floor as everyone looked at her.

At last she said it out loud. "You spineless bastards. All you care about is those pieces of paper. Three people died in the abbey today and you're drooling over a bunch of old words." She snatched the book from Siobhan's hands and flipped page after page, wrinkling them, until she found what the Redeemer said in Kansas City. "The soldiers therefore, when they had crucified him, took his garments, and they made four parts, to every soldier a part." She looked at Luke John, Erin, Eleanor. "Do any of you Readers understand that?"

"Annie," Siobhan said.

"Shut up, Siobhan. The Redeemers use those Pages to torture and kill Readers. It's like their instruction manual. That's why I couldn't find one in the classroom. It's all here." She smacked the book with her hand. "After they recited this, they cut off my clothes and left me naked on their wood. Exactly what they did to the Readers this morning." Her legs wouldn't hold her. She sank to the floor, her hand slipping off the book. "They said the image sentence again. Something about an image and a son. They said it like it described the Readers on the wall."

"What do you mean, Annie?" Bess said.

"If your Pages are about a person with a weird name, then he—she—inspired the Redeemers. Too bad about the way that person died. Too bad for Readers. Too bad for me." She rubbed her arms over and over, but it didn't warm her. *I can't get warm. I'm dead.* "I should've saved them. I should've gone in earlier. Spent less time in the cellar. Thought about how they were screaming and bleeding and dying up there." She stopped, but a moment later the words gushed from her mouth. "Bleeding. That's right. Here's what your brother didn't tell you, Bess. They have these beautiful gold wineglasses on the floor. After the Readers have hung on the walls for awhile, the Redeemers—" she swallowed— "the Redeemers take the full glasses and divide the, blood among enough little cups for everyone. Then they, then they all drink it."

No one spoke. Susan shifted on the couch. Jack sat beside Annie on the floor. "Is that why you threw up in the hall?"

Annie shuddered at the gentleness in his voice. She'd break down if he kept being sweet to her. "Yeah. I didn't want them to hear me. I didn't want to be nailed up there again." Tears blurred her vision. "I'm a coward. I could've saved them, but instead I only saved my own skin." She rocked back and forth, arms pulled into her chest again.

"Grandma," George said, "I can take the books to Cal on Friday. His bookseller's a smart lady."

"No!" Annie jerked up. "Not the bookseller. Redeemers help us, I almost forgot." She grabbed the Page book and dug her nails into the covers. "When they drank the—blood—from the little cups, they tipped them up to get every drop."

Susan gasped, and Ben, standing in the kitchen doorway, muttered, "Matthew's balls."

"Their hoods fell off," Annie said, "and I saw their faces. I saw Jacob. I saw Zachary."

"Who?" Jack said.

"Jacob, our bookseller in Kansas City. The Redeemers knew

when to kidnap me there because they did it after I showed Hank's Page to Jacob. They found me in Topeka because Zachary grabbed my arm and pushed up my sleeve. He saw the scar." She held all their eyes in turn. "The booksellers are Redeemers."

"Impossible," James said from the hearth.

Dead Annie flamed to life. She pushed to her feet, reached James in two strides, and slapped him across the face. "Piece of sheep shit." She turned to the rest of the family. "All of you think the same. As long as you're safe everyone else can get plowed under. If there was justice in the world, the Redeemers would guzzle your blood tomorrow. All of you." She snatched the Matthew book from George.

"Annie?" he said.

"Drop this Reader garbage before you turn into two-faced rats, like your parents and my best friends who wrote that letter and these two here who latched onto me so the Redeemers would take me and leave them alone." She spun on her bare heel and seized the Page book. "If I'd known my husband was one of you, I wouldn't have wept when the Redeemers killed our baby." Her voice faltered, but she straightened her back and glared at Ben, Susan, and George. "If you do stay Readers, I hope none of you have children. Readers are a disease that will kill the world. The sooner you die off, the better."

Annie stalked down the back hall and wrenched open the door. She didn't feel dead any longer. Cold rain stuck her hair to her neck and the brimming cart tracks in the road soaked her bare feet.

She ran the length of the street, splashing muddy water over her clothes. "Listen to me, Readers! I'm not dead! Hide while you can, because I'm dragging you down with the Redeemers! I promise you this in the memory of little Hank."

When she reached the inn, the sight of her filthy feet on the steps made her pause. *I can't go in looking like this. I have no idea what happened to my boots, either.*

Her frantic elation collapsed. "What did I say to Susan? Pigs on stage, this rain is cold." She flattened herself against the wall under the porch roof. "I should've covered these books." The underside of her sleeve was drier than the rest of her, so she used it to wipe the covers. "The adults are sheep shit, but the young ones aren't like them yet. They won't understand what I said, even after seeing the scars yesterday."

The rain thinned, but the wind picked up. Annie sneezed. Her lacerated scalp stung.

"I sure picked a memorable way to decide I'm not dead." She heard the Readers screaming and bit her lips. "Hold it in. You'll never be a regular person again, but you can act like it. Fix the cell and stuff everything back in there." She sheltered the books from a last gust of wind-blown rain. "I have to go back and apologize. My mother raised me with better manners."

She walked back to the carpenter's, staying out of the worst of the puddles. "Not all Readers are worthless. Hank wasn't. I have to believe that."

Jack careened around the corner, splashing water every which way. Annie stood still. He crashed into her but held on. They stayed upright.

"Matthew's balls, Annie, why do you keep running away?"

"I was coming back."

"Try staying put for a change." His long hair dropped water over both of them. "You're barefoot, it's like ice out here, and you are the most unreasonable woman I've ever met." He took a long breath. "Are you all right?"

Annie lifted one shoulder. "It was too much in there, the abbey and then James. He didn't see the blood and hear the screams or the Redeemers singing."

Jack bit his lip. "Are you sure you saw those booksellers?"

She pulled away. "I'm furious and terrified and guilt-ridden and sick to my stomach, but I'm not a liar, Jack."

He raised his hands in a gesture of surrender. "I'm sorry. I know you're not lying. You should hear the fight going on back there. Only James was holding out when I came after you. Bess is lecturing everyone on the logic of it all, and Susan and George and Ben think you're as wonderful as Matthew. You know what I mean."

Annie shivered. "I'm just a cook who got caught in something too big for her."

Jack pulled her closer, sandwiching the books between them. "You know what nobody else knows and you have more guts than any ten people I could name. You and these books are the beginning of freedom. Are you coming back with me?"

"Not if you compare me to Matthew again. He saved the world to kill Readers."

"Yeah, but history isn't completely off-balance. Matthew taught us how to keep civilization going. He did that right."

"And that makes me, what? Matthew's apprentice?" Annie

shivered again.

"No, no. It makes you the most important teacher on the Smoky River."

Annie leaned into his embrace and he tightened it. "I need some help, you know. I don't understand all this Page stuff. The Matthew book is written like it too."

"I'm at your service, missus."

"Wait." She looked up at him. "I'm going after the Readers as well as the Redeemers. Walk away now if you still want to be one of them."

"I know you are. I'm staying with you."

Annie nodded. *Hero time over. Time to work.*

Jack smiled down at her. "Come and teach your first class."